澄清聲明

親愛的讀者：

倍斯特出版事業有限公司鄭重聲明，大陸中國紡織出版社與本社無業務往來。

近來發現本社之公司Logo，出現於中國紡織出版社之貝斯特英語系列書籍，該出版社自 2012年11月1日起之所有出版品與本社並無任何關係；鑑於此事件，懷疑有人利用本社之商業信譽，藉此誤導大眾，本社予以高度關注。特此聲明，以正視聽。

倍斯特出版事業有限公司　敬啟

倍斯特出版事業有限公司
Best Publishing Ltd.

叫我一聲
"Well-educated"
Taiwanese

NEWS
英語增進表達力!!

Talks On
News English—Sharpen
Your Expression!!

English

以相關新聞英語類談話議題與老外商談搏感情，
成為商業社交對談的佼佼者，
你就是Number One的勝出代表！

新聞主題多元豐富：中英文主題式文章，使你的知識視野大開，英語表達更上一層樓。

問題與討論：書中備有與主題相關的問題，擴大思考層面，加深學習印象，供學習與討論。

主題對話範例：實際模擬新聞英語的相關主題對談，讓你學以致用，產生更有深度的問答。

同義字與名詞：掌握在不同的專業領域，應如何使用正確的詞彙表意。

志達◎著

作者序

　　運用新聞事件或有興趣之題材去增加自己的英文能力，應該是一種比較實際且有效之方式。因此我決定撰寫壹本有關之英文工具書，冀望藉此有益莘莘學子及英文同好，拋磚引玉，略盡綿薄。

　　本書內容著重英文之關鍵用字，句型範例，問題討論及對話，另同義名詞所衍生涵義，以增進英文功力。尤其讓學習者能夠正確傳達意思外，同時提升彼此交談內容及深度。又各篇文章單元所列舉之新聞詞彙及專業用語乃我們目前日常生活或職場正式範疇，廣加愛用，歷久彌新。

　　俗云『聞道有先後，術業有專攻』，在學習英文過程中也可稱謂之『百尺竿頭，更進一步』。在台灣尚未有較佳『英文大環境』前提下，有志學好英文或喜愛英文語言者，自己要建立起堅強之英文學習意志，求知求新，日新又新。

　　筆者自從事英文相關工作已歷卅餘載，至今猶保持當年學子精神，發現自己不懂之英文單字或文句，有「文」必錄，追根究底。繼續涉獵各式英文相關項目，或自行賞閱或進行翻譯，日漸精進，樂趣自在。

　　最後，我要特別感激倍斯特公司用心籌劃及出版本書。另承辦同仁戮力不懈，鼎力相助，使拙著得以如期付梓。

　　祝各位 開卷有益 樂活學習！

陳志達 謹誌于台北
2013年11月9日

特約編輯序

閱讀是一種習慣，是一種輕鬆的生活方式，不該是一種沉重的負擔，這是我們出版這本《用 News 英語增進表達力》的初衷，透過（八）大主題，共（三十六）篇簡顯易懂的文章，希望能幫助讀者輕鬆養成閱讀英文書報的習慣。

本書包含各種生活中常見的資訊訊息，從食衣住行到休閒育樂，甚至國際時事，這裡應有盡有，可說是各種常見英語章節的集散地。我們把每篇文章依段落提供中文翻譯，幫您迅速搞懂文章結構，增加吸收資訊的效率。

我們在文章後面提供常用字彙、單字搭配的例句，簡單有趣，讓您在閱讀文章之餘，能迅速掌握關鍵詞彙，無形中提高英文閱讀能力。模擬文章主題的對話例句，簡短易讀，就像在看影視劇場，不但增進英語對話能力，更豐富您的談話內容。還有我們特別挑選的同義字、類義詞，讓您記一個字，同時也記住一連串字，有效累積額外的單字詞彙。

現代社會中資訊傳達的速度，已超出我們的想像，繁忙的上班族和學生，難得有有時間靜下心來，慢慢閱讀一篇文章。這本《用 News 英語增進表達力》就是希望能協助您輕鬆強化英文閱讀能力，讓您能在極短的時間內，有效吸收必須的英文資訊。

焦豪洵

編者序

　　很感謝作者於百忙之中撥冗來寫作本書，將紮實且豐富的新聞經驗，用極鍊達的英語撰寫出來。作者與編者都在成書的過程中，尋找對讀者最有切身需要的題材，加以撰述，希望可以讓讀者在一讀本書時，可以一邊訓練語言，一邊陶冶身心。本書的英語用字，在您細讀後就可以發現十分的有學習性，而內文也非常的有啟發性。對於想要增進自己的中英文造詣且對於時事有更通透的了解的讀者，不但透過書中的主題式文章，且因著本書提供的一些可以進一步開放性思考的問題介紹，讓讀者的思想與和人之間的話題與應答，更有想法與開拓性。特別是有時會不知道如何用英語表達一些較困難或較有深度的話題，如何用字與表述，透過閱讀本書，更加培養充分的字彙與新聞性題材的表達能力。讓您要以英語和人進一步溝通時，不再退卻，反倒可以因著有好的預備，讓人刮目相看，將您的英語討論與表達力更進一步的提升，也因而增進您的商務社交能力。請善用本書，讓您的英語可以源源不絕，清楚用英語表達自己的想法。

倍斯特編輯部

目 次 CONTENTS

Part 1　談政治情勢

Part 2　談經貿發展

Part 1 談政治情勢
Talks About Political Situations

Unit　01　梅克爾所領軍的歐盟
（Merkel Displays Leadership in EU）

🖇 巾幗不讓鬚眉

德國首位女性總理（Angela Porothe Merkel）

Angela Dorothe Merkel became chancellor of Germany in 2005, assuming the first female prime ministry in history and a federal leader from East Germany. Following former British Prime Minister, Margaret Thatcher, Merkel now ranks as the most influential female politician in Europe and is called "the Iron Lady of Germany."

梅克爾於 2005 年開始擔任德國史上首位女性聯邦總理，也是第一位出身前東德地區的聯邦總理。梅克爾是歐洲繼英國前首相柴契爾夫人後，最影響力的女性政治家暨領導人，也有人稱之為「德國鐵娘子」。

成長背景（Growth Background）

Merkel was born on July 17, 1954 in Hamburg with the full name of Angela Dorothea Kasner. "Merkel" is the surname of her first husband while it is still kept after divorced. Her father was a clergyman of the Lutheran Church. After she was born, the family moved to Templin, about 80 kilometers north from East Berlin, as her father received a new assignment from the church, and Merkel completed her primary education there. She majored in physics at the Carl Marks University in Leipzig (1973-1978) and acquired her Ph.D. in quantum chemistry (1990).

梅克爾 1954 年 7 月 17 日誕生於漢堡，全名安格拉 · 多羅特婭 · 卡斯納（Angela Dorothea Kasner）。梅克爾是她第一任丈夫的姓氏，離婚後保留下來。她父親是一位路德教會牧師，在她出生後不久，由於父親從教會接到新的任命，全家移居東德東柏林以北 80 公里的

Politics

Commerce

Jobs

Sports

Healthy

Society

Career

Life

Templin，她在那裡完成初等教育。她在萊比錫卡爾‧馬克思大學攻讀物理學（1973 年－ 1978 年），之後在科學院物理化學中央學會工作學習（1978 年－ 1990 年），後來取得博士學位，研究領域是量子化學。

Ever since the Berlin Wall was collapsed in 1989, Merkel had devoted herself to the burgeoning democratic movements. She obtained a deputy spokesman post in the new government as East Germany held its first (and also was a final) democratic election by the end of same year. When two Germanys were unified in December of 1990, Merkel served as the minister of women and youth under the cabinet of Helmut Kohl (chancellor, 1982-1998), and she was the minister of environmental protection and nuclear safety in 1994. Merkel chaired the Christian Democratic Union (CDU) of Germany during the period of June 1996 to May 2000. However, Merkel's political career was elevated by Kohl, who once called Merkel as das Mädchen (means little lady in English). Today, several media have even cited Merkel as "Kohl's little lady".
1989 年柏林圍牆推倒之後，她投入到蓬勃發展的民主政治運動中。1989 年底東德第一次（也是最後一次）民主選舉後，她得到新政府一個副政府發言人的職務。1990 年 12 月兩德統一後，她成為科爾內閣中婦女青年部部長。1994 年出任環境和核能安全部長。1993 年 6 月至 2000 年 5 月任德國基督教民主聯盟（基民盟）主席。梅克爾的政治生涯得益於前聯邦總理赫爾穆特 ‧ 科爾的提拔。科爾有一次叫她小姑娘，因此很多媒體也把梅克爾叫做「科爾的小姑娘」。

Joachim Sauer, the second husband of Merkel, owns a Ph.D. degree and is a professor of quantum chemistry at Humboldt University, Berlin. They met in 1981 when Sauer instructed Merkel in her postdoctoral research and formally married until 1998. Merkel entered politics and Sauer continued his scientific researches after Germany was unified, however.

她現任（即第二任）丈夫是畢業並任教於德國洪堡大學博士教授、量子化學家 Joachim Sauer，兩人是 1981 年認識的，當時 Sauer 是她的博士研究生導師。直到 1998 年，兩人才正式結婚。兩德統一之後，梅克爾從政，紹爾繼續科研事業。

總理（Chancellor）

Merkel worries EU is unable to define the common interests in the "future trade war", adding that Europe has realized its purpose of "peace and freedom" with the cold war. "What I think is that Europe has to learn so many things instead of wasting too much energy on others like building an exclusive bike passageway between Portugal and northwestern part of Germany," she laments.

梅克爾擔心歐盟未能定義「未來貿易戰」的共同利益，現在歐洲的冷戰以保持「和平和自由」的目的已經實現。「這就是我認為的，歐洲需要學習很多東西，不是把太多精力放到諸如『要不要在葡萄牙修建與德國西北部相同的自行車專用道』這樣的事情上。」

EU plans to levy punished tariffs on products exported from China as solar energy panel and certain telecommunications products are sold at very low prices and unreasonable. This unfair competition will damage manufacturers in EU eventually. Merkel said that she would exert Germany's economic influences to persuade EU from conducting such punishment, explaining that a trade war with China will bring no benefits to EU. Germany insists that EU and China should negotiate to solve the trade disputes at earliest possibilities.

歐盟近來打算對中國銷歐產品課徵整罰性關稅。太陽能板及部分通訊產品，廉價不合理，不公平競爭傷害歐盟業者。梅克爾說她會運用德國的經濟力量，勸說歐盟不要這樣做。因為與中國貿易戰，對歐盟沒有好處。德國主張歐盟與中國應該盡快協商，化解貿易爭端。

Second only to the U.S., EU accounts for the second largest trade partner of China. EU's two-way trade amount with China totaled € 430 billion in 2012, with solar energy panels representing 7% of China's exports to EU.

歐盟是目前僅次於美國的中國第二大貿易夥伴。去年大陸與歐盟雙邊貿易金額達 4300 億歐元，太陽能板佔中國銷歐產品比重達百分之七。

Meanwhile, Merkel agrees with the change of model regarding volunteered nations joining in EU. "In Germany, we always face the risk of a slower pace. We need to accelerate the speed of reform," Merkel concludes.

另外，梅克爾贊同國家自願參與模式需要變革。「在德國，我們總是面對『總是慢一拍』的危險。我們要加速變革。」

A biography of Merkel was published by the "Blid," a leading media in Germany, revealing that even if CDU wins the parliament election in the autumn of 2013 and Merkel resumes her chancellorship, she may resign in 2015 as she will be over 60 years old and has taken the office for ten years by the date. "The service term of 10 years should be the ceiling for either the chancellor or a federal leader", Merkel once said so to her trusted aides.

德國「畫報」(Blid) 近期已出版梅克爾傳記，書中提及即使基民黨在今年 (2013) 秋天贏得國會勝選，梅克爾續任總理，2015 年她可能請辭。因為 2015 年 7 月 17 日她已年過六旬，也任職總理達 10 年。梅克爾曾經告訴她的親信，不論是擔任總理或聯邦首長，任職 10 年應屬最長期限。

歐盟簡介（EU Brief）

"總有一天，到那時，……，所有的歐洲國家，無須丟掉你們各自的特點和閃光的個性，都將緊緊地融合在一個高一級的整體裡；到那時，你們將

Politics

Commerce

Jobs

Sports

Healthy

Society

Career

Life

構築歐洲的友愛關係……"
　　　　　——維克多・雨果 (Victor Hugo, 1802-1885, French Writer)

Headquartered in Brussels, Belgium, EU (European Union) was developed from European Communities (EC) but has now combined both political and economic entities in an united organization. As of January 2007 when both Romania and Bulgaria were approved to join in EU, the number of member countries has reached 27 covering a total population of over 480 million, and is regarded as the world's most powerful economic entity in a single region.

總部設在比利時首都布魯塞爾，歐洲聯盟（簡稱歐盟，European Union-EU）是由歐洲共同體 (European communities) 發展而來的，是一個集政治實體和經濟實體於一身、在世界上具有重要影響的區域一體化組織。2007 年 1 月，羅馬尼亞和保加利亞兩國加入歐盟，成為一個涵蓋 27 個國家總人口超過 4.8 億的當今世界上經濟實力最強、一體化程度最高的國家聯合體。

🔗 重要單字暨新聞辭彙（Key Vocabulary & News Glossary）

- Chancellor *(n.)* 總理
- assume *(v.t.)* 擔任
- rank *(v.t.)* 列名
- burgeoning *(adj.)* 蓬勃的
- European Union 歐洲聯盟
- levy *(v.t.)* 課徵
- conduct *(v.t.)* 實施
- trade disputes 貿易糾紛
- volunteer *(n.)* 志願
- biography *(n.)* 傳記
- political ／ economic entity 政治／經濟實體

🔗 單字及句型範例（Vocabulary & Sentence Examples）

1. They ranked high in their class. 他們在班上名列前茅。
2. Los Angeles formed a backbone of the burgeoning movement in the punk history. 洛杉磯成為龐克蓬勃運動史上之支柱。

Politics

Commerce

Jobs

Sports

Healthy

Society

Career

Life

3. A trade dispute between the EU and the U.S. over EU preferences for bananas from former colonies. 在有關歐盟較偏愛前殖民地香蕉方面，歐盟與美國之間爆發了貿易糾紛。

4. He volunteered for the hard and unprofitable job. 他自願作苦差事。

5. Taiwan is the 15th largest economic entity in the world. 台灣名列全世界第 15 大經濟體。

📎 問題與討論（Questions & Discussions）

Q 1. 為何梅克爾是歐洲最具影響力的女政治家及領導人並被稱為德國鐵娘子？試簡述她的成長背景，其成功有何值得世人學習或借鏡之處？

Q.1 Why Merkel now ranks as the most influential female politician and leader in Europe and is called the Iron Lady of Germany? Try to brief her growth background and how can people learn or emulate from her success?

Q 2. 梅克爾有歷練過哪些政府部門主要職務或政黨工作？她在正式成為德國總裡後，媒體上有發表過哪些有關歐盟或德國之重要談話？

Q.2 How many major jobs Merkel has experienced in government agencies or political party in Germany? What important talks about EU or Germany are revealed on media during her chancellorship?

Q 3. 對歐盟組織及現況您有多少認知？

Q.3 How much do you know about EU and its current situations?

📎 主題對話範例（Dialogue Examples）

Example 1

A：I am very interested about Merkel's leadership and influences in Germany and Europe.

B：Merkel is important in the political field, especially her influences in Germany or EU.

Example 2

A：Do you know the growth background of Merkel, the Iron Lady of Germany?

B：Would you like to comment on Merkel's political efforts and achievements after two Germanys are united?

Example 3

A：EU's common interests in the future trade war, for example?

B：Why Merkel objects to build an exclusive bike passageway between Portugal and northwestern part of Germany?

Example 4

A：EU proposes to levy punished tariffs on China's exports. What are your views on the so-called "unfair trade competition" and "harm to manufacturers in EU"?

B：Issues on two-way trade between EU and China, including EU's trade protectionism?

同義字與名詞（Synonym & Terminology）

1. chancellor（總理）⇨ premier ⇨ prime minister
2. assignment（任命）⇨ appointment ⇨ mission
3. spokesman（發言人）⇨ spokesperson
4. unified（統一）⇨ integrate ⇨ unite
5. environment（環境）⇨ conditions ⇨ circumstances
6. levy（課徵）⇨ collect ⇨ impose
7. trade amount（貿易總額）⇨ sum of money in trade
8. change（變革）⇨ transform ⇨ reform
9. biography（傳記）⇨ life story ⇨ memoirs
10. resume（續任）⇨ continue ⇨ proceed ⇨ carry on
11.headquarters（總部）⇨ base ⇨ central station ⇨ main office
12.population（人口）⇨ inhabitants ⇨ people

📎 英譯中練習：（參閱主題文章）

English ⇨ Chinese Translation Practice：(Refer to the theme article)

1. Following former British Prime Minister Margaret Thatcher, Merkel now ranks as the most influential female politician in Europe and is called the Iron Lady of Germany.（英譯中）

   ....

   ....

2. "Merkel" is the surname of her first husband while it is still kept after divorced.（英譯中）

   ....

   ....

3. Ever since the Berlin Wall was collapsed in 1989, Merkel had devoted herself to the burgeoning democratic movements.（英譯中）

   ....

   ....

4. EU plans to levy punished tariffs on products exported from China as solar energy panel and certain telecommunications products are sold at very low prices and unreasonable.（英譯中）

   ....

   ....

5. Headquartered in Brussels, Belgium, EU (European Union) was developed from European Communities (EC) but has now combined both political an economic entities in an united organization.（英譯中）

   ....

   ....

Unit 02 為何全球示威抗議的聲音不斷？
(Why Ever-Growing Protesting Voices in the World?)

📎 一波未平，一波又起

2011 年埃及革命（2011 Egypt Revolution）

The 2011 Egypt Revolution, which was also called "the January 25 Revolution of Egypt", broke out by the people who started a series of demonstrations, parades, gatherings, and strikes on the street as protesting activities against the government. An organization named April 6th Youth Movement assigned the January 25, the date happened to be the policemen holiday, for the beginning of the demonstration.

2011 年埃及革命也稱為埃及 125 革命，是指從 2011 年 1 月 25 日開始的，由埃及民眾所進行的一系列街頭示威、遊行、集會、罷工等抗議活動向政府表達不滿。由於當日正值埃及法定警察假日，所以一個名為 4 月 6 日青年運動的組織選定該日作為示威活動開始的日子。

The protest was most fierce in Cairo and Alexandra and obvious protests also occurred in other cities, attracting over one million people to participate in. They requested President Hosni Mubarak to step down. The protest was the largest of its kind in terms of a democratic demonstration in 30 years after Egypt took place the "Bread Riot" in 1977.

抗議示威活動在開羅和亞歷山大最為激烈，在埃及的其他城市也有明顯的抗議示威活動。超過一百萬人參與了此次抗議，他們要求埃及總統穆巴拉克下台。此次大規模示威成為了自 1977 年埃及發生「麵包暴動」以來近 30 年內發生的規模最大的民主化的示威運動。

The Egypt Revolution was regarded as part of the anti-government

Unit 2　為何全球示威抗議的聲音不斷?　▶

Politics

Commerce

Jobs

Sports

Healthy

Society

Career

Life

protest of the Arabian World during 2010-2011 and took place few weeks right after "the Jasmine Revolution" in Tunisia. Some protestors even brought the national flag of Tunisia as a symbol of its influences. Surrounded by the rude police force, protestors were discontented of Egypt's state emergency law, the lack of free selection, and freedom of speech. They were also unsatisfied against serious political corruptions, high unemployment rate, as well as economic issues such as low wages and high commodity prices.

作為 2010 － 2011 年阿拉伯世界的反政府示威的一部分，此次大規模示威活動在突尼西亞茉莉花革命的數周后開始，部分示威者還攜帶了突尼西亞國旗以作為他們的影響力的標誌。示威者圍繞埃及警察粗暴執法，不滿國家緊急安全法，公民缺乏自由選舉權和言論自由權，政治嚴重腐敗等政治問題以及失業率嚴重，低工資和高物價等經濟問題展開抗議。

Above all, the organizers of demonstration asked President Mubarak to resign his presidency and bring to an end of martial law by the army, as an attempt to gain freedom and justices. Eventually, they hoped to build up a responsible government selected by civilians and let it to handle all resources of Egypt.

示威活動組織者的主要要求包括：要求胡斯尼‧穆巴拉克下台，軍隊結束戒嚴，終止緊急狀態法，獲得自由和正義的權利，組建一個負責任的民選政府，並由他們管理整個埃及的資源。

As of January 29, the protest caused the death toll of 105 demonstrators, leaving at least 750 policemen and 1,500 protestors injured, according to the report. Cairo, the capital of Egypt, was described as a "war zone" together with conflicts and violent incidents continuing in Suez, the port city. Thus, the government imposed a curfew but protestors did not abide by the order, however.

據報導截至 1 月 29 日，至少有 105 名示威者死亡，超過 750 名警察和

1500 名示威者受傷。埃及首都開羅在此次事件中被形容為「戰區」，港口城市蘇伊士一直有衝突和暴力事件發生。政府實行了宵禁，但實際上示威者並不遵守。

Evaluations from the international society were mixed as many nations appealed to a peaceful protest action and expected certain reforms could be performed in Egypt. Most western countries conveyed their concerns about the situation but issued travel warnings and started to evacuate their individual domestic citizens from Egypt at the same time.
國際社會應對抗議活動的評價有好有壞，許多國家均呼籲希望抗議活動能夠和平進行，並希望能進行一些改革。大部分西方國家的政府還對局勢表示關切。與此同時，大多數政府已經發出了旅遊警告，並且開始從埃及疏散本國公民。

Facing the ever-growing pressure from all parties, Mubarak claimed that he himself and his son would not run for the presidential election scheduled in September. Through the national TV station, Vice President Omar Suleimen announced that Mubarak has resigned his presidential duty and handed over his power to Egypt's highest committee of armed force. Egypt held a national referendum on March 19, with the contents covering reforms in presidential election, and agreements of other nine issues, including the presidential election in 2011 or early 2012.
面臨各方越來越大的壓力，穆巴拉克宣布他和他的兒子將不會參與將於九月舉行的重新選舉。2 月 11 日，副總統奧馬爾蘇萊曼透過國家電視台宣布，穆巴拉克已經辭去總統職務並將權力移交給埃及武裝部隊最高委員會。3 月 19 日，埃及舉行埃及憲法修正案全民公決，內容包括總統選舉改革、是否同意今年底或明年初舉行大選等九項議題。

發生背景（Demonstration Background）

Egypt President Mohamed Anwar Sadat was assassinated in 1981 and

Hosni Mubarak succeeded and carried out a half-presidential system, paving the way for Mubarak to become a president that ruled the longest time in Egypt. Together with the National Democratic Party, Mubarak kept the dictatorship and held the nation under the emergency ever since. Thus, Mubarak was criticized as a "pharaoh" of Egypt by media.

自從 1981 年薩達特總統遇刺後，胡斯尼‧穆巴拉克上台，實行半總統制，他也是埃及歷史上執政時間最長的總統。穆巴拉克和他的國家民主黨一直保持著一黨專政制度，並且將國家一直處於緊急狀態。穆巴拉克由於其獨裁統治而經常被媒體和其他批評聲音比做「埃及的法老」。

國家緊急安全法 State Emergency Law

The State Emergency Law of Egypt was enacted in 1967 after the "Six-day War", which happened in June 1967 between Israel and her neighboring nations. With only a short break of 18 months in early 1980s, the management of Egypt was always under the state emergency law, the longest martial law in the world.

埃及國家緊急狀態安全法是在 1967 年「六日戰爭」後頒布的。自 1967 年以來，除了 1980 年代早期有過 18 個月的中斷以外，國家一直處於「緊急狀態法」管理之下（這是世界上最長的一次戒嚴）。

According to the law, the power of police is enlarged but the constitutional rights of citizens are suspended. The censorship of policemen is legalized and the government can put people into detention with an unlimited time in custody. The law also forbids any and unapproved political activities (including street protests) to be conducted by non-government organizations. About 17,000 people were detained and it is estimated that the number of political prisoner reached up to 30,000 persons.

根據這個法律，警察的權力被擴大，公民的憲法權利被暫時終止，警

察的審查被合法化，同時政府可以無理由對個人實施無限期監禁。這
個法律嚴格限定了非政府組織和未經批准的政治組織的活動（包括街
頭示威等活動）。因此導致大約 1.7 萬人被扣押，估計監獄裡的政治犯
更高達 3 萬人。

外交關係 Diplomatic ties

Western governments, including the U.S., believed that the Mubarak
regime was an important ally in the Arabian World. After the war with
Israel in 1967 and 1973, Egypt signed an agreement in the David Camp
of the U.S. in 1978 and reached a peace accord in the second year. This
aroused controversies in the Arabian World, however.

包括美國在內的西方政府認為穆巴拉克政府在巴以和談中是一個重要
的阿拉伯盟友。在 1967 年與 1973 年與以色列爆發戰爭後，埃及於
1979 年簽署了和平條約。埃及在 1978 年簽署了大衛營協議，並且在
一年後簽署了和平條約，這在阿拉伯世界引發爭論。

Both Israel and Egypt received rescues worth billions of U.S. dollars
from the U.S. per year. In addition with the economic assistances, Egypt
was also granted with about US$1.3 billion of military aids from the
U.S. Most Egyptian people, especially the younger generation, said that
the Mubarak served for the western interests instead of interests of local
people.

以色列和埃及每年都會收到來自美國的數十億美元的援助。除了經濟
和發展援助之外，埃及每年還會收到美國約 13 億美元的軍事援助。許
多埃及民眾，特別是埃及的青年人，認為穆巴拉克服務於西方的利益
而不是本國人民的利益。

According to a report, about 40% of people (Egypt's total population
is less than 80 million) earned only US$2 per day in 2010, and most
of people have to rely on food subsidies for their survivals. The basic

Unit 2　為何全球示威抗議的聲音不斷?　▶

Politics

Commerce

Jobs

Sports

Healthy

Society

Career

Life

problem of Egypt results from the unemployment due to its expanded population, the report said.

據報導 2010 年大約 40%（埃及總人口不到 8000 萬）的埃及人生活在每天收入只有兩美元的水平，其中有一大部分人要依賴食物補助而生存。據研究數據，埃及的基本問題在於由於人口膨脹而導致的失業。

2003 年 2 月 15 日全球反戰行動
（Global Anti-war Campaign, February 15, 2003）

Happened on February 15, 2003, the global anti-war campaign mainly opposed the U.S. military coalition in Iraq, attended by all anti-war people around the world on the same day. According to a BBC report, over 60 nations with a total of between six million and 10 million people participated in the protest. Other statistics show that about 8 million and 30 million people were involved in the campaign.

2003 年 2 月 15 日全球反戰行動是反對美國在伊拉克的軍事行動的聯合行動，各國反戰人士約定於同一天發起抗爭。據 BBC 估計有超過 60 個國家，共約 6 百萬至一千萬人參與抗爭，其它方面的估計則達 8 百萬至 3 千萬人之譜。

The largest scaled protest was held in Europe, with about three million persons attending in Rome. This record was ranked by Guinness Book of Records in 2004 as the largest anti-war parade in the world. The war-weariness was high in the Middle East area but its scale was comparably small. In the Chinese world, it is estimated that about 1,000 people attended the protest in Hong Kong, compared with a small scale protest in Macau.

規模最大的示威發生在歐洲。大約有 3 百萬人參加了在羅馬的抗爭，此紀錄被 2004 年金氏世界紀錄大全列為史上最大的反戰遊行。反戰情緒在中東地區達到高峰，但其示威規模較小。在華人世界，香港的示威據估計有 1 千人左右，澳門也有小規模的遊行。

Not any protests were reported in mainland China. In Taiwan, there were only 500 persons protested in front of American Institute in Taiwan (AIT) due to regulations of gathering law are loose and most Taiwanese are apathetic about the anti-war campaign.

中國大陸未發生任何示威；台灣對集會遊行的規定雖然較鬆，卻只有 500 餘人在美國在台協會旁示威，多數民眾仍對反戰運動冷感。

London: The anti-war alliance of Britain initiated the parade in London, claiming that it was the largest parade of its kind in history. Police estimated that about a total of 750,000 people attended the parade while the organization said that there were about two million people. The slogan of parade is "No War in Iraq, Free Palestine".

倫敦：英國的反戰聯盟在倫敦發起遊行，並聲稱這是倫敦史上最大的遊行。警方估計約有 75 萬人，主辦單位則估計有大約 200 萬人。遊行口號為「不要伊拉克戰爭，要巴勒斯坦的自由」。

Canada: There were 70 cities erupted the protest in Canada, with Montreal accounting for the largest scale. More than 100,000 people walked to the street under the temperature of -30℃ .

加拿大：在加拿大的 70 個城市爆發了示威，其中以蒙特婁的示威規模最大，有 10 萬人在零下 30 度的寒冬中走上街頭。

The U.S.: A total of 150 cities held the protest, according to Columbia Broadcasting. In New York, there were about 100,000 people gathered in front of United Nations, including relatives of victims in the 911 terrorists attack. By the end of parade, the number of people was reported to reach between 300,000 and 400,000.

美國：根據哥倫比亞廣播公司統計，在美國共有 150 個城市發生了示威。在紐約，約有 10 萬人集合在聯合國大樓前，其中包括一群九一一襲擊事件的罹難者家屬。在遊行最後，人數達 30 至 40 萬人。

Politics

Commerce

Jobs

Sports

Healthy

Society

Career

Life

Japan: Before the date of the anti-war campaign, 25,000 people attended in Tokyo, compared with abut between 2,000 and 3,000 persons in Seoul, South Korea.

日本：東京在前一天有 25000 人參加遊行。南韓：首爾有 2 千至 3 千人參加遊行。

Iraq: Several tens of thousands people attended a parade in Bagdad and protestors carried posters of President Saddam Hussein and burned the American flag. Some protestors even took along with their rifles. Hussein called the day as "the world's anger day". The military action on Iraq was getting started on March 20, 2003.

伊拉克：數萬名伊拉克人參加巴格達的遊行，遊行者帶著薩達姆・海珊的海報並焚燒美國國旗，許多遊行者也攜帶步槍。薩達姆・海珊稱這天為「世界憤怒日」。對伊拉克的軍事行動於 2003 年 3 月 20 日開始。

✑ 重要單字暨新聞辭彙（Key Vocabulary & News Glossary）

- demonstration (n.) 示威
- assign (v.t.) 指定
- fierce (adj.) 激烈的
- state emergency law
  國家緊急安全法
- corruption (n.) 腐化
- unemployment rate 失業率
- martial law 戒嚴法
- curfew (n.) 宵禁

- coalition (n.) 聯合
- Guinness Book of Records
  金氏世界紀錄大全
- American Institute in Taiwan (AIT)
  美國在臺協會
- 911 terrorists attack
  九一一恐怖攻擊
- United Nations (UN) 聯合國

📎 單字及句型範例（Vocabulary & Sentence Examples）

1. We watched the demonstration from our windows. 我們從窗口看示威遊行。
2. After a fierce battle the enemy was forced to retreat. 激戰之後，敵人被迫撤退了。
3. Unemployment rate projected to pose up to 4.7%. 失業率預估微幅上移到 4.7 個百分點。
4. Police have imposed curfew. 警察實施宵禁。

📎 問題與討論（Questions & Discussions）

Q 1. 2011 年埃及革命如何發生，其主要結果如何？ 總統穆巴拉克因此下臺，對埃及或世界有無帶來任何衝擊？

Q.1　How did the 2011 Egyptian Revolution take place, and what are major consequences? After President Mubarak stepping down, will the revolution bring any impacts to Egypt or to the world?

Q 2. 對於埃及一直處於緊急狀態法管理之下（世界上最長的一次戒嚴），您有何看法？長期實施宵禁是否造成一個國家之政治腐化或失業率也因此而提高？

Q.2　What are your comments on the state emergency law of Egypt, the longest one in the world? Will a long term curfew create corruption or increasing unemployment rate to a country?

📎 主題對話範例（Dialogue Examples）

Example 1

A：Did the 2011 Egyptian Revolution bring real reforms to Egypt?
B：What is the difference between a dictator and a president selected by people?

Politics

Commerce

Jobs

Sports

Healthy

Society

Career

Life

Example 2

  A：Did you participate in any demonstration or protest in the past? Please specify it.

  B：I have experienced demonstration or protest in Taiwan and/or other countries.

同義字與名詞（Synonym & Terminology）

1. protest（抗議） ⇨ object ⇨ dissent
2. assign（指派） ⇨ appoint ⇨ name ⇨ choose
3. fierce（激烈的） ⇨ violent ⇨ raging ⇨ vicious
4. campaign（運動） ⇨ drive ⇨ movement ⇨ crusade
5. coalition（聯合） ⇨ alliance ⇨ league
6. gathering（集會） ⇨ crowd ⇨ party
7. apathetic（冷淡） ⇨ impassive ⇨ unemotional ⇨ unfeeling
8. claim（聲稱） ⇨ demand ⇨ require
9. anger（憤怒） ⇨ wrath ⇨ ire

📎 英譯中練習：（參閱主題文章）

English ⇨ Chinese Translation Practice：(Refer to the theme article)

1. The protest was the largest of its kind in terms of a democratic demonstration in 30 years after Egypt took place the "Bread Riot" in 1977.（英譯中）

  ....

  ....

2. About 17,000 people were detained and it is estimated that the number of political prisoner reached up to 30,000 persons.（英譯中）

  ....

  ....

Unit 03　中國之「一國兩制」
（China's "One Country, Two Systems"）

解讀中國的特殊政治體制

Being a Taiwanese, we must know the "One Country, Two Systems" policy as we stand across the strait and take a broad view of the world. Initiated by Deng Xiao-ping （1904-1997）, former President of the Peoples' Republic of China （PRC）, the policy mainly aims to create a peace unification of China and serves as a basic solution package to tackle with the "Taiwan Issue". Within various political environments in China, the "special administration district" is allowed to build up as an actual government but the original social system in each district should not be interfered. Both Hong Kong and Macau had put into practice of this political system soon after their sovereignty transfers to PRC in 1997 and 1999, respectively.

生為台灣人，對立兩岸，放眼天下，我們必須了解「一國兩制」。此政策最早係由大陸前國家主席鄧小平首先提出，主要目的為實現中國和平統一目標，並針對「台灣問題」之基本解決方案。大陸允許政治環境不同之地區設立特別行政區，對這些地方原有之社會體系等不予干涉。香港和澳門於 1997 與 1999 主權回歸大陸後，已分別實施此政治制度。

The "One Country, Two Systems" policy is based on a "One China" principle and emphasizes that PRC is the only legal government that represents China at the same time. China has now carried out the socialism with Chinese characteristics and a centralized democracy system. However, Hong Kong and Macau have not followed suit the socialism but instead keeping their own capitalisms after the transfer. With the exception of national defense and diplomacy, the above two "special administration districts" can enjoy high autonomies and rights in international affairs. Thus, "Hong Kong people govern Hong Kong, high autonomy" and "Macau people govern Macau, high autonomy".

所謂「一國兩制」乃以「一個中國」為原則，同時強調「中華人民共和國是代表中國的唯一合法政府」。中國大陸實行中國特色社會主義及民主集中制，但是在香港、澳門皆不實行社會主義，主權移交後保持其原有的資本主義。並可以享有除國防和外交外，其他事務高度自治及參與國際事務的權利，稱為「港人治港，高度自治」及「澳人治澳，高度自治」。

Hong Kong and Macau have already practiced the system but the issue between the "China reunification" and "Taiwan independence" is controversial in Taiwan. In 1996, the island conducted its direct presidential election, making it the first time since the Republic of China (ROC) was established in 1912 and the first of its kind in five thousand years that a national leader is elected by people in Taiwan and Chinese regions in the world. Thus, Taiwanese people may not accept the "One Country, Two Systems" policy in the short term period or an expected future.

雖然香港和澳門已實行「一國兩制」，惟台灣民眾在中國統一或台灣獨立的問題上仍意見分歧。台灣在 1996 年開始總統直選，是中華民國建國以來第一次總統、副總統的公民直選，更是台灣與華人地區五千年來首次以民選的方式產生的國家元首。因此，台灣人民在短期間或可預計之未來，應該不會接受或實施所謂「一國兩制」。

歷史沿革 Chronology

Historically, PRC conducted the" One Country, Two Systems" policy during the early period of the nation. Chinese Communists did not touch

the system of farm slavers in Tibet until 1959, for example.
其實中共在建國之初，也實行過一國兩制，即在 1959 年以前他們並不
觸及西藏地方施行的農奴制度。

When the government of ROC moved to Taiwan in 1949, the Communist
Party of China tried to adopt the policy of "liberalizing Taiwan by force.
"In 1956, PRC Central Committee Chairman Mao Ze-dong (1893-1976)
expected to use the "Third Kuomintang-Communist Corporation" to
solve the "Taiwan Issue." Chairman Mao met with Indonesian President
Sukamo in 1961 and remarked the permit to let Taiwan keep its original
social system, the first time in history. "We allow Taiwan to maintain
its original social system and wait Taiwanese to solve this problem
themselves," Mao elaborated. This is the earliest model of "One Country,
Two Systems". In 1963, PRC Prime Minister Zhou En-lai (1898-1976)
summarized the Taiwan policy into the "One Outline, Four Items" policy,
concluding the "One Country, Two Systems" subsequently.
1949 年中華民國政府遷台時，中國共產黨起初採取「武力解放台灣」
的方針。1956 年，中共中央主席毛澤東提出以「第三次國共合作」來
解決台灣問題。1961 年 6 月，毛澤東在與印尼總統蘇卡諾會談時，首
次談及容許台灣保持原來的社會制度。他說「我們容許台灣保持原來
的社會制度，等台灣人民自己來解決這個問題。」這就是一國兩制的
最早雛形。之後在 1963 年，國務院總理周恩來將中國政府對台政策歸
納為「一綱四目」，其中已經隱含後來「一國兩制」的意思。

實現狀況與民調 Implementation and poll

Based on a recent poll made by Hong Kong University, people who
trusted the "one country, two systems" represented 54.9%, higher than
39.7% of those who are non-confidenced and the confidence with
the Beijing regime climbed up to 35.4% as of September 2013. The
confidence of Hong Kong people with the future of Hong Kong dropped

Unit 3 　中國之「一國兩制」 ▶

Politics

Commerce

Jobs

Sports

Healthy

Society

Career

Life

to 54.4% at the same time, down from 72.7% recorded in July 1977.
根據港大民意研究計劃的民調顯示，2013 年 9 月，對「一國兩制」信
任者（54.9％）高於不信任者（39.7％）。2013 年 9 月，對北京政府
的信任度回升至 35.4％。香港人對香港前途的信心由 1997 年 7 月的
72.7% 下滑至 2013 年 9 月的 54.4％。

Macau handed over it regime to China on December 20, 1999. Macau
has followed the special district basic law for the "One country, Two
systems" policy.
澳門主權於 1999 年 12 月 20 日移交中國，按《澳門特別行政區基本
法》實行一國兩制。

質疑 Call in question

Despite the "One country, Two systems" is carried out in Hong Kong
and Macau, people questioned that this system has existed in name only.
Many commentaries said that Hong Kong has nominally owned its laws
and speech freedom but obeyed orders from the central government in
Beijing so as to suppress dissidents and tighten up the free speech.
雖然「一國兩制」已名義上在港澳實行，但是也有人質疑「一國兩制」
是名存實亡。很多網路或報章雜誌的評論認為香港名義上有自己的法
律，也有言論和表達自由，但是往往有打壓異見人士和逐步收緊言論
自由的舉動。

Former Republic of China President Lee Teng-hui and Chen Shui-bian
criticized that the "One country, Two systems" policy made Hong Kong
to fall back its democracy, erode its basic human rights, speed up the
hollowing out of local industries, and increase the unemployment rate
sharply. The crux of Hong Kong's political and economic issues lies on
the deprived of its autonomy and subject.
前任中華民國總統李登輝和陳水扁都批評「一國兩制」使香港民主倒

退、基本人權屢受侵蝕、產業空洞化加速、失業率大幅提高。香港政經困境的真正癥結是香港喪失自主性與主體性。

📎 重要單字暨新聞辭彙（Key Vocabulary & News Glossary）

- initiate *(v.t.)* 開創
- peace reunification *(n.)* 和平統一
- the Peoples' Republic of China (PRC) 中華人民共和國
- special district *(n.)* 特別行政區
- socialism with Chinese characteristics 中國特色社會主義
- centralized democracy system *(n.)* 民主集中制
- capitalism *(n.)* 資本主義
- sovereignty transfer *(n.)* 主權移交
- autonomy *(n.)* 自治
- diplomacy *(n.)* 外交
- Taiwan independence *(n.)* 台灣獨立
- Central Committee (of the Communist Party of China)（中國共產黨）中央委員會
- Tibet 西藏

📎 單字及句型範例（Vocabulary & Sentence Examples）

1. The planning department initiated the money-making project. 企劃部開創該項賺錢方案。
2. A true democracy allows free speech. 真正的民主國家允許言論自由。
3. The neighboring country demanded sovereignty over the island. 鄰國要求對該島擁有主權。
4. The new ambassador is highly experienced in international diplomacy. 新外交官在國際外交方面經驗豐富。
5. India gained independence from Britain in 1947. 印度於一九四七年脫離英國獲得獨立。

Politics

Commerce

Jobs

Sports

Healthy

Society

Career

Life

📎 問題與討論（Questions & Discussions）

Q 1. 您同意中國大陸實施所謂『一國兩制』政策嗎？此制度是否有助於實現中國之和平統一？

Q.1 Do you agree to the "One Country, Two Systems" policy proposed by mainland China? Whether this policy enables to help the peace unification of China or not?

Q 2. 在一國兩制架構下，香港和澳門皆已設置特別行政區，對此您有何看法？

Q.2 Under the framework of "One Country, Two Systems," Hong Kong and Macau have built up individual special administration districts. What is your comment on this issue?

Q 3. 台灣人民早已開始正副總統直選，您認為對中國大陸老百姓而言或其他華人地區，這部份有何重要象徵意義？

Q.3 Taiwanese people have started to directly elect the president and vice president by voting. Does this represent any important meanings to people in mainland China or in other Chinese regions of the world?

Q 4. 真有所謂『台灣問題』嗎？您對『台灣獨立』問題有無任何評論或高見？

Q.4 "Taiwan Issue" really exists or not? Do you have any comments or opinions about the "Taiwan independence" issue?

📎 主題對話範例（Dialogue Examples）

A：I think the "One Country, Two Systems" policy of the Communist Party of China only plays as a template to buy off the public.

B：If Taiwan falls into the trap of tactics, mainland China may break its promises after the unification.

A：Why Hong Kong and Macau are supposed to serve as a mirror of peace unification of China?

B：If Hong Kong and Macau become successful with the "One Country, Two Systems" policy, Taiwan may follow suit? Or it is totally impossible to be an option for most Taiwanese people, and your reasons?

A：Your personal observations on Tibet or Dalai Lama?

B：Any comments on Communist Party's "socialism with Chinese characteristics" and "centralized democracy system"?

同義字與名詞（Synonym & Terminology）

1. system（制度）⇨ plan ⇨ design ⇨ scheme
2. target（目標）⇨ object ⇨ goal ⇨ aim
3. solution（解決）⇨ explanation ⇨ answer
4. legal（合法的）⇨ authorized ⇨ permitted ⇨ lawful
5. independent（獨立的）⇨ unconnected ⇨ autonomous ⇨ self-reliant
6. solve（處理）⇨ clear up ⇨ work out ⇨ figure out
7. summarize（總結）⇨ brief ⇨ outline

⬭英譯中練習：（參閱主題文章）

English ⇨ Chinese Translation Practice：(Refer to the theme article)

1. Initiated by Deng Xiao-ping, former President of the Peoples' Republic of China (PRC), the policy mainly aims to create a peace unification of China and serve as a basic solution package to tackle with the "Taiwan Issue."（英譯中）

2. The "One Country, Two Systems" policy is based on a "One China" principle and emphasizes that PRC is the only legal government that represents China at the same time.（英譯中）

....

....

3. Hong Kong and Macau have already practiced the system but the issue between the "China reunification" and "Taiwan independence" is controversial in Taiwan.（英譯中）

....

....

3. Thus, Taiwanese people may not accept the "One Country, Two Systems" policy for the moment or in the short period or an unexpected future.（英譯中）

....

....

4. When the government of ROC moved to Taiwan in 1949, the Communist Party of China tried to adopt the policy of "liberalizing Taiwan by force."（英譯中）

....

....

Politics

Commerce

Jobs

Sports

Healthy

Society

Career

Life

Unit 04　小馬哥需要硬起來？
（President Ma Needs More Political Guts?）

📎 台灣的政治領袖面對很大的考驗

執政能力 Governing Capacities

On May 19, 2012, one day before the inauguration of President Ma Ying-jeou's second term, an opinion surveyed by the United Daily News show that only 23% of Taiwanese people are satisfied with governing capacities of Ma, compared with 22% from the TVBS poll, a new low in recent years. Meanwhile, the percentage of no confidence to the administration team of Ma increased to 53%.

馬英九總統於 2012 年 5 月 19 日連任就職前夕，根據當時聯合報民調顯示，馬英九執政滿意度僅為 23%，TVBS 民調顯示馬英九執政滿意度創下 22% 的新低；另不信任度更高達 53%。

出身背景 Growth Background

Born on July 13, 1950 in Hong Kong, Ma Ying-jeou is a Taiwanese politician and law scholar, and concurrently president of the Republic of China and chairman of ruling party Kuomintang (KMT). Ma is also a representative individual of post KMT civil war generation. He and his parents immigrated to Taiwan in 1951 and completed his law bachelor degree at National Taiwan University, and later obtained law master of New York University and Doctor of Laws of Harvard University.

馬英九（1950 年 7 月 13 日－）是臺灣政治人物與法學學者，也是現任中華民國總統兼執政黨國民黨主席，為國民黨內戰後世代的代表人物。他在香港出生後，於 1951 年隨雙親移民臺灣，日後取得臺灣大學法律學士、紐約大學法學碩士和哈佛大學法學博士。

Politics

Commerce

Jobs

Sports

Healthy

Society

Career

Life

After returning to Taiwan In 1981, Ma soon entered governmental departments and worked in central authorities of KMT. In the past, he served as Minister of Justice, Vice Chairman of Mainland Affairs Committee, Chairman of Research Development Evaluation Committee, Taipei Mayor, and the 4th term KMT chairman, respectively. In 2008, he was elected as president of ROC for the first time and successfully resumed his second term in 2012.

1981 年返回臺灣後,馬英九旋即進入政府部門與國民黨中央工作。曾任法務部部長、陸委會副主任委員、研考會主任委員、臺北市市長、國民黨第四任黨主席等職。2008 年首次當選中華民國總統,並於 2012 年成功連任。

九月政爭(September Political Struggle)

Taipei's political circle played a "raging fire" power struggle in September of 2013. According to a public poll, 51.7% of people believed that the juridical was intervened due to President Ma and KMT struggles. However, 22.7% viewed that the president had displayed his political guts in order to safeguard justice.

2013 年台北政壇正如火如荼上演「九月政爭」,根據最新民調結果顯示,51.7% 的民眾認為馬英九總統是為了政治鬥爭而介入司法。22.7% 則認為馬總統是基於維護正義展現其魄力。

Based on monitoring evidences, the Special Investigation Panel (SIP) under the Supreme Prosecutor Office pointed out that both former Minister of Justice Tseng Yung-fu and Legislative Speaker Wang Jin-ping illegally lobbied a juridical case. In a press conference, President Ma criticized Wang over the scandal. A poll revealed that 41.6% of people conceded that the exposure of the lobbying scandal is a political struggle inside the KMT party. 13.8% attributed the struggle to officials in juridical departments. Another 13.6% agreed that the struggle was a

blow to privileges. However, 31% had not yet declared their positions.
高檢署特偵組根據監聽結果，指出前法務部長曾勇夫與立法院長王金平關說司法案件。馬總統也隨即召開記者會，指責王金平關說。有41.6% 的民眾認為揭發此事，主要是國民黨內的政治鬥爭，13.8% 認為是司法機關的官員內鬥，13.6% 認為是為了打擊特權關說，31.0% 則未明確表態。

President Ma's satisfaction poll was left with only 11% after the struggle, the lowest level since he took office in 2008. Former President Chen Shui-bian (Democratic Progress Party, 2000-2008) recorded a historical low of 10% during the period of "Red Guards" demonstration.
馬英九總統經過這次「九月政爭」後，民調僅剩 11%，這是他自從 2008 年上任以來最低的滿意度，以創下就任來的最低點。幾乎已經逼近前總統陳水扁，在「紅衫軍」時倒扁時期的 10%。

- In an interview with *China Times* as Ma was elected as KMT chairman on Aug. 5, 2005, he claimed that the national position of Taiwan should be as following:
  1. Supports: "Against communists but not against China, against (Taiwanese) independence but not promotion of (China) unification," "No unification talks unless political rehabilitations on the Tiananmen Square Incident are reached", the strait belongs to "One China, Two districts," Taiwan and China are not under the "one-side-one-country or two countries" status but are in a status of "one country, two districts."
  2. Opposes: "Legal-principled Taiwan Independence," "Rectifying the name for constitution," and "the Republic of Taiwan."
  3. Explanation of Taiwan status: Speech freedom
- 2005 年 8 月 5 日，馬當選國民黨主席，接受《中國時報》專訪時稱：
  1. 支持：「反共不反中，反獨不促統」、「六四不翻案，統一不可

Unit 4　小馬哥需要硬起來? ▶

Politics

Commerce

Jobs

Sports

Healthy

Society

Career

Life

談」，兩岸屬「一中兩區」。兩岸「既非一邊一國，也不是兩個
國家」，而是「一國兩區」。

2. 反對：「法理台獨」、「正名制憲」、「台灣共和國」。

3. 解釋台灣現狀：言論自由。

- In a speech delivered on the 2008 presidential inauguration held
in Taipei Little Dome, Ma reiterated the relationship across the
strait: "Three No's Policy," which indicates "no unification, no
independence, no force." Under the framework of ROC constitution,
Taiwan maintains its current status followed by the "1992 Consensus,"
which allows "One China with respective interpretations," Ma added.
However, he opposed to the "One country, Two systems" policy
initiated by China.

- 2008 年 5 月 20 日，在台北小巨蛋舉行的就職慶祝大會，發表就職
演說。再次重申「三不政策」──「不統、不獨、不武」的兩岸關
係，在中華民國憲法架構下，維持九二共識後的臺灣海峽的現狀，
即「一個中國，各自表述」（一中各表），反對中共所提之「一國
兩制」。

- In a TV debate and press conference held for the 2012 presidential
election, Ma clearly stated that the Republic of China is generally
known as Taiwan in the world and Both ROC and Taiwan are nations.
He also took Britain as an example: The United Kingdom of Great
Britain and Northern Ireland is also called the United Kingdom. In this
open occasion, Ma mentioned that "Taiwan is my country" for the first
time.

- 2011 年 12 月 3 日，在第一場 2012 總統大選電視辯論及會後記者會
時，首度明確表明：「臺灣」是為「中華民國」的國家簡稱與國際
通稱，兩者皆是國家，並舉例「英國」為「聯合王國」或「大不列
顛及北愛爾蘭聯合王國」的簡稱與通稱，也是馬英九第一次在公開
場合中提到「台灣是我的國家」。

• President Ma's second term will be ended on May 20, 2016.

• 馬英九總統的第二個任期將於 2016 年 5 月 20 日結束。

對釣魚台問題的看法 Views on Diaoyu (Senkaku) Islands Issues

Commemorating the 60th anniversary of the coming into force of the Treaty of Peace between the ROC and Japan and a seminar held on Aug. 5, 2012, the "East China Sea Peace Initiative" was submitted by President Ma as Taiwan's views regarding issues on Diaoyu (Senkaku) Islands, also known as the Pinnacle Islands. The main idea: self-restraint, and not to raise opposing actions.

1. Suspends controversies; not to give up dialogues and communications
2. Abides by international laws and deals disputes with peace
3. Seeks consensus, planning "the East China Sea Standards of Conduct"
4. Builds up a mechanism for the cooperative development of resources in the East China Sea.

2012 年 8 月 5 日，在「中日和約生效 60 週年紀念特展暨座談會」中提出「東海和平倡議」，主旨為：自我剋制，不升高對立行動。

1. 擱置爭議，不放棄對話溝通
2. 遵守國際法，以和平方式處理爭端
3. 尋求共識，研訂「東海行為準則」
4. 建立機制，合作開發東海資源

After the above remark is made public, most scholars in Taiwan consented to the view, explaining that President Ma's proposal may serve as a graceful way to back out the embarrassing situation among China, the U.S., and Japan. But the opposition DPP doubted that it was a two-faced tactics: to please Japan in one hand and assert Taiwan's sovereignty over Diaoyu Islands in another hand. And all of these moves are political speculations.

談話一出之後，臺灣學者大多表贊同，認為馬的說法是為中國、美國與日本在此僵局中找到了下台階；但在野的民進黨質疑此為兩面手法：一面對外討好日本，另一面又在對內宣示釣島主權，是政治操作。

民調與媒體評論 Opinion poll and media comments

With the topic of "Ma, the bumbler", the Britain-based Economist magazine released a commentary about Taiwan's latest political situation on November 17, 2012. The Associated Press reported that the Ma administration was "amid a widespread perception of administration bungling and personal remoteness." This results in a support rate of only 15%, a new low after Present Ma took the presidency and a "setback for the beleaguered government of President Ma Ying-jeou."

英國經濟學人（The Economist）雜誌 2012 年 11 月 17 日，在網路上刊登一篇關於台灣政情的最新評論，不過標題為「笨蛋，馬英九」。美聯社於 2013 年 9 月 7 日報導由於馬政府被普遍公認的「行政笨拙」及馬英九與人民脫節背離，導致他的支持率僅剩 15％，創上任五年多以來的新低，對已「坐困圍城」的馬政府而言，更是一大挫折。

According to a poll made by the Era TV after the September political struggle, President Ma's satisfaction reached at only 9.2% among 1,039 sampling investigation, a historical low. This reflects that the general public has asked Ma to step down the presidency.

根據年代新聞民調中心於 2013 年九月政爭發生後 9 月 13 日至 9 月 14 日間所做的民調，在 1039 份樣本裡，馬英九總統施政滿意度僅達 9.2％，創歷來新低，反映民眾要求他下台。

✐重要單字暨新聞辭彙（Key Vocabulary & News Glossary）

- poll *(n.)* 民意調查
- Kuomintang (KMT) 國民黨
- political circle 政壇
- struggle *(n.)* 鬥爭
- intervene *(v.i.)* 干預
- Special Investigation Panel 特偵組
- lobbying *(n.)* 關說
- scandal *(n.)* 醜聞
- privileges *(n.)* 特權
- politician *(n.)* 政治人物
- immigrate *(v.t.)* 遷移（入）
- Democratic Progress Party (DPP) 民進黨
- Diaoyu Islands (the Pinnacle Islands) 釣魚島

✐單字及句型範例（Vocabulary & Sentence Examples）

1. The Bank of England had been intervening in foreign exchange markets. 英格蘭銀行對外匯市場進行了干預。
2. Let me reiterate that we have absolutely no plans to increase taxation. 讓我再一次重申我們絕對沒有增稅的計劃。
3. Lobbying a bill through Congress is a common practice in the U.S. 在美國，進行遊說使議案在國會通過是常有的事。

✐問題與討論（Questions & Discussions）

Q 1. 為何馬總統執政滿意度民調近年來一直偏低？政府經營團隊是否出了些問題？

Q.1 Why the poll about President Ma's governing capacity is low in satisfaction in recent years? Are there any troubles with the governmental administration team?

Unit 4　小馬哥需要硬起來? ▶

Politics

Commerce

Jobs

Sports

Healthy

Society

Career

Life

Q 2. 您如何看待國民黨「九月政爭」?馬總統和王金平院長在該事件中
　　表現各為何?

Q.2　How do you evaluate the "September Power Struggle" of KMT? How
　　do you comment on the performance of President Ma and Legislative
　　Speaker Wang Jin-ping?

📎 主題對話範例 (Dialogue Examples)

A：People said that President Ma is incompetent at governing capacities
　　even after his presidency for the second term. Do you agree to this
　　view or not, and why?

B：Do you agree the poll is fair enough to evaluate President Ma's
　　governing capacities? If not, why?

A：Would you like to comment on the "September power struggle" of
　　KMT?

B：Discussions on political struggle of other foreign nations, if possible.

同義字與名詞 (Synonym & Terminology)

1. poll (民調)　⇨ canvass ⇨ survey ⇨ vote ⇨ questionnaire
2. representative (代表)　⇨ delegate ⇨ envoy
3. authority (權力)　⇨ jurisdiction ⇨ dominion ⇨ sovereignty
4. safeguard (保護)　⇨ shield ⇨ screen ⇨ bulwark ⇨ precaution
5. exposure(揭發)　⇨ disclosure ⇨ revelation ⇨ expose
6. reiterate (重述)　⇨ repeat ⇨ recount ⇨ retell

📎 英譯中練習:(參閱主題文章)

English ⇨ Chinese Translation Practice:(Refer to the theme article)

1. In a press conference, President Ma criticized Wang over the scandal.
　　(英譯中)

....

....

Unit 05 歐巴馬 vs. 曼德拉
（Obama vs. Mandela）

🔖 兩位走在世界前線的政治巨人

歐巴馬讚曼德拉激勵全世界 Obama: Mandela inspires the world

President Jacob Zuma of South Africa welcomed the state visit of U.S. President Barack Obama and said that the first African-American president has owned dreams for millions of people in Africa. President Obama praised that former president Nelson Mandela of South Africa has inspired the world. An epochal meeting between President Obama and Mandela was overshadowed by the illness of Mandela in bed, however. President Zuma noted that both Obama and Mandela are the first black presidents in their country, concluding the two presidents have already met each other, historically speaking. He added that both persons have dreams for numerous people in Africa.

南非總統雅各朱瑪歡迎美國總統歐巴馬到訪，他表示美國這第一位非裔總統帶有眾多非洲人民的夢想。歐巴馬則推崇曼德拉激勵了全世界。對於因南非前總統曼德拉臥病而蒙上陰影的此次劃時代訪非之行，朱瑪表示曼德拉和歐巴馬分別是南非與美國的第一位黑人總統，兩人「因歷史而交會」。他說：「你們兩位都帶有眾多非洲人民的夢想。」

South Africa was the second stay of President Obama's visit in Africa, making it the most important trip since he resumed the U.S. president five years ago. During the first term of presidency in 2009, Obama visited Ghana as his first visit to Africa. As mainland China continues to expand its influences over Africa, President Obama is criticized fiercely by outsiders that he has not valued Africa as expected, despite his father came from Kenya.

南非是歐巴馬此次非洲之行的第二站，而這是他將近五年前出任美國

44

總統以來，最重要的訪非之行。第一次是 2009 年造訪迦納，當時是他擔任美國總統的第一任期。由於中國大陸不斷擴大對非洲的影響力，父親原籍肯亞的歐巴馬遭外界嚴厲批評不夠重視非洲。

Earlier, Obama decided not to visit Mandela in the hospital in Pretoria, but he would still meet with the family of Mandela. Zuma said to Obama: "Our talks were held during the illness of the beloved Mandela, who builds up the democracy in South Africa. As I know, he is also your hero." Obama complimented Mandela on his moral courage, citing Mandela as a power to inspire the world.

歐巴馬稍早已決定不去普勒托利亞的醫院探視病情嚴重的曼德拉，但仍將會見曼德拉的家人。朱瑪對歐巴馬說：「我們的會談是在南非敬愛的前總統曼德拉臥病時進行，曼德拉是為南非創建民主的總統。我知道，他也是您心目中的英雄。」歐巴馬今天盛讚曼德拉的道德勇氣，他說，曼德拉是激勵全世界的一股力量。

歐巴馬總統成長背景（Growth Background）

A Democratic Party politician, Obama owns both black and white bloods. He became the first African-American president in 2008, and successfully gained the second term of his presidency in 2012.

美國民主黨籍政治家，第 44 任美國總統，為第一位非裔美國總統，同時擁有黑與白血統。2008 年初次當選美國總統，並於 2012 年成功連任。

Obama was born in Honolulu, Hawaii on Aug. 4, 1961 and spent most of his childhood and teenage in both Indonesia and Hawaii. With a top student honor, he graduated from the Law School at Harvard University in 1991. He was elected as Senator of Illinois in 1996 but failed to run for a seat in the House of Representatives in 2000. He continued his senator work and obtained another success in 2002. After delivering

a keynote speech in a Democratic representative conference in 2004,
Obama became a famous political figure in the U.S.

歐巴馬 1961 年出生於美國夏威夷州檀香山，童年和青少年時期分別在
印尼和夏威夷度過。1991 年歐巴馬以優等生榮譽從哈佛法學院畢業。
1996 年當選伊利諾州參議員。2000 年競選美國眾議院席位失敗，後一
直從事州參議員工作，且於 2002 年獲得連任。2004 年在美國民主黨
全國代表大會上發表主題演講，因此成為全美知名的政界人物。

After Obama held the office, he began to conduct an overall economic
recovery plan of the U.S., including reforms in energy, immigration, civil
medical care, education, and taxes. In military, he positioned to withdraw
troops from both Afghanistan and Iraq. Moreover, he expressed the
goodwill to the Islam World instead of accompanying with forces.

歐巴馬就任總統後全面實施恢復美國經濟的經濟復興計劃，對能源、
移民、公民醫療保健、教育、稅政等領域進行變革；軍事上主張從阿
富汗和伊拉克撤軍，並向伊斯蘭世界表示友善而非以武力相伴。

Meanwhile, President Obama signed an accord "the Prague Treaty"
with Russia as an effort to cut nuclear weapons. The Nobel Committee
awarded him with a peace prize on October 9, 2009.

另外，歐巴馬總統還和俄國簽署削減核武器的《布拉格條約》。2009
年 10 月 9 日獲得諾貝爾委員會頒發的諾貝爾和平獎。

The oil leaking incident happened in the Gulf of Mexico in 2010 was
the most grim challenge for President Obama. In the 57th presidential
election held on November 6, 2012, Obama beat the Republican-
nominee Willard Mitt Romney and successfully resumed his second
term.

2010 年，發生在墨西哥灣的漏油事件使他面臨執政能力的嚴峻挑戰。
2012 年 11 月 6 日，第 57 屆總統大選中，歐巴馬擊敗共和黨候選人羅
姆尼，成功連任。

Unit 5 歐巴馬 vs. 曼德拉 ▶

Politics

Commerce

Jobs

Sports

Healthy

Society

Career

Life

In 2013, President Obama faced the crises in both Egypt and Syria.

2013 年，面臨埃及和敘利亞危機。

納爾遜 • 曼德拉（Nelson Mandela）

Nelson Rolihlahla Mandela was born on July 18, 1918 in Transkei, South Africa. He was elected as the first president of South Africa during 1994-1999 after the country taking effect its parliamentary democracy. Before he was president of South Africa, Mandela was enthusiastic to oppose the racial segregation and posted as a leader of "Umkhonto we Sizwe", the National Assembly of Africans.

納爾遜 • 羅利拉拉 • 曼德拉 1918 年 7 月 18 日生於南非川斯凱，曾於 1994 年至 1999 年間任南非總統，也是透過全面代議制民主選舉所選出的首任南非元首，在他任職總統前，曼德拉是積極的反種族隔離人士，同時也是非洲人國民大會武裝組織民族之矛的領袖。

When Mandela led the anti-racial segregation movement, the court of South Africa convicted him with accusations such as conspiracies to overthrow the government. He was sentenced to prison for 27 years, with about 18 years being jailed in Robben Islands. He was called with a nickname of "Madiba," which is an honor title for the elder member in the family of South Africa. This appellation now becomes the synonym of Mandela.

當曼德拉領導反種族隔離運動時，南非法院以「密謀推翻政府」等罪名將他定罪，曼德拉在牢中服刑了 27 年半，其中有約 18 年在羅本島度過。在南非，他普遍被暱稱為馬迪巴（Madiba），其是曼德拉家族中長輩對他的榮譽頭銜。這個稱謂也變成了曼德拉的同義詞。

After he was released in 1990, Mandela exerted all his strength to lead South Africa's multiple ethnic groups in the transition of democracy. He was highly praised by all works of life, including the quenchers in the past, for his outstanding efforts to end the racial segregation.

1990 年出獄後，曼德拉推動多元族群民主的過渡期，挺身領導南非。
自種族隔離制度終結以來，曼德拉受到了來自各界的讚許，包括從前
的反對者。

Over the past four decades, Mandela received more than 100 awards,
including the remarkable Nobel Peace Prize in 1993. In 2004, the
broadcasting company of South Africa held an election for "SABC3's
Great South Africans," Mandela was elected as the greatest person in
South Africa.

曼德拉在 40 年來獲得了超過一百項獎項，其中最顯著的便是 1993 年
的諾貝爾和平獎。2004 年，南非廣播公司舉辦了最偉大的南非人票選
活動，結果曼德拉被選為最偉大的南非人。

🔗 重要單字暨新聞辭彙（Key Vocabulary & News Glossary）

- state visit 國事訪問
- inspire *(v.t.)* 激勵
- African-American 非裔美國人
- praise *(v.t.)* 讚美
- epochal *(adj.)* 劃時代的
- overshadow *(v.t.)* 投上陰影
- senator 參議院議員
- the House of Representatives 眾議院
- keynote speech 專題演講
- parliamentary democracy 代議制度
- racial segregation 種族隔離
- Nobel Peace Prize 諾貝爾和平獎

🔗 單字及句型範例（Vocabulary & Sentence Examples）

1. The publishers praised his novel pretty highly.
   出版商們對他的小說評價甚高。
2. Her new book will overshadow all her earlier ones.
   她的新書將會使她以前寫的書都黯然失色。

📎 問題與討論（Questions & Discussions）

Q 1. 歐巴馬與曼德拉之成就帶給世人有何啟發，對美國及南非有何重要影響？

Q.1　What inspirations to people regarding the success achieved by President Obama and Mandela and their important affections on the U.S. and South Africa?

📎 主題對話範例（Dialogue Examples）

A：Up to now, President Obama has visited Africa by only twice. What are the U.S. interests in Africa?

B：People said that President Obama has paid less attention to Africa than expected, compared with mainland China. The competition of the two superpowers in Africa and its future trend?

同義字與名詞（Synonym & Terminology）

1. influence（影響）　⇨ sway ⇨ affect ⇨ move
2. leader（領袖）　⇨ chief ⇨ head ⇨ doyen ⇨ principal
3. racial segregation（種族隔離）　⇨ segregation between races ⇨ apartheid

📎 英譯中練習：（參閱主題文章）

English ⇨ Chinese Translation Practice：(Refer to the theme article)

1. When Mandela led the anti-racial segregation movement, the court of South Africa convicted him with accusations of conspiracies to overthrow the government.（英譯中）

   ....

   ....

Part 2 談經貿發展
Talks about Economic Development

Unit　01　QE3 救市真有用？

（Does QE3 Really Work?）

📎 QE3 執行得如何呢？

美國聯邦準備理事會 QE 3 政策（QE3 of U.S. Fed）

The Federal Reserve System (Fed) of the U.S. announced the practice of QE3, the third round quantitative easing. Major contents include: to purchase US$40 billion worth of mortgage-backed bonds per month, to continue reverse operations, and to maintain the low interest rate level extending from 2014 to 2015. The U.S. stock market warmly welcomed the announcement with Dow Jones Average closing at an upturn of over 200 points.

美國聯邦準備理事會宣布執行第三輪貨幣量化寬鬆政策（QE3），其主要內容包括：每個月購買機構抵押貸款擔保證券 400 億美元，同時繼續執行扭轉操作，以及延長維持低利率水準的承諾，從原來的 2014 年延長至 2015 年。該措施宣布後，美國股市立即熱烈反應，道瓊指數收盤跳漲逾 200 點。

The Fed Chairman Ben S. Bernanke said that the decision finalized for QE3 was adequate, defending that he was worried about the employment status and Fed's latest policy would lower the unemployment rate. He submitted three points to retort against critics on the policy, including (1.) The Fed purchases only financial assets instead of commodities or labor services. (2.) Low interest rates are unfavorable to depositors, and deposits will be improved if the economy turns to be strong. (3.) The Fed has not triggered the inflation as the commodity price is relatively stable for the moment.

聯準會主席柏南克極力捍衛這個決策的適當性，他表示就業情況讓人深感擔憂，因而 Fed 採取了一項新的政策，盡可能壓低失業率。他並提出三點說明反駁對 Fed 積極政策的批評：(1.) Fed 僅買金融資產，不買商品和勞務；(2.) 低利率對存款人不利，等經濟轉強，存款人的情況就會好轉；(3.) Fed 並未引發通貨膨脹，物價仍相對穩定。

Former Fed economist Catherine Mann said that Fed expects to accelerate the economic growth, especially in the increase of work opportunities but the capability of QE is limited in this regard. Statistics show that two previous QEs injected a fund of US$2.3 trillion in the market, reducing10-year government bond yields by one percentage point and creating about two million jobs. The current scale of QE3 is small but it will create job opportunities. As of the end of August, a total of 12.5 million Americans are still jobless, however.

前 Fed 經濟學家曼恩表示，Fed 希望經濟成長加速，尤其是增加更多工作機會，但 QE 在這方面的能力，實在有限。因為根據資料顯示，前兩次的 QE 總額高達 2.3 兆美元，對市場挹注大量的資金，10 年期公債殖利率因而下降了約 1 個百分點，創造了約 200 萬個工作機會。現在 QE3 的規模較小，雖然也可以多少創造出一些工作機會，但至 8 月為止，美國仍有 1,250 萬人失業。

The practice of QE1 and QE2 led to a sharp currency appreciation and became nightmares for most newly industrialized countries. Financial officials at Brazil once warned that a worldwide monetary war has begun and the government would levy taxes on hot money as a strategy to stop the inflow of mass capitals.

QE1 和 QE2 的執行導致新興工業國家的貨幣大幅升值，也成為新興國家的夢魘。當時巴西財政官員還因此大聲疾呼，全球貨幣戰爭開打了，同時對流入的熱錢採取課徵稅負的措施，以阻止大量資金的湧入。

The New Taiwan Dollar (NTD) followed the appreciation trend to reach 4.43% during the period of QE1, which started in November 2008 and ended in March 2010. And the NTD appreciated by 6.43% when QE2

Politics

Commerce

Jobs

Sports

Healthy

Society

Career

Life

was effective from November 2010 to June 2012. After QE3, Taiwan's exports may suffer as NTD still stands at the high level against the greenback, which is under an environment of continued depreciation.

我國新台幣的走勢也是如此，在 2008 年 11 月至 2010 年 3 月的 QE1 期間，新台幣升值了 4.43％；在 2010 年 11 月至 2011 年 6 月的 QE2 期間，新台幣升值了 6.43％。在 QE3 之後，而且在美元持續走貶的環境下，新台幣恐怕會維持相對高檔的價位，這對於正要全力促進出口的台灣，乃是極為不利的因素。

Generally, QE3 brings hectic trading in international stock markets and is a favor factor to Taiwan's economy. The government and the private sector should upgrade the competitiveness of local industry and keep an eye on the long term impacts of QE3.

QE3 的確帶來全球股市和國內股市的熱絡，對台灣經濟當然是一項利多。政府和民間仍要關注國內產業競爭力的提升並認真看待 QE3 長期帶來的影響，持續發展應有的努力。

何謂「量化寬鬆」（What is Quantitative Easing?）

The quantitative easing (QE) is a monetary policy manipulated by the central bank to increase the money supply and is simplified as an indirect way of printing money. Through certain manipulations in the market, the central bank purchases securities and increases capitals of the banking institutions in the settlement account of the central bank, thus inputting new circulations in the financial system.

量化寬鬆是一種貨幣政策，由中央銀行通過公開市場操作以提高貨幣供應，也被簡化地形容為間接增印鈔票。其操作是中央銀行通過公開市場操作購入證券等，使金融機構在央行開設的結算戶口內的資金增加，為銀行體系注入新的流通性。

Politics

Commerce

Jobs

Sports

Healthy

Society

Career

Life

The "quantitative" means to create certain amount of money as desired, and the "easing" aims to reduce the capital pressure of the bank. By using the increased money, the central bank enables to buy governmental bonds, to lend money to institutions of bank savings, and / or to purchase assets from other banks. All these moves will lessen the earning of governmental bonds and overnight interest rates. Thus, the central bank expects that the banking and financial institutions will be more interested to offer loans for their returned profits and ease the capital pressure in the market.

「量化寬鬆」中的「量化」指將會創造指定金額的貨幣,而「寬鬆」則指減低銀行的資金壓力。中央銀行利用憑空創造出來的錢在公開市場購買政府債券、借錢給接受存款機構、從銀行購買資產等。這些都會引起政府債券收益率的下降和銀行同業隔夜利率的降低,央行期望銀行會因此較願意提供貸款以賺取回報,以紓緩市場的資金壓力。

When the supply of money is easy or the purchased asset (such as treasury bonds) depreciates somewhat due to the inflation, the implementation of QE may make the money be inclined to depreciate. In order to reduce the risk of currency depreciation, the government usually makes the debut of QE in the deflation stage. However, continued QE moves may result in the inflation and worsen it.

當銀根已經鬆動,或購買的資產將隨著通脹而貶值(如國庫債券)時,量化寬鬆會使貨幣傾向貶值。由於量化寬鬆有可能增加貨幣貶值的風險,政府通常在經歷通縮時推出量化寬鬆的措施。而持續的量化寬鬆則會增加惡性通脹的風險。

QE3 即將退場? QE3 to leave market?

The decision-making department of U.S. Fed is now reviewing the economic setback caused by the recent government shutdown. In the first meeting presided over by Chairman Ben Bernanke and his successor

Janet Yellen, the Federal Open Market Committee has decided to wait more evidences of economic momentum are announced.

美國聯邦準備理事會決策部門檢討面對政府停擺的相關資料以及其所造成的經濟倒退。廣泛的共識是，在與聯準會主席柏南奇官方欽定接班人葉倫首次召開的會議中，聯邦公開市場委員會將再度選擇等待呈現經濟力道的更多證據出爐。

The decision expects to extend speculations of the time when QE3 leaves the market. Fed initiated the purchase of bonds with an amount of up to US$85 billion per month but Bernanke declined predictions of market and only promised to take action under the support of economic data.

這將延長有關 QE3 何時開始逐漸退場的揣測遊戲。QE3 是聯準會每月總額 850 億美元的購債刺激經濟計畫。不過，柏南奇審慎拒絕市場的預期，承諾只在有經濟數據支持的情況下才會採取行動。

📎 重要單字暨新聞辭彙（Key Vocabulary & News Glossary）

- quantitative easing (QE) 量化寬鬆
- the Federal Reserve System (Fed) 聯邦準備理事會 (美國央行)
- Dow Jones Average 道瓊工業指數
- labor service 勞務
- percentage point 百分點
- yield *(n.)* 殖利率
- newly industrialized countries (NICs) 新興工業國家
- greenback *(n.)* 美鈔
- appreciation *(n.)* 升值
- depreciation *(n.)* 貶值
- inflation *(n.)* 通貨膨脹
- deflation *(n.)* 通貨緊縮
- hectic *(adj.)* 熱絡的

Politics

Commerce

Jobs

Sports

Healthy

Society

Career

Life

📎 單字及句型範例（Vocabulary & Sentence Examples）

1. The U.S. Fed approved the practice of third round quantitative easing (QE) as its continued efforts to save the market. 美國聯準會同意實施第三輪量化寬鬆，以作為其繼續拯救市場之努力。

2. The appreciation of the dollar against the yen is in your favor. 美元對日元的增值對你有利。

3. I had a hectic day in the office. 我在辦公室裡忙亂了一天。

4. Millions of people were thrown into unemployment. 數百萬人被迫失業。

5. The government did nothing to curb inflation. 政府沒有採取措施遏制通貨膨脹。

📎 問題與討論（Questions & Discussions）

Q 1. 您可否簡單扼要解釋何謂『量化寬鬆』，以及此財經政策所造成之重要影響？

Q.1　Could you briefly explain the meaning of quantitative easing (QE) and the important influences caused by this financial policy?

Q 2. 美國聯邦準備會為何要採取第三輪量化寬鬆政策，此舉對美國經濟有何助益或會引起其他國家之任何財經衝擊？

Q.2　Why the U.S. Fed decided to carry out the third round of quantitative easing (QE3)? Do you think the move may benefit the U.S. economy or incur any financial impacts to other countries in the world?

Q 3. QE3 對未來台灣出口或經濟有何影響？您會建議政府採取哪些應對措施？

Q.3　What are the major impacts of QE3 to Taiwan's exports or its economic performances in the future? What proposals will you suggest to the authorities concerned, if any?

4.　報載 QE3 即將要退場，並將會引起全球經濟各方面之重要影響，對此您有何評論？

Q.4　It is reported that QE3 may soon leave the market and this will incur certain impacts on the global economy in all respects. How do you comment on this matter?

🖉 主題對話範例（Dialogue Examples）

A：The U.S. QE policy is an important financial move and it may also cause unexpected impacts on the world economy in the future.

B：I think the Fed's QE policy is vital to the U.S. economy; at least it works to cut the unemployment rate.

A：Aided by the QE3, the current economy of the U.S. may gain momentum and roll again in its right guideway.

B：What is the importance of U.S. Fed and its policy to the world?

A：The NTD appreciated during the practice of QE1 & 2 and this has affected the competitiveness of Taiwan's exports.

B：The Central Bank of China (CBC) is suggested by local export-oriented manufacturers to depreciate NTD in order to increase their competitiveness in the world market.

同義字與名詞（Synonym & Terminology）

1. announce（宣佈）⇨ proclaim ⇨ broadcast ⇨ report ⇨ state ⇨ declare
2. purchase（購買）⇨ buy ⇨ shop
3. mortgage（抵押）⇨ pledge ⇨ guaranty ⇨ security
4. maintain（維持）⇨ keep ⇨ uphold ⇨ possess
5. extend（延長）⇨ stretch ⇨ lengthen ⇨ increase ⇨ enlarge
6. adequate（適當的）⇨ satisfactory ⇨ sufficient
7. asset（資產）⇨ accounts ⇨ wealth
8. accelerate（使增速）⇨ hurry ⇨ hasten ⇨ quicken ⇨ speed up

🖉 英譯中練習：（參閱主題文章）

English ⇨ Chinese Translation Practice：(Refer to the theme article)

1. The Federal Reserve System (Fed) of the U.S. announced the practice of QE3, the third round quantitative easing.（英譯中）

   ....

   ....

2. Fed expects to accelerate the economic growth, especially in the increase of work opportunities but the capability of QE is limited in this regard. （英譯中）

   ....

   ....

3. After QE3, Taiwan's exports may suffer as NTD still stands at the high level against the greenback, which is under an environment of continued depreciation.（英譯中）

   ....

   ....

4. The government and the private sector should upgrade the competitiveness of local industry and keep an eye on the long term impacts of QE3.（英譯中）

   ....

   ....

Politics

Commerce

Jobs

Sports

Healthy

Society

Career

Life

Unit 02　您今天 Google 了嗎？

（Have you googled yet today?）

🖇 讓生活更加便利的網路世界

Google 谷歌

An U.S.-based multinational high-tech enterprise, Google Inc. endeavors in internet searching, cloud calculations, and advertising technologies. It develops and offers mass internet products and services, and gains profits mainly from its AdWords service.

谷歌公司是一家美國的跨國科技企業，致力於網際網路搜尋、雲端運算、廣告技術等領域，開發並提供大量基於網際網路的產品與服務。其主要利潤來自於 AdWords 等廣告服務。

Google was founded by Larry Page and Serge Brin when both were studying for the science & engineering Ph D. degree at Stanford University. Thus, they are also called the "Google Guys." Established on Sept. 4, 1998 as a private company, Google designs and manages the "Google search engine" and starts to use the Google website beginning in the second half of 1999.

谷歌由當時在史丹佛大學攻讀理工博士的賴利・佩吉和謝爾蓋・布魯共同建立，因此兩人也被稱為「Google Guys」。1998 年 9 月 4 日，Google 以私營公司的形式創立，設計並管理一個網際網路搜尋引擎「Google 搜尋」；Google 網站則於 1999 年下半年啟用。

Google's shares were listed on NASDAQ on Aug. 19, 2004. The official mission of the company is to organize the world's information and makes it universally accessible and useful. But the company's informal slogan is "Don't be evil," which was shouted out by Amit Patel, a company engineer, and supported by Paul Buchheit. Called Googleplex, the headquarters is located at the Mountain View, County of Santa Clara, California of the U.S.

2004 年 8 月 19 日，谷歌公司的股票在納斯達克上市。創始之初，Google 官方的公司使命為「整合全球範圍的訊息，使人人皆可存取並從中受益」；而非正式的口號則為「不作惡」，由工程師阿米特・帕特爾所創，並得到了保羅・布赫海特的支援。Google 公司的總部稱為「Googleplex」，位於美國加州聖塔克拉拉縣的山景城。

It is estimated that Google has managed with millions of servers within its worldwide data centers and processed innumerable searching requests per day, plus the data management of about 24 PB (1PB = 1,000 TB = 1,000,000 GB) users. In addition to the core web searching, Google has spurred relevant businesses such as R&D projects, acquisitions, and joint ventures in order to meet the fast growth.

據估計，谷歌在全世界的資料中心內運營著超過百萬台的伺服器， 每天處理數以億計的搜尋請求，和約二十四 PB 拍位元【1PB = 1,000 TB（百萬兆）= 1,000,000 GB（千兆）】使用者生成的資料。 Google 自創立開始的快速成長同時也帶動了一系列的產品研發、併購事項與合作關聯，而不僅僅是公司核心的網路搜尋業務。

Google offers abundant on-line software services, including cloud discs, Gmail, and social web services such as Orkut, Google Buzz, and Google+. Other products include Google Chrome (web browser), Picasa (picture editing software), and Google Talk (real time communication tool). The Android (operation system) and Google Chrome OS for small notebooks are also available.

谷歌公司提供豐富的線上軟體服務，如雲端硬碟、Gmail 電子郵件，包括 Orkut、Google Buzz 以及 Google+ 在內的社群網路服務。Google 的產品同時也以應用軟體的形式進入使用者桌面，例如 Google Chrome 網頁瀏覽器、Picasa 圖片整理與編輯軟體、Google Talk 即時通訊工具等。另外，Google 還進行了行動裝置的 Android 作業系統以

Politics

Commerce

Jobs

Sports

Healthy

Society

Career

Life

及小筆電的 Google Chrome OS 作業系統的開發。

Alexa, an international well-known web information analyzing company, said that the domain name of google.com had now accounted for the world's largest website in terms of accesses. Google has several domains in other nations, including google.co.in, google.de, and google.com.hk and the access of YouTube, Blogger, and Orkut are ranked within the top 100s.

網站資訊分析網 Alexa 資料顯示，谷歌的主域名 google.com 為全世界存取量最高的站點，除此之外，Google 搜尋在其他國家或地區域名下的多個站點（google.co.in、google.de、google.com.hk 等），及旗下的 YouTube、Blogger、Orkut 等的存取量都在前一百名之內。

搜尋引擎（Search Engine）

"Google Search" is the most important and popular function of Google, serving as the highest usage rate in internet search engine for many nations. According to statistics released by comScore in November 2009, Google represented a search engine market share of 65.6% in the U.S.

谷歌搜尋是 Google 公司重要也是最普及的一項功能，是多個國家內使用率最高的網際網路搜尋引擎。根據 comScore2009 年 11 月公布的市場統計，Google 在美國搜尋引擎市場上佔有率為 65.6%。

Meanwhile, Google provides at least 22 special functions such as synonym, weather forecast, time zone, share price, map, and earthquake, movie, airport, and sports score. Additional services also include conversion table, currency exchange, digital conversion, package tracking, and area code. A language translation service is available, followed by voice and picture searches in 2011.

同時，谷歌搜尋還提供至少 22 種特殊功能，如同義詞、天氣預報、時區、股價、地圖、地震資料、電影放映時間、機場、體育賽事比分等。

Google 搜尋在搜尋與數位相關的訊息時又會有另一些特殊功能：如單位換算、貨幣換算、數位運算、包裹追蹤、地區代碼。同時，Google 也為搜尋頁面提供語言翻譯功能。2011 年，Google 先後推出語音搜尋和圖片搜尋。

Although Google is a favorite to the general public, some organizations issued the voice of criticism. In 2003, New York Times claimed that Google has infringed its copyrights by accessing contents of the newspaper's website, for example. However, the Nevada District Court judged and overthrew the accusation.

儘管 Google 搜尋很受大眾喜愛，但也有組織對它發出批評的聲音。2003 年，紐約時報聲稱谷歌對其網站抓取與形成的快取侵害了網站內容的版權。在這個問題上，內華達地方法院審理了相關的案件，推翻了指控。

📎 重要單字暨新聞辭彙（Key Vocabulary & News Glossary）

- endeavor *(v.i.)* 努力
- internet searching 網路搜尋
- cloud calculation 雲端計算
- found *(v.t.)* 建立
- website *(n.)* 網站
- listed *(adj.)* 股票登記上市的
- NASDAQ 納斯達克股市
- accessible *(adj.)* 可得到的
- innumerable *(adj.)* 數以億計的
- search engine 搜尋引擎
- PB (petabyte) *(n.)* 10 億兆位元
- social web service 社群網路服務
- domain name 域名

📎 單字及句型範例（Vocabulary & Sentence Examples）

1. He endeavored to streamline the plant organization.
   他努力使工廠組織簡化而更有效地運作。
2. The pilgrims founded a colony in Plymouth.

清教徒們在普利茅斯創建了一殖民地。

3. Medicine should not be kept where it is accessible to children.
藥品不應放在兒童容易拿到的地方。

4. There is no website configured at this address.
此網址並未配置任何網站。

5. Police searched everyone present at the scene of crime. 警察搜查了在犯罪現場的每一個人。

6. These names are to be listed in the catalog. 這些名字將列入目錄。

7. innumerable troubles 無數煩惱的事

8. I can't answer your question about photography. It's not in my domain. 我無法回答你有關攝影的問題。我不做那一行。

9. This action infringed the constitution. 這種行為違反了憲法。

10. The publisher sold the copyright on the novel to a movie producer. 出版商將這本小說的版權賣給了電影製造商。

11. Fascism had lawlessly overthrown the democratic government.
法西斯非法推翻了民主政府。

📎 問題與討論（Questions & Discussions）

Q 1. 您覺得 Google 現階段之功能對您有何助益？試想沒有 Google 的世界。

Q.1　Do you think Google's functions are helpful to you, and why? Image the world without Google?

Q 2. 雅虎與臉書在台灣之搜尋引擎市佔率比谷歌高。您認為 Google 在台灣將來會沒落嗎？

Q.2　Google's market share of search engine in Taiwan is lower than that of Yahoo and Facebook Do you think Google will be effete in Taiwan in the future?

📎 主題對話範例（Dialogue Examples）

A：Google is the world's largest leading search engine company and a listed firm in NASDAQ. Did you buy Google shares, and the reason?

B：Google may face the inspection of Antitrust Act of the U.S., just like AT&T or Microsoft which were once asked to separate businesses to avoid the monopolization?

A：Google has become increasingly successful in search engine and prospects are promising.

B：People said that the working environment of Google is so attractive and comfortable to employees.

A：Do you think Google is illegal in accessing information from other websites, especially in the copyright of contents?

B：I think that the official mission of Google is good but its informal slogan is better, and what are your comments on the Google slogan?

同義字與名詞（Synonym & Terminology）

1. endeavor（努力）⇨ strive ⇨ attempt ⇨ try
2. list（名冊）⇨ enumeration ⇨ schedule ⇨ record ⇨ register
3. available（可得到的）⇨ handy ⇨ convenient ⇨ obtainable
4. represent（展現）⇨ exhibit ⇨ show ⇨ demonstrate

📎 英譯中練習：（參閱主題文章）

English ⇨ Chinese Translation Practice：(Refer to the theme article)

1. In addition to the core web searching, Google has spurred relevant businesses such as R&D projects, acquisitions, and joint ventures in order to meet the fast growth.（英譯中）

　　...

　　...

Politics

Commerce

Jobs

Sports

Healthy

Society

Career

Life

Unit 03 巴西未來的行情
（Brazil's Future Market Price）

📎 不容小覷的經貿未來

巴西（Brazil）

Originating its name from the "Brazilwood", the Federative Republic of Brazil is the largest nation in Latin America and owns a total population of about 192 million (2011 statistics) ranking as the No. 5 largest in the world. Aided by plenty of natural resources and sufficient labor forces, Brazil's gross domestic product (GDP) leads Latin America and stands at the sixth place in the world. As Brazil was a colony of Portugal in history, Portuguese represents the official language of Brazil.

國名源於巴西紅木，巴西聯邦共和國是拉丁美洲最大的國家，總人口數約一億九千兩百萬（2011 年統計數字），居世界第五。得益於豐厚的自然資源和充足的勞動力，巴西的國內生產總值位居南美洲第一，世界第六。由於歷史上曾為葡萄牙的殖民地，巴西的官方語言為葡萄牙語。

Brazil accepted over five millions of immigrants from both Europe and Japan during the 19th century and the early period of 20th century and started to be industrialized since 1930s. Brazil moved its capital from Rio de Janeiro to Brasilia in 1960. And a military coup broke out in 1964 and the right-winged dictatorship ruling was ended until 1985.

19 世紀後期到 20 世紀前期，巴西接納了超過 500 萬來自歐洲和日本的移民並於 20 世紀 30 年代開始工業化。1960 年，巴西首都由里約熱內盧遷往巴西利亞。1964 年巴西發生軍隊政變，建立了右翼軍人獨裁統治，直到 1985 年才結束。

Politics

Commerce

Jobs

Sports

Healthy

Society

Career

Life

With a premise of adjusting both financial policies and economic structure, Brazil was granted with a loan of US$41.5 billion from the International Monetary Fund (IMF) in November 1998. The central bank of Brazil announced that the Brazilian Real would no longer be pegged against the U.S. dollar in January of 1999. This depreciation measure was adopted to cope with the sluggish economic growth of Brazil then.

1998 年 11 月，巴西從國際貨幣基金主導的國際援助項目獲得了 415 億美元的貸款，前提是調整財政政策和經濟結構。1999 年 1 月，巴西中央銀行宣布雷亞爾與美元脫鉤。這一貶值措施緩和了當年經濟增長回落的趨勢。

In 2001, the central bank of Brazil used a high interest rate policy to ease the pressure of inflation and its GDP dropped to below 2%. An unbalanced income distribution still indicates the major economic issue of Brazil, however.

2001 年，在主要市場增長放緩，中央銀行採取高利率政策應對通貨膨脹壓力，國內生產總值增長率降至 2% 以下。嚴重的收入分配不均仍然是巴西經濟的主要問題。

新興市場（Newly Emerging Market）

The population serves as an important factor to affect the economic development of the nation. As long as a nation has the huge population and its labor forces in on the basis of rising turn, the nation enables to maintain itself at a high economic growth level, plus high domestic requirements. Brazil now possesses the best economic growth potentials in the world.

人口是影響一個國家經濟發展最重要的因素，只要有勞動人口上升未結束的基礎，和高度內需產值的龐大人口國家，經濟都可以維持在高檔。巴西是目前全球經濟潛力最好的國家。

Brazil's GDP reached US\$2.5 trillion in 2011, exceeding US\$2.4 trillion recorded by Britain to become the sixth largest economic entity in the world. The "Economist" magazine of Britain predicted that Brazil may have the opportunity to surpass France and promote as the top five economic power of the world in 2013.

2011 年，巴西的 GDP 已達 2 兆 5,000 億美元，超越英國的 2 兆 4,000 億美元，成為全球第六大經濟體。英國《經濟學人》雜誌更預估，巴西有機會再 2013 年就可超越法國，晉升為全球前五大的經濟體。

Brazil now enjoys an annual GDP growth rate of 5.4% to reach about US\$12,000. Despite the U.S. subprime mortgage crisis, Brazil's economy soon recovered within six months in 2010. The domestic market requirement accounts for 62% of GDP, a high percentage compared with exports.

巴西的 GDP 年平均增長率達到 5.4％，人均 GDP 現已達到 12,000 美元左右水準。2010 年是美國次級房貸之後的第 2 年，半年內迅速恢復。巴西國內的內需市場有 62%，出口占整體的 GDP 產值比例低。

From the point view of foreign exchange rates, the Brazilian Real maintains a trend of sharp appreciation, and the opportunity is very high as the Brazilian currency will be equal to the value of the U.S. dollar in the near future.

從匯率的角度來看，巴西 Real 匯率長線還有大幅升值的機會，未來巴西幣再度跟美元等價的機率是非常高的。

Brazil's labor force has risen and is expected to maintain the trend until 2025. This, together with huge local consumer market requirements, paves the way for the fast economic growth for Brazil, especially after the subprime mortgage crisis. Judged by the industrial structure criteria, Brazil posts the lowest risk environment for investors in recent years.

巴西的勞動人口上升期非常長，可以維持到 2025 年左右，加上龐大的

Unit 3　巴西未來的行情 ▶

Politics

Commerce

Jobs

Sports

Healthy

Society

Career

Life

內需消費市場，巴西的經濟在次級房貸復甦以後成長會更快速。另綜觀巴西的產業結構，近幾年內應是風險較低的投資環境。

六成巴西人自認處於社會底層 60% Brazilians resign to low life

A recent survey shows that 43% of Brazilians are satisfied with their existing economic performances but 62% of interviewees have resigned themselves to the low life. And 26% believed that the economic trend of the nation would be better.

一項報告指出，儘管 43% 的受訪巴西人對個人經濟現況感到滿意，62% 自認處於社會階層底層。26% 相信國家經濟走勢看好。

Latinobarometro, a non-government organization based in Chile, interviewed 20,204 persons in 18 nations (except Cuba) in Latin America in June this year and 25% replied that their domestic economy was good. Argentina, Nicaragua, and Brazil represented a same proportion of 26%, followed by Equator, with 57%; Uruguay, with 47%; Panama, with 44%; and Chile, with 34%.

智利非政府組織 Latinobarometro 今年 6 月在拉丁美洲 18 國（古巴除外）調查訪問 2 萬 204 人，25% 認為本國的經濟狀況良好；阿根廷、尼加拉瓜與巴西的比例都是 26%、厄瓜多 57%、烏拉圭 47%、巴拿馬 44%、智利 34%。

The survey shows that one third of Latin American people are satisfied with their economy situation, with Brazil standing at a ratio of 43%; followed by Equator, with 52%; Uruguay, with 50%; and Argentina, with 44%. Only 8% of Brazilians confessed that they are in high life, 28% in the middle level, and 62% in low life.

調查指出，1/3 的拉丁美洲人對目前個人經濟現況感到滿意，巴西比例 43%、厄瓜多 52%、烏拉圭 50%、阿根廷 44%。只有 8% 的巴西人自認處於社會經濟階層的高階位置，28% 中階、62% 低階。

📎 重要單字暨新聞辭彙（Key Vocabulary & News Glossary）

- population *(n.)* 人口
- gross domestic product (GDP) 國民生產總額
- immigrants *(n.)* 移民
- military coup 軍事政變
- newly emerging market 新興市場
- foreign exchange rate 匯率
- grant *(vt.)* 授予
- the International Monetary Fund (IMF) 國際貨幣基金

- peg *(vt.)* 釘牢
- sluggish *(adj.)* 緩慢的
- The Economist （英國）《經濟學人》雜誌
- subprime mortgage crisis （美國）次級房貸危機
- risk *(n.)* 風險
- consumer market 消費市場

📎 單字及句型範例（Vocabulary & Sentence Examples）

1. The population of this country rose by 10 percent.
   這個國家的人口增長了百分之十。
2. Canada has many immigrants from Europe. 加拿大有許多歐洲移民。
3. GDP, the total value of all goods and services produced in a country, in one year, except for income received from abroad 國內生產總值。
4. The firm granted him a pension. 公司同意給他一筆養老金。
5. He was ready for any risks. 他準備冒一切風險。

📎 問題與討論（Questions & Discussions）

Q 1. 在金磚四國中（巴西、俄羅斯、印度與中國），巴西咸被認為具有最佳投資環境與最低風險，對此您有何看法？

Q.1 Among the "BRICs" (Brazil, Russia, India, and China), Brazil is regarded the nation posed with the best investment environment and the lowest risk. How do you comment on this view?

Q 2. 您曾經投資過巴西？其成效如何？

Q.2　Have you ever invested in Brazil so far? Could you reveal the results of your investment?

Q 3. 您最近對巴西市場有無新投資計畫？ 有看上哪些標的物？

Q.3　Do you have any new investment projects in Brazil? And what are your targets?

Q 4. 您有無朋友或親戚基於何種原因移居巴西？據您所知，他們在那裡過的好嗎？

Q.4　Do you have any friends or relatives who have immigrated to Brazil, and on what reasons? As your understanding, are the guys living cool in Brazil?

🔖 主題對話範例（Dialogue Examples）

A：Brazil is the largest nation in Latin America and has abundant natural resources, including water and mines.

B：Brazil maintains a stable economic growth rate in recent years, especially in GDP.

A：The investment environment in Brazil is excellent, especially for foreign investors.

B：The Brazilian government adopts an open investment policy and this should solicit more investors in the future.

A：Brazil accepted over five million immigrates from Europe and Japan. Did the policy trigger the dynamic progress of the nation?

B：Brazil still has so many slum housings in the country. Do you think this issue can be solved following its fast economic growth in the future?

Politics

Commerce

Jobs

Sports

Healthy

Society

Career

Life

同義字與名詞（Synonym & Terminology）
1. population（人口）⇨ inhabitants ⇨ people
2. resources（資源）⇨ property ⇨ goods ⇨ possessions ⇨ wealth
3. move（搬動）⇨ lift ⇨ carry ⇨ take ⇨ send
4. grant（授予）⇨ give ⇨ donate ⇨ present ⇨ bestow ⇨ award
5. sluggish（緩慢的）⇨ lethargic ⇨ slow-moving ⇨ inactive
6. promote（晉升）⇨ encourage ⇨ inspirit ⇨ boost ⇨ build up
7. loan（貸款）⇨ lend ⇨ advance ⇨ give
8. risk（風險）⇨ chance ⇨ hazard ⇨ gamble ⇨ venture

英譯中練習：（參閱主題文章）

English ⇨ Chinese Translation Practice：(Refer to the theme article)

1. Aided by plenty of natural resources and sufficient labor forces, Brazil's gross domestic product (GDP) leads Latin America and stands at the sixth place in the world.（英譯中）

....

....

2. Brazil accepted over five millions of immigrants from both Europe and Japan during the 19th century and the early period of 20th century and started to be industrialized since 1930s.（英譯中）

....

....

3. With a premise of adjusting both financial policies and economic structure, Brazil was granted with a loan of US$41.5 billion from the International Monetary Fund (IMF) in November 1998.（英譯中）

....

....

4. The "Economist" magazine of Britain predicted that Brazil may have the opportunity to surpass France and promote as the top five economic power of the world in 2013. （英譯中）

....

....

5. From the point view of foreign exchange rates, the Brazilian Real maintains a trend of sharp appreciation, and the opportunity is very high as the Brazilian currency will be equal to the value of the U.S. dollar in the near future. （英譯中）

....

....

Politics

Commerce

Jobs

Sports

Healthy

Society

Career

Life

Unit 04 **App 令人好愛不釋手**
（Fondling with App）

📎 帶來樂趣且又輕便

「App」到底是什麼？（What is App?）

"App" abbreviates from "application" and originally means the application program or application software. When someone says "A-P-P" to me, it means to use of the "WhatsApp" software, which is a real time and free message service, and has now become increasingly popular in Taiwan.

「App」乃是英文「Application」的縮寫，而「Application」原義是「應用程式」或「應用軟體」。常聽說「A-P-P 給我」是指所謂使用 WhatsApp 即時通的軟體，這款免費簡訊軟體，目前在台灣非常相當受到歡迎。

Any smart phones installed with WhatsApp are able to telex messages free of charges. Thus, when a person mentions: "I am A-P-P chatting with someone"; he or she means the use of "WhatsApp" for talks. Precisely, "App" defines the broad sense instead of only "WhatsApp."

任何智慧型手機只要有裝上 WhatsApp，就可以和朋友免費簡訊。所以說「我跟他用 A-P-P 聊天」就是在用 WhatsApp 聊天。正確來說，「App」是一個廣泛的定義，不是單指 WhatsApp。

As smart phones have become popularized in recent years, the word "App" has started to appear in our daily life as that of the "PC" did decade ago. The software in the PC is all "App." If you purchase a new PC, you may pursue for the use of the best software so as to create the hardware value. The situation is just about the same way in smart phones nowadays.

由於智慧型手機近年來已日漸普及，「App」這個字眼已開始出現在我們的生活當中，就如同十多年前，個人電腦開始普及一般。但電腦中的各種軟體廣義來說也是「App」。當你有了一台新電腦，你都將追求使用好的軟體，讓電腦硬體的存在產生價值，智慧型手機也是如此。

The word "App" covers the application software in smart phones. After you own an iPhone or iPad, you need to find your own "App" to meet requirements. For example, what kinds of "App" are used by office clerks? Use iPhone to listen to music, 10 essential "App" for students, and iPhone photo "App," and so on.

但目前大家講「App」這三個英文字母簡稱，泛指的是智慧型手機內的應用程式。所以購入 iPhone 或者 iPad 後，務必尋求適合自己使用的「App」。例如：上班族該用什麼「App」？用 iPhone 聽音樂囉！，十種學生必備「App」，iPhone 攝影 App 必選！

Presently, all smart phones in the market are available for the use of "App." The so-called smart phone is allowed to install or remove "App," like that of a PC.

目前市場所定義的「智慧型手機」皆可使用「App」。所謂的「智慧型手機」就是一台可以隨意安裝和移除應用軟體「App」的手機，就像電腦那樣。

However, "App" is not convertible to all smart phone brands mainly due to the different use of OS (operation system). Take PC for instance, the Windows system adopts the Yahoo "App", and, accordingly, is not able to install in the iOS system for Apple PC. But if a new version is convertible for the iOS of Mac PC, the Yahoo "App" can be used in Mac PC. The same reason happens in smart phones.

「App」在各廠牌智慧型手機中並不通用，這就牽扯到使用的 OS

（作業系統）是否一樣了。拿電腦來比喻：「Windows 系統」使用的 Yahoo 即時通（App），在蘋果電腦的「iOS 系統」中並無法安裝使用。但若開發出相容於 iOS 作業環境的 Mac 版就可以。手機亦是如此。

智慧型手機「OS」四巨頭 Four Smart Phone「OS」Giants

At present, the four smart phone OS giants are: Apple's "iOS", representing a market share of 27%; Google's "Android", taking a lion's share of 42% (shared by multiple plants); Microsoft's "Windows Mobile", 5.7% (shared by multiple plants); and RIM's "Black Berry", 21% (belonged to Black Berry only). The remaindering 4.3% is shared by Nokia's "Symbian", "Palm", and others.

目前智慧型手機「作業系統」四巨頭為：Apple「iOS 作業系統」，佔 27%（iPhone 專屬），Google「Android 作業系統」，佔 42%（多廠合佔），Microsoft「Windows Mobile 作業系統」，佔 5.7%（多廠合佔），RIM「Black Berry 作業系統」，佔 21%（黑莓機專屬）。其餘 4.3% 由 Nokia (Symbian) 及 Palm 等廠家分佔。

App 專屬銷售平台 App Sales Platforms

Each OS has built up exclusive sales platforms. After the third party develops the "App" software, they will be put in individual platforms for sales, as follows: "App Store" for iOS (Apple), "Android Market" for Google, "Windows Marketplace" for Windows Mobile (Microsoft), "App World" for Black Berry (RIM), and "Nokia Ovi" for Nokia, respectively.

各作業系統均有屬於自己獨立的銷售平台，第三方軟體業者將「App」完成後，就會把它放至其專屬平台販售。目前各家銷售平台如下：iOS (Apple) 為「App Store」，Android (Google) 為「Android Market」，Windows Mobile (Microsoft) 為『Windows Marketplace」，Black Berry (RIM) 為「App World」，以及 Nokia 為「Nokia Ovi」。

Statistics from the non-profited Industrial Economics & Knowledge Center (IEK) under the Industrial Technology Research Institute (ITRI) of Taiwan show that Apple's "App" downloads totaled 10 billion times in 2010. It is estimated that the amount will rise for sharply to 75 billion times in 2014, creating the revenue worth US$580 billion. "App Store" has attracted some 80,000 software developers around the globe and another 20,000 counterparts have ventured into the development of "Android" system.

另外，我國工業技術研院產業經濟與趨勢研究中心統計數字顯示，2010 年蘋果「App」下載次數為一百億次，2014 年，預估將達七五〇億次，營收將達五千八百億美元。蘋果「App Store」目前已經吸引了全球近八萬位軟體開發業者，另一陣營「Android」系統也有兩萬餘人陸續投入應用軟體之開發。

📎 重要單字暨新聞辭彙（Key Vocabulary & News Glossary）

- application program 應用程式
- telex messages 簡訊
- smart phones 智慧手機
- decade *(n.)* 十年
- pursue *(vt.)* 追求
- essential *(n.)* 必備的
- install *(vt.)* 安裝
- remove *(vt.)* 移除
- convertible *(adj.)* 可轉換的
- Industrial Economics & Knowledge Center (IEK)
  產業經濟與趨勢研究中心
- the Industrial Technology Research Institute (ITRI)
  工業技術研院
- venture *(vt.)* 冒險

📎 單字及句型範例（Vocabulary & Sentence Examples）

1. the first decade of the 21st century 二十一世紀最初十年。
2. Hard work is essential to success. 成功必須努力工作。
3. The policemen pursued the bank robbers. 警察追趕搶劫銀行的罪犯。

4. He's going to install an air-conditioner in the house.
   他要在這屋子裡裝冷氣機。
5. She removed the painting to another wall. 她把畫搬到另一面牆上。

📎 問題與討論（Questions & Discussions）

Q 1. 您目前大部分喜愛用哪些 App ？ 這些 App 各方面有何特色，可否分享之？

Q.1　What kind of App you prefer to use for the moment, and could you specify their features or share your experiences in this regard?

Q 2. 您對智慧手機了解有多少，以及您最愛之功能？

Q.2　How much do you understand smart phones, and your favorite functions?

Q 3. 蘋果 iPhone5 已上市，這款新智慧手機應該可支援很多「App」？

Q.3　Apple has already marketed iPhone 5. This new smart phone should support many "Apps" as expected?

📎 主題對話範例（Dialogue Examples）

A：How many kinds of "App" have you used up to now?
B：I prefer to use different "App" for certain purposes.
A：Do you know the difference between OS of smart phones?
B：How many OS platforms are now available in the market?
A：Prospects for the "App" market are bright in the years to come.
B：The market potentials of "App" have attracted so many investors to venture into the business.

同義字與名詞（Synonym & Terminology）
1. application（應用）　⇨ use ⇨ utilization ⇨ employment

Politics

Commerce

Jobs

Sports

Healthy

Society

Career

Life

2. pursue（追求）　⇨ chase ⇨ follow ⇨ seek
3. essential（必備的）　⇨ needed ⇨ necessary ⇨ important ⇨ vital
4. install（安裝）　⇨ place ⇨ fix
5. remove（移除）　⇨ withdraw ⇨ extract ⇨ eject ⇨ expel
6. convertible（可轉換的）　⇨ transmutable ⇨ transformable ⇨ changeable
　　⇨ alterable

📎 英譯中練習：（參閱主題文章）

English ⇨ Chinese Translation Practice：(Refer to the theme article)

1. When someone says "A-P-P" to me, it means to use of the "WhatsApp" software, which is a real time and free message service, and has now become increasingly popular in Taiwan.（英譯中）

....

....

2. As smart phones have become popularized in recent years, the word "App" has started to appear in our daily life as that of the "PC" did decade ago. （英譯中）

....

....

3. "App" is not convertible to all smart phone brands mainly due to the different use of OS (operation system).（英譯中）

....

....

4. "App Store" has attracted some 80,000 software developers around the globe and another 20,000 counterparts have ventured into the development of "Android" system. （英譯中）

....

....

Unit 05 柏南克～美國財政幕後操盤手
（Bernanke ~ U.S. Finance Manipulator）

🖇️大權在握，位高權重

班・柏南克 Ben Shalom Bernanke

Born in Augusta, Georgia, Ben Shalom Bernanke is an American-Jewish economist and chairman of the Federal Reserve System（Fed, the U.S. Central Bank）. He taught in Princeton University for 17 years and acted as Director of the Department of Economics.

出生於美國喬治亞州奧古斯塔・班・柏南克為美國猶太裔經濟學家，也是現任美國聯邦準備理事會（美國中央銀行）主席。他曾在普林斯頓大學任教過十七年，也擔任過該校經濟學系系主任。

In 2002, Bernanke was appointed by President George W. Bush as a board director of Fed and became chairman of the economic advisory committee to President in June 2005. He was nominated to succeed Alan Greenspan as the new Fed Chairman in October 2005. Due to his outstanding performances to help the U.S. tide over its fiercest economic crisis since "the Recession", Bernanke was selected as "Person of the Year" by the Time Magazine in 2009.

2002 年被小布希總統任命為美聯儲理事。並於 2005 年 6 月起任職總統經濟顧問委員會主席。在同年 10 月被任命為下任美國聯邦準備理事會主席，以接替格林斯潘職位。2009 年，柏南克因為帶領美國度過大蕭條以來最惡劣的經濟危機中有傑出之表現，被《時代雜誌》評選為「年度風雲人物」。

時代雜誌年度風雲人物 Person of the Year（Time Magazine）

Bernanke is a famous economist with major researches in monetary

policy and macroeconomics history and is concurrently an academician of the American Academy of Arts and Science and a fellow of the Econometric Society. He published principle of macroeconomics and microeconomics, which are mainly served as the purpose of textbooks.
柏南克身為聞名的宏觀經濟學家，其主要研究興趣： 貨幣政策和宏觀經濟史。他同時是美國藝術與科學學院院士和計量經濟學會會士，編著過《宏觀經濟學原理》、《微觀經濟學原理》等教科書。

Decided by a voting of 70 against 30 on Jan. 28, 2010, the U.S. Senate approved Bernanke to serve another term of office for four years.
美國國會參議院於 2010 年 1 月 28 日以 70 票對 30 票，表決通過確認柏南克連任，任期 4 年。

「量化寬鬆」紓解美國金融危機？（QE Bails out U.S. Financial Crisis?）

Facing a newly emerged "Recession" since 1933, it is a must to keep the market in circulation, thus avoiding an overall collapse of the U.S. economy. To this end, Fed agreed to print more U.S. dollars as an effort to meet the purpose—known as the QE policy.
面對 1933 年來首度可能形成之「大蕭條」，為避免美國經濟全面崩潰，必須保持市場流動性。聯準會並且同意，如果有需要，就可以通過大量印刷鈔票來增加流動性，及目前正實施眾所周知之『量化寬鬆』政策。

However, the 2008 global economic crisis has become a history. As far as the U.S. is concerned, all of its economic indicators, including the employment market, have improved considerably. The spirit of both precise policy and bold action adopted by Bernanke to fight against the crisis is acknowledged by the world.

Politics

Commerce

Jobs

Sports

Healthy

Society

Career

Life

2008 年全球金融危機已成歷史，就美國而言，各項經濟指數及就業市場等也逐漸好轉。柏南克所採取明確政策及果敢行動，襲退逆境，其精神已為世人肯定。

Fed expects to maintain a long term, low interest rate and the basic interest rate will be close to zero even after the unemployment rate declining to the target of 6.5%, said Chairman Bernanke when he attended the National Economists Club and delivered a speech recently. He defended his QE policy and stood at the same front with his successor Janet Yellen.

Fed 將維持長期低利率，甚至在失業率降至目標 6.5% 後，基準利率仍將繼續維持在趨近零水準。柏南克於全國經濟學人聯誼會（National Economists Club）發表演說，強力為超低利率及債券收購計劃等超寬鬆貨幣政策辯護，與即將接棒的現任副主席葉倫（Janet Yellen）站在同一陣線。

失業率降低 保持低利 Maintains Low Interest Rate

When the asset purchasing project of Fed is ended, the interest rate will maintain at a level of close to zero. This low interest rate policy will continue even the unemployment rate has declined to 6.5%, Chairman Bernanke said.

柏南克說：「資產購買計劃結束，聯邦基金利率可能會在相當長一段時間維持趨近零的水準，於失業率降至 6.5% 後，仍持續保持低利率。」

🔖 重要單字暨新聞辭彙（Key Vocabulary & News Glossary）

- manipulator *(n.)* 操盤手
- Federal Reserve System
  美國聯邦準備理事會（簡稱 Fed）
- inaugurate *(vt.)* 就職
- spouse *(n.)* 配偶
- alma mater 母校
- D.S.E. (Doctor of Science in
  Economics) 經濟學博士
- specialty *(n.)* 專長
- Jewish *(adj.)* 猶太人的
- economic crisis 經濟危機
- the Recession（經濟）大蕭條

- person of the year 年度風雲人物
- the American Academy of Arts
  and Science 美國藝術與科學學院
- the Econometric Society
  計量經濟學會
- academician *(n.)* 院士
- fellow *(n.)* 會士
- principle of macroeconomics
  宏觀經濟學原理
- principle of microeconomics
  微觀經濟學原理
- the U.S. Senate 美國國會參議院

🔖 單字及句型範例（Vocabulary & Sentence Examples）

1. the man behind the scenes, the man behind the curtain 幕後黑手
2. He was inaugurated as President. 他正式就任總統。
3. Her specialty is biochemistry. 她的專業是生物化學。
4. They are my fellows at school. 他們是我的同學。
5. The money helped him to tide over a temporary embarrassment.
   那筆錢幫助他解決了暫時的經濟困難。

🔖 問題與討論（Questions & Discussions）

Q 1. 作為美國最高貨幣政策主管機關的舵手，柏南克如何以「量化寬鬆」來解除其經濟危機？

Q.1　As chairman of Fed, how Bernanke used the quantitative easing (QE) policy to tide over the economic crisis of the U.S.?

Q 2. 為避免美國經濟全面崩潰，柏南克認為如果有需要，就可以通過大量印刷鈔票來增加流動性，因此 Fed 決定實施第三輪量化寬鬆政策。對此新最新措施，您有何看法？

Q.2　In order to avoid an overall economic collapse of the U.S., Fed decided to carry out the third round quantitative easing (QE3). What is your comment on this recent decision?

Q 3. 您如何評價柏南克之創意或領導力，尤其他獲選為 2009 年時代雜誌風雲人物？

Q.3　How do you evaluate Bernanke's innovation or leadership, especially when he was selected as Person of the Year by Time in 2009?

Q 4. 聯準會「量化寬鬆」遲早必然會退出．但確定時機不知落在何時以及其後續之影為何？

Q.4　Fed will soon or latter withdraw its QE policy, but what is the right time and future impacts?

📎 主題對話範例（Dialogue Examples）

A：Bernanke used the QE policy to stimulate the U.S. economy, and this financial measure has improved certain economic indicators and the unemployment rate.

B：The Fed announced the QE3 to keep the circulation of the market by printing more U.S. dollars.

A：Bernanke was selected as the Person of the Year by Time. The reason: innovation and leadership.

B：To cope with the economic crisis, the Fed of U.S. adopts the third round of QE.

A：If Fed quits its QE, there will be a panic among people.

B：Bernanke is a hero in QE but the mission is not so perfect as expected.

Politics

Commerce

Jobs

Sports

Healthy

Society

Career

Life

同義字與名詞（Synonym & Terminology）
1. inaugurate(就職) ⇨ begin ⇨ install ⇨ introduce ⇨ launch
2. appoint（任命） ⇨ elect ⇨ nominate ⇨ designate ⇨ choose
3. nominate（指派） ⇨ appoint ⇨ assign ⇨ place, ⇨ designate
4. succeed（接替） ⇨ replace ⇨ supply ⇨ come after
5. outstanding(傑出的) ⇨ important ⇨ great ⇨ eminent
6. performance(表現) ⇨ achievement ⇨ accomplishment ⇨ work ⇨ deed

📎 英譯中練習：（參閱主題文章）

English ⇨ Chinese Translation Practice：(Refer to the theme article)

1. Bernanke was appointed by President George W. Bush as a board
   director of Fed and started to become chairman of the economic advisory
   committee to President in 2002.（英譯中）

   ....

   ....

2. Due to his outstanding performances to help the U.S. tide over its fiercest
   economic crisis since "the Recession", Bernanke was selected as "Person
   of the Year" by the Time Magazine in 2009.（英譯中）

   ....

   ....

3. Bernanke is a famous economist with major researches in monetary
   policy and macroeconomics history and is concurrently an academician
   of the American Academy of Arts and Science and a fellow of the
   Econometric Society.（英譯中）

   ....

   ....

Part 3　談就業趨勢和就業率
Talks About Job Currency

Unit 01 你想創業嗎？
(Your Career Start-Up?)

📎圓自己的一個夢

台灣全球創業週（Taiwanese Global Entrepreneurship Week）

Regarded as the world's largest-scaled social activity relating to career start-ups, the Taiwanese Global Entrepreneurship Week (GEW) is held in November each year, inviting a total of over 120 nations to participate in. Under the guidance of both the Small and Medium Enterprise Administration (SMEA) of the Ministry of Economic Affairs (MOEA) and the Taiwan-based China Youth Career Development Association Headquarters, Taiwan joined in GEW in 2010. All governmental agencies concerned are invited to attend relevant GEW activities, an effort to promote the development of career start-ups in Taiwan.

「全球創業週」是目前全球全球最大創業活動社群，於每年 11 月中舉行，並邀請全世界共有 120 多個國家參與盛會。台灣係於 2010 年正式加入『全球創業週』，此創業活動由經濟部中小企業處指導，並由中華民國青年創業協會總會負責承辦。本活動期間，全台各有關單位均受邀出席，以期共襄盛舉！

Statistics show that Taiwan ranks as the world's first place in terms of the "entrepreneur spirit," which also serves as important drives behind the economic development of the island over the past decades. This "start-up DNA" must be continued and the MOEA decided to keep its cooperation tie with the social network of GEW.

數據顯示，台灣「創業家精神」全球排名第一，也是我國經濟發展的重要命脈。為了讓這個「創業 DNA」能夠延續下去，經濟部決定與全球最大創業活動社群「全球創業週」合作。

In his delivered speech, Vice President Wu Den-yih encouraged career start-ups to hold far sighted views and focus on market demands. "The government will render its full support for career start-ups. This move expects to help them to create the maximum contribution for the country," Wu indicated.

副總統吳敦義於出席「全球創業週」時致詞，勉勵有志創業者要有遠見，並鎖定市場需求，政府一定會給予全力支持。吳副總統表示，「讓創業者創業有成，對國家社會做出最大的貢獻」。

On the theme of "Global Entrepreneurship: A Driving Force in Economy," an International Innovation and Entrepreneurship Forum is also held as an event accompanied with GEW activities. In addition to GEW, experts from the Global Entrepreneurship Monitor (GEM), the International Council for Small Businesses (ICSB), and the Asia Council for Small Businesses (ACSB) are invited to share their international entrepreneurship trends and analyze global economic development factors. All of these moves have aimed at enhancing the entrepreneurial power of Taiwan.

另配合『全球創業週』在台活動，國際創業創新論壇以「全球創業風潮 引領經濟起飛」為專題，邀請來自於全球創業趨勢專家，包括全球創業週 (GEW)、全球創業觀察 (GEM) 、國際中小企業聯合會 (ICSB)、亞洲中小企業聯合會 (ACSB) 等，分享國際創業趨勢，並剖析全球經濟發展之癥結點，以期進一步提升台灣之創業實力。

創業台灣計劃 "Start-Up Taiwan!" Plan

The MOEA has integrated its services for youth career start-ups into a single window beginning in 2013. To this end, a "start-up Taiwan!" plan is initiated to create an excellent start-up environment in Taiwan. Thus, "Let all good start-ups happen in Taiwan".

經濟部於 102 年起，開始整併青年創業輔導服務，打造創業服務單一窗口。共同推動台灣創業服務引擎，優化創業環境，讓所有的創業好事盡在台灣。

Meanwhile, the Small and Medium Enterprise Administration supports to incubate new emerging businesses. Relevant assistances to loans are offered as efforts to promote the growth of career start-ups in Taiwan.

同時，中小企業處也積極鼓 創新育成新興產業。另協助有關資金融通，以持續推動我國創業風氣之成長！

台灣國際文化創意產業博覽會
Taiwan International Cultural and Creative Industry Expo

The Taiwan International Cultural and Creative Industry Expo is another important event connecting with career start-ups in recent years. This event is jointly sponsored by the Ministry of Culture and the General Chamber of Commerce of the ROC. Starting from 2010, the "Taiwan Culture & Creativity Award" is offered to enhance the energy of Taiwan's culture and creativity industry, honor outstanding creative talents, and encourage enterprises to value the importance of innovations. The selected items are introduced in both domestic and overseas sales arenas, thus making the world to see the esthetics of culture from Taiwan.

近年來與國內創業有關之活動，另有「台灣國際文化創意產業博覽會」，係由行政院文化部主辦，及中華民國全國商業總會承辦。本博覽會主要為提升台灣之文創產業能量，拔擢優秀的創意人才，鼓勵企業重視研發創新。並於 2010 年起，拓過「台灣文創精品獎」選拔，藉以拓展海內外市場，並讓全世界看到台灣文化之美。

Companies from different fields of the industry are invited to compete for the award, with which to influence on the market. The spiritual theme of the award extends to "the quality lifestyle of the Chinese people," an

Politics

Commerce

Jobs

Sports

Healthy

Society

Career

Life

attempt to encourage innovations and build up commercial models.
文創精品獎活動招募台灣文創各領域企業參與賽事，以利本獎項持續
建立市場影響力。精神主軸延續定義為「華人優質生活」，持續鼓勵
用心於創新思維、建構商業模式的文創產業。

重要單字暨新聞辭彙（Key Vocabulary & News Glossary）

- start-up *(n.)* 建立
- the Small and Medium Enterprise Administration (SMEA) 中小企業處
- the Ministry of Economic Affairs (MOEA) 經濟部
- entrepreneur(n.) 企業家
- focus *(vt.)* 使集中
- render *(vt.)* 給予
- accompany *(vt.)* 伴隨
- enhance *(vt.)* 提高
- integrate *(vt.)* 使合併
- incubate *(vt.)* 培育
- expo *(n.)* 博覽會
- arena *(n.)* 競爭場所
- innovation *(n.)* 創新

單字及句型範例（Vocabulary & Sentence Examples）

1. start up a new bus company　建立新的公共汽車公司。
2. I can't focus my thoughts today.　今天我思緒無法集中。
3. We are ready to render them assistance.　我們樂意援助他們。
4. He wished her to accompany him.　他希望她陪他。
5. It has been very difficult to integrate all of the local agencies into the national organization.　將所有的地方機構合併為全國性的機構一直非常困難。

⌕ 問題與討論（Questions & Discussions）

Q 1. 您曾參加過台灣「全球創業週」活動嗎，此項活動對您創業是否有幫助？

Q.1　Have you ever attended the Taiwanese Global Entrepreneurship Week (GEW) and will this help you in career start-ups?

Q 2. 您有打算自己創業嗎，有何具體規劃？

Q.2　Do you have any plans of your career start-up?

Q 3.「創業維艱，守成不易」。對此論點您有何看法？

Q.3　"It is easy to start an enterprise but difficult to maintain it." What are your views on this argument?

⌕ 主題對話範例（Dialogue Examples）

A：I plan to visit the "Taiwanese Global Entrepreneurship Week (GEW)" this year but I was wondering what I can benefit from the activity.

B："Better be a head of a dog than tail of a lion." I would like to take chances for career start-ups, if possible.

A：Customers are important to an enterprise. To locate your customers is important for career start-ups.

B：To start a new business is difficult, especially in soliciting clients and orders.

A：The cultural and creative has become a booming industry in Taiwan.

B：Innovations are important in the cultural and creative industry.

同義字與名詞（Synonym & Terminology）

focus（集中） ⇨ concentrate ⇨ adjust

render（給予） ⇨ give ⇨ present ⇨ grant

integrate（合併） ⇨ amass ⇨ combine ⇨ merge

initiate（發起） ⇨ introduce ⇨ arrange

accompany(伴隨) ⇨ escort ⇨ squire ⇨ esquire
enhance（提高） ⇨ improve ⇨ better ⇨ enrich ⇨ uplift
integrate（合併） ⇨ equalize ⇨ balance ⇨ coordinate

英譯中練習：（參閱主題文章）

English ⇨ Chinese Translation Practice：(Refer to the theme article)

1. Statistics show that Taiwan ranks as the world's first place in terms of the "entrepreneur spirit," which also serves as important drives behind the economic development of the island.（英譯中）

   ....

   ....

2. The government will render its full support for career start-ups. This move expects to help them to create the biggest contribution for the country.（英譯中）

   ....

   ....

3. The selected items are introduced in both domestic and overseas sales arenas, thus making the world to see the esthetics of culture from Taiwan. （英譯中）

   ....

   ....

Unit 02　西班牙和希臘青年就業前景不勝唏噓

（Spain and Greece Sigh in Uncertain Youth Prospects）

📎 畢業即失業的困境

歐債危機（European Debt Crisis）

　Mainly affected by the euro debt crisis, the job opportunity in the labor force market of Spain and Greece had kept declining, making their unemployment rates, especially in the youth sector, to climb up significantly. The two European Union (EU) member countries sighed in uncertain prospects of their young people.

由於歐元區主權債務危機，使西班牙與希臘的勞工市場工作機會持續下降。致使這兩個歐盟國家的青年失業率同時也跟隨著不斷攀升，影響就業前景，令人不勝唏噓。

Latest statistics from authorities show that a total of 6.2 million people in Spain were jobless, or an unemployment rate of 27.2%, as of the end of March, 2013. The figure was a new high in 19 years and ranked it as the No. 1 place among all EU nations. Greece followed next by reaching an overall unemployment of about 27%.

根據西班牙政府最新數據顯示，到 2013 年 3 月底，西班牙總共有 620 萬人失業，使失業率達到 27.2%，為近十九年來最高，在所有歐元區國家中高居榜首。 西班牙的高失業率，在歐洲僅有希臘能與之相比，希臘目前整體失業率也有 27% 左右。

In Spain, the youth with the age of between 16- and 24-year old registered an individual unemployment rate of 57.2%, compared with 34.2% for the youth of between 25- and 34-year old in Greece. The unemployment rate of between 15- and 24-years old skyrocketed to 59.3% in Greece, indicating that over 30% of the youth were unable to get jobs. Thus, many people are concerned about prospects of the youth and it may result in breakout of social impacts.

在西班牙 16 歲至 24 歲之年輕族群中，目前失業率達 57.2%。在希臘，25 歲至 34 歲青年人失業率也有 34.2%，另 15 歲至 24 歲者之失業率更高達 59.3%。顯示以上這些年齡階層中，平均超過三成以上青年沒有就業，許多人也憂慮青年人之就業前景，可能也會因此而爆發另一波社會衝擊。

As the fourth largest economic entity in EU, Spain now enjoys a big and important economic scale than that of Greece. Despite both nations have adopted retrenchment measures to reduce the debt issue, they have suffered losses from budget deficits and the economic stagnation, thus leading to a flow of high unemployment for the youth.

西班牙為歐元區第四大經濟體，其經濟規模較希臘大且重要。惟此二國家苦於預算赤字與經濟停滯，雖然均採取了撙節措施以減緩債務問題，但國加之經濟卻也因蒙受損失，並連帶引發年輕人之高失業潮。

西班牙增加青年就業機會（Spain Adds Youth Employment）

The Partido Popular party of Spain won a landslide victory in the 2012 election and started the practice of several bold and decisive economic measures. Of the major policy, it focused on the promotion of economy, increase of employment opportunities, rebuilding up confidence of consumers, stability of financial markets, thus avoiding structural risks.

2012 年，西班牙「人民黨」贏得大勝取得執政後，開始大刀闊斧執行多項經貿措施。以促進經濟、增加就業機會、重建消費者信心、穩定金融市場及避免潛在性結構危機為其施政重點。

One thing worth mentioning is that the company with staff less than 250 is exempted from the social insurance expenditures if it adds new jobs to hire young employees with the age of under 30, and a 75% of subsidy is offered each for the company with employees over 250. This move, together with other important labor force reforms, expects to lower down the unemployment.

尤其值得一提，針對 250 名員工以下之公司，若新增就業機會聘僱 30 歲以下之青年，免除其雇主應負擔之全部社保費用，250 名員工以上之公司則補助 75%。加上勞動市場一些重要改革，以企盼降低失業率。

Meanwhile, Morgan Stanley predicted that the banking and financial institutions in Spain require an extra capital of 5 billion euro (or about US$6.61 billion) for the bailout, and the amount may enlarge to 16 billion euro (or US$21.15 billion) if it suffers the worst situation. The Spanish government or the European Financial Stability Facility is likely to offer the assistance for this purpose.

另外摩根士丹利預估西班牙銀行業將需要額外的 50 億歐元（66.12 億美元）紓困資金，而如果在最糟之情況下，紓困資金則會擴增至 160 億歐元（211.58 億美元）。西班牙政府或透過歐洲金融市場穩定基金未來將可能提供該項協助。

Spanish belongs to an industrialized nation, occupying a developed market scale. Its GDP (Gross Domestic Product) stood at US$32,000 in 2011.

西班牙屬於已開發的工業國 ，擁有較發達的市場經濟規模。2011 年人均國內生產毛額 (GDP) 約有 32,000 美元。

希臘：貪腐的政府（Greece: A Corrupted Government）

In an investigation conducted by the World Bank regarding the corruption among the world's rich nations, Greece was evaluated as the last place in 16 nations in EU. The Transparency International also

Unit 2　西班牙和希臘青年就業前景不勝唏噓 ▶

Politics
Commerce
Jobs
Sports
Healthy
Society
Career
Life

found out that Greece encountered the most serious corruption among 27 EU member countries, a same situation as that of Peoples' Republic of Bulgaria and Romania.

在一項世界銀行針對富裕國家控管貪腐成效的調查中，希臘在歐元區 16 國敬陪末座。國際透明組的調查也發現，希臘的貪腐情形在歐盟 27 國中最嚴重，與保加利亞、羅馬尼亞不相上下。

The Brookings Institute, a think tank based in Washington D.C., also pointed out that the Greece government lost over 20 billion euro per year, or about 8% of GDP, mainly due to its corruption and briberies. As of February of 2010, Greece owed a total debt of 300 billion euro, which almost triggered an entire collapse of euro in 2011 as other EU nations worried about the debt crisis would incur impacts eventually.

華盛頓智庫，布魯金斯學會的一項研究結果顯示，賄賂、獻金和其他公職腐敗致使希臘政府每年損失 200 多億歐元，相當於希臘 GDP 的 8%。 2010 年 2 月，希臘政府欠債 3 千億歐元，其他歐元區國家擔心希臘的危機會對他們造成重大衝擊，釀成歐洲主權債務危機 ，在 2011 年幾乎導致歐元區瓦解。

People in Greece now must work until 65 years old to apply for the retirement, compared with 50 years old available in the past. Meanwhile, the salary for the government functionary is cut by an average of 12%, plus the reduction of unemployment benefits and relevant welfares.

過去，50 多歲就能退休的希臘人，以後得要工作到 65 歲才可以退休。希臘公務員平均減薪 12%，另外還減少失業救濟金及相關福利。

📎 重要單字暨新聞辭彙（Key Vocabulary & News Glossary）

- sigh *(vi.)* 嘆息
- debt *(n.)* 債
- unemployment rate 失業率
- breakout *(n.)* 爆發
- retrenchment *(n.)* 緊縮
- stagnation *(n.)* 停滯
- landslide victory 獲大勝
- exempt *(vt.)* 免除
- subsidy *(n.)* 補貼

- bail out 紓困
- deficit *(n.)* 赤字
- the European Financial Stability Facility
  歐洲金融市場穩定基金
- corruption *(n.)* 貪腐
- World Bank 世界銀行
- think tank 智庫
- government functionary 公務人員

📎 單字及句型範例（Vocabulary & Sentence Examples）

1. We heard her sigh with relief. 我們聽到她寬慰地歎了一口氣。
2. Landslide, a victory in an election in which one person or party gets a lot more votes than all the others. 一面倒的勝利，（競選中）一方選票佔壓倒性多數。
3. The city is riddled with corruption. 該城腐敗成風。
4. The director of the factory felt no individual responsibility for the deficit. 廠長個人不覺得應對工廠虧損負責。
5. The prospects of the car industry are brightening. 汽車工業前途看好。

📎 問題與討論（Questions & Discussions）

Q 1. 西班牙與希臘的經濟近年情況不佳，是引發其高失業率或其他主因而造成？

Q.1 The high unemployment rate in both Spain and Greece was mainly caused by the poor economic situation in recent years, or by other reasons?

Unit 2　西班牙和希臘青年就業前景不勝唏噓　▶

Politics

Commerce

Jobs

Sports

Healthy

Society

Career

Life

Q 2. 對於歐元區發生主權債務危機，您有何看法？您是否贊成歐盟目前採取的處理方式？試列舉重點說明之。

Q.2　Do you have any comments on the euro debt crisis? Are you agreed or not to the method that EU has handled in the crisis? Try to elaborate your points.

📎 主題對話範例（Dialogue Examples）

A：The high unemployment in both Spain and Greece is a tough issue, and this has related to the youth job opportunity.

B：The future prospects of Spain and Greece are determined on the attitude of how EU handles in the debt issue of the two nations.

A：Will EU give up either Spain or Greece due to their debt issues in the future?

B：I agree that Spain may have the opportunity to recover from its economic difficulties but not Greece, which is riddled with corruption.

同義字與名詞（Synonym & Terminology）

exempt（免除）⇨ free ⇨ release ⇨ excuse

budget(預算）⇨ ration ⇨ allowance ⇨ schedule

high unemployment (lots of people without a job) (高失業率)

📎 英譯中練習：（參閱主題文章）

English ⇨ Chinese Translation Practice：(Refer to the theme article)

1. Mainly affected by the euro debt crisis, the job opportunity in the labor force market of Spain and Greece had kept declining, making their unemployment rates, especially in the youth sector, to climb up significantly. （英譯中）

....

....

Unit 03 台灣 vs. 南韓：
薪資怎差這樣多？

（Taiwan vs. South Korea:

Why the Salary Difference Is So Big?）

📎 值得令人省思之處

南韓月薪 6 萬贏台灣 2 萬 4（South Korea Monthly Salary NT$60,000 Surpasses Taiwan's NT$24,000）

According to a survey made public recently by the career website "Incruit" in South Korea, the social freshman of South Korea has started with an average monthly pay of 27.13 million Korean Won, or about NT$60,000, in the first year. The survey from 104 Manpower Bank showed that Taiwan's new office clerks are paid with about NT$24,000 per month and a pay of between NT$19,000 and NT$25,000 represents a lion's share of about 50%.

根據南韓就業網站 Incruit 最新公布的調查結果顯示，南韓社會新鮮人平均第一年月薪平均為 2713 萬韓元，折合台幣一個月薪資約 6 萬多元左右。而根據 104 人力銀行發表的調查顯示，台灣新上班族每月平均起薪約 2 萬 4 千元，與去年相當。而薪資落在 1 萬 9 千元至 2 萬 5 千元中間，則佔大多數，有 5 成左右。

In South Korea, the price of Starbuck TS coffee is sold at about NT$180 per cup, compared with NT$130 per cup in Taiwan, indicating that the commodity price of South Korea is higher than Taiwan by about 1.4 fold, or an equivalence of NT$40,000 in pay. Over 70% of graduated students in Taiwan are still looking for their jobs up to now, down 12% compared with the same period a year ago.

以南韓一杯星巴克價錢約 180 元台幣，與台灣一杯約 130 元台幣來換算，南韓物價高台灣約 1.4 倍，換算台灣薪資也有近 4 萬元台幣。台灣今年 (2013) 剛畢業的社會新鮮人逾 7 成都還在找工作，不過跟去年同期相比減少了 12%。

South Korea's GDP (gross domestic product) surpassed that of Taiwan beginning in 2005 and is estimated to reach US$21,000 in 2013, far exceeding US$18,000 recorded by Taiwan. Meanwhile, the unemployment stood at about 3% in South Korea, compared with over 6% in Taiwan as of the end of July 2013.

南韓國民年均所得 (GDP) 從 2005 年超越台灣後，預估在今年會突破 2 萬 1 千美元，遠超過台灣的國民年均所得 1 萬 8 千美元；另外，南韓失業率目前約 3%，反觀台灣 7 月份失業率已破 6%。

Latest statistics from the Directorate General of Budget, Accounting, and Statistics (DGBAS) under the Executive Yuan (the Cabinet) reported that the real salary is estimated to reach NT$36,000 per month in Taiwan in 2013, backing toward to the same level 16 years ago, or about 10% less in comparison with 10 years ago. A survey also concluded that the "temporary employee service" has become a major reason behind the low wage situation in Taiwan, making no mention of the "22K salary package" system adopted since the 2008 global financial crisis. And a report from the National Science Council of the Executive Yuan said that the average pay of temporary employee service was paid with only NT$26,800 per month, a curb for a higher pay structure in Taiwan.

主計總處最新統計，今年的實質平均薪資三萬六千元，一口氣倒退回十六年前的水準，還比十年前少六％，更讓人擔憂的是，除了「22K」之外，「派遣」已經成為拉低台灣薪資的主要原因之一，行政院國科會調查派遣平均薪資，只有二萬六千八百元，是另一個箍住年輕人薪水的魔咒。

五十七萬派遣工一勞工界的一群孤兒（570,000 Temporary Workers—A Bundle of Orphans in Labor Force）

Legally, the manpower (brokerage) company does not have to pay any insurance, bonus, and welfares such as days off for temporary workers, or even the fee for the temporary employment service. Those temporary workers do not have any promotion channels or name cards as the manpower company does not "admit" the existing of these employees.
法律上，派遣（仲介）公司不用支付派遣工保險、獎金、休假等福利，甚至資遣派遣工時，要派公司連資遣費都不用出。派遣工也沒有任何升遷管道，他們連名片也沒有，因為公司根本不「承認」有這些員工。

Taiwan's labor force in the temporary employment service increased significantly after the 2008 financial tsunami. Statistics from local scholars and the Council of Labor Affairs revealed that number of temporary workers increased from some 70,000 persons in 2002 to 570,000 persons in 2012, up 700%. The number of temporary workers exceeds the total of 400,000 foreign labors in Taiwan but the work of these temporary employees is not protected, becoming a bundle of orphans in the labor force.
二〇〇八年金融海嘯後，台灣的派遣人力大幅增加。學者及勞委會也統計，臨時性或派遣勞工人數從二〇〇二年的七萬多名，暴增了七倍，到去年的五十七萬名，早就超越外勞的四十萬名，但他們的工作，甚至比外勞更沒保障，儼然成為一群勞工界的孤兒。

政府是最大派遣戶 The Gov't Is Largest User of Temporary Workers

Ironically, the government has become the largest user of temporary workers and paid 30% to 40% wages lower than the private sector, another factor to worsen the salary in Taiwan. The Control Yuan (the watchdog under the constitution of the ROC) surveyed that the Council of Agriculture and its governed agencies hired 2,803 temporary workers, compared with the Ministry of Economic Affairs, 2,433 persons, and the Ministry of Education, 1, 174 persons, ranking as the top three organizations. The whole central government agencies have hired a total of over 10,000 persons as their temporary employees.

不只是民間企業愛用派遣，更誇張的是，政府竟然才是全國最大派遣戶，而且還用低於合理薪資三到四成的超低價，讓台灣的薪資更進一步崩壞。根據監察院前年調查政府派遣勞工問題時發現，農委會及所屬機關派遣勞工達 2803 人、經濟部有 2433 人、教育部有 1174 人，高居各部會前三名。整個中央機關，派遣勞工竟超過萬人。

The ECA International, a human resources supply company in Britain, predicted that Taiwan's salary adjustment range may hit 4% in 2014, a slight growth from 3.5% in 2013. The adjustment rate of Taiwan ranks as the 11th place in the Asia-pacific region and the world's 30th place.

根據英國人力資源分配方案供應商 ECA International 調查指出，預期台灣明年的調薪幅度大約是在 4%，相較於今年的 3.5% 略有增長調。薪幅度在亞太地區排名第 11 名，全球則是排名第 30 名。

重要單字暨新聞辭彙（Key Vocabulary & News Glossary）

- salary (n.) 薪資
- surpass (vt.) 超越
- career website 就業網站
- freshman (n.) 新鮮人
- Korean Won 韓圜
- manpower bank 人力銀行
- a lion's share 大部分
- commodity price 物價
- equivalence (n.) 相等
- exceed (vt.) 超越
- the Directorate General of Budget, Accounting, and Statistics (DGBAS) 主計處
- the Executive Yuan (the Cabinet) 行政院 (內閣)
- 22K salary package system 22K 薪資制度
- the National Science Council 國科會
- tsunami (n.) 海嘯
- the Council of Labor 勞委會
- ironically (adv.) 諷刺地
- the Control Yuan 監察院
- the Council of Agriculture 農委會
- the Ministry of Education 教育部

📎 單字及句型範例（Vocabulary & Sentence Examples）

1. She surpassed her brother in mathematics. 她在數學方面超過了她的兄弟。

2. David got the lion's share of the family's property because he is most be loved by his father. 大衛得到家中大部分財產因為他最受到父親的寵愛。

3. He finally got a job in a company paying good salaries. 他終於在一家薪水高的公司裡找到一份工作。

4. The sales exceeded my expectation. 銷售超過了我的預料。

5. ironically, 讓人哭笑不得的是　　in an ironic way 用諷刺的方式。

6. He is a freshman in the show business. 他在演藝界是一名新手。

7. An average of two students are absent each day.
　每天平均有兩個學生缺席。

8. In Thailand rice is an important commodity for export.
　米是泰國的一項重要出口商品。

9. Mary was graduated from Oxford. 瑪麗畢業於牛津大學。

10. The police estimated the number of demonstrators at about 5,000.
　　警方估計示威者的人數為五千左右。

11. The public demanded a curb on military spending.
　　公眾要求限制軍事開支。

12. To save brokerage fee, he decided to manage his own stocks.
　　為了節約佣金, 他決定自己管理自己的股票。

📎 問題與討論（Questions & Discussions）

Q 1. 南韓和台灣社會新鮮人起薪差太多，您對這件事有何看法？

Q.1 The salary difference of social freshman between South Korea and Taiwan is so big, and how do you comment on this issue?

Q 2. 南韓國民所得比台灣高出許多，此是否意味台灣在整體競爭力已落後南韓？

Q.2 South Korea's GDP has exceeded that of Taiwan, which means the overall competitiveness of Taiwan has lagged behind South Korea?

Q 3. 南韓平均物價也比台灣高，這部份對於南韓上班族是否造成某種程度之壓力，縱使他們之平均所高於台灣之薪水階級？

Q.3 The commodity price of South Korea is higher than that of Taiwan. This has incurred certain pressure for the people of office clerks in South Korea despite they gain much higher pays than their counterparts in Taiwan?

Q 4. 您知道台灣實施所謂 22K 薪資制度？對該項政策您有何評論？

Q.4 Do you understand the "22K salary package system" in Taiwan. What are your comments on this policy?

🖇 主題對話範例（Dialogue Examples）

A：The pay for graduated students in Taiwan is very low for the time being, compared with South Korea.

B：It is difficult for graduated students to find jobs in Taiwan as over 70% are still jobless after graduating from the school, according to latest statistics.

A：The government hires too many temporary employees and this affects the salary structure of Taiwan.

B：The "22K salary package system" seems not a fair policy and it needs to be evaluated soon.

A：Taiwan solicits more tourist than South Korea due to its low commodity prices.

B：The commodity price in Seoul is too high, compared with Taipei.

同義字與名詞（Synonym & Terminology）
1. salary（薪資）⇨ wages ⇨ pay
2. exceed（超越）⇨ surpass ⇨ better ⇨ excel
3. share（分配）⇨ divide ⇨ proportion ⇨ apportion
4. commodity（商品）⇨ product ⇨ ware ⇨ article
5. tsunami（海嘯）⇨ a tidal wave; financial tsunami ⇨ 金融海嘯 (風暴)
6. insurance（保險）⇨ security ⇨ guaranty
7. bonus（獎金）⇨ extra ⇨ premium
8. welfare（福利）⇨ advantage ⇨ benefit ⇨ interest

📎 英譯中練習：（參閱主題文章）

English ⇨ Chinese Translation Practice：(Refer to the theme article)

1. Taiwan's new office clerks are paid with about NT$24,000 per month and a pay of between NT$19,000 and NT$25,000 represents a lion's share of about 50%.（英譯中）

   ....

   ....

2. A survey also concluded that the "temporary employee service" has become a major reason behind the low wage situation in Taiwan, making no mention of the "22K salary package" system adopted since the 2008 global financial crisis.（英譯中）

   ....

   ....

3. Ironically, the government has become the largest user for temporary workers and paid 30% to 40% wages lower than the private sector, another factor to worsen the salary in Taiwan.（英譯中）

   ....

   ....

4. The ECA International, a human resources supply company in Britain, predicted that Taiwan's salary adjustment range may hit 4% in 2014, a slight growth from 3.5% in 2013.（英譯中）

....

....

Politics

Commerce

Jobs

Sports

Healthy

Society

Career

Life

Unit 04 綠能事業新天地
（Green Energy Business——A Brand New World）

📎 極富潛力的新興產業

台灣「綠能產業」 Green Energy Industry in Taiwan

As part of efforts to promote a "rising green energy industry" in Taiwan, the Bureau of Energy of the Ministry of Economic Affairs has selected seven items, including solar cells, LED photonics, wind power generation, bio-fuels, hydrogen power and fuel cells, energy information/communications, and electric vehicles as strategic sectors to offer vital assistances since 2009. This project leads the local green industry to a low-carbon and high value-added development and aims at transforming Taiwan into a major green energy nation in the world.

經濟部能源局於 2009 年起推動的「綠能產業旭升方案」中，即選定七項綠能產業重點輔導，包括太陽光電、LED 光電照明、風力發電、生質燃料、氫能與燃料電池、能源資通訊與電動車輛。此計畫目標希望引領台灣產業朝向低碳與高值化發展，使我國列入世界之綠色能源產業大國。

Based on the proposal, Taiwan expects to be a green energy technology and production nation within 10 years and ranks as the world's third largest manufacturer in solar cells and the world's largest supplier in both LED modules and wind power electrical system. Taiwan turned out NT$414.9 billion worth of green energy products in 2011, with solar cells and LED representing significant market shares in the world.

此計畫目標在於 10 年內將台灣打造成為一綠能源技術與生產大國，並成為全球前三大太陽電池生產大國、全球最大 LED 光源及模組供應國以及全球風力發電系統之供應商。目前台灣的綠能產業，於 2011 年產值約達 4,149 億元，太陽光電、LED 照明光電等產業已在全球市場具顯著比重。

According to the *2011 annual report on world competitiveness* released by the Lausanne International Institute for Management Development of Switzerland, Taiwan enables to employ its green technology potentials to create the global competitiveness and is evaluated the 11th place in the world. This indicates that Taiwan's green energy industry has obtained the international acknowledgement and the world competitiveness.
根據瑞士洛桑國際管理學院「2011 世界競爭力年報」中，台灣在各國運用綠色科技創造競爭優勢的潛力評比排名全球第十一。顯示台灣綠能產業已獲國際肯定具全球競爭力。

In a wide sense, those industries that offer products or services to conserve energy and reduce carbon emissions are categorized as the green industry. It can be divided into major sectors, as follows:
- Low-carbon energy (hydrogen fuel cell production and nuclear power generation)
- Renewable energy (solar, wind, hydro- , and marine power generation)
- Energy conservation and carbon reduction (replacement, refitting and renovation of materials; energy-saving equipment)
- Greenhouse gas reduction (recycling, re-usage and storage of greenhouse gases)
- Management of energy conservation and carbon reduction (carbon-asset management and consultation; inspection and certification of energy conservation)

廣義上，凡是所生產的產品或提供的服務能達到節能減碳效益者，都可歸屬於綠色產業。主要範疇涵蓋低碳能源產業（如：氫能燃料電池產業、核能產業）、再生能源產業（如：太陽能產業、風力發電產業、水力發電產業、海洋能產業等）、節能減碳產業（如：材料替換或改裝、節能設備等）、溫室氣體減量產業（如：溫室氣體回收再利用產業、溫室氣體封存產業）與節能減碳管理產業（如碳資產管理顧問產業、節能驗證產業等）。

Despite both LED and solar cells are facing the challenge of oversupply in the world's green energy marketplace, the government is still optimistic about the two sectors. To this end, a project for the production value of NT$1.15 trillion in 2015 has been submitted recently.
儘管 LED、太陽能產業正面臨全球產能供過於求的嚴峻挑戰，不過政府部門仍對這兩大產業抱以厚望。另已提出 2015 年產值挑戰新台幣 1.15 兆元的目標。

Taiwan's green industry has now focused on solar cells and LED, with solar cells taking a share of 48.7% out of the total production value; and LED, with 46% in 2011, respectively. Solar cells enjoyed a highest growth rate of 93% and LED, with 73% in 2010. As the market was not so booming as expected, the growth rate dropped slightly in 2011.
台灣綠能產業以太陽光電與 LED 照明光電為主，在 100 年以太陽光電與 LED 照明光電為最多，分別佔總產值之 48.7% 與 46.0%。各綠能產業之產值趨勢為逐年增加，其中以 99 年增加之幅度最大，太陽光電於 99 年成長 93%，LED 亦成長了 73%，而在 100 年由於受市場景氣影響，產值微幅下降。

Besides of the production value contribution, the local green energy industry offers a stable job opportunity to Taiwan at the same time. In 2010, the solar cell industry released a total workforce of over 20,000 persons, compared with LED, with an employment of 30,000 persons. The chain clustered with solar cell industry has recruited over 160 manufacturers and produced 4.3GWp of solar cell products in 2011, second only to mainland China, according to Photon International statistics.
綠能產業除在產值上對台灣有貢獻，在就業上亦提供穩定之工作機會。

2010 年，太陽光電所提供之就業人數超 2 萬人，LED 更達到 3 萬人以上。台灣太陽光電產業整體產業鏈共計有超過 160 家生產廠商投入生產製造，Photon International 統計，台灣太陽電池 2011 年產量達 4.3GWp，居全球第 2 位，僅次於中國大陸。

Meanwhile, the production value of Taiwan's LED components reached NT$186.7 billion in 2011, up 15% from 2010, and is estimated to climb to NT$224 billion in 2012. And its production scale has become the world's top three supply sources.

台灣 LED 元件產業 2011 年產值逾新台幣 1,867 億元，較 2010 年成長 15%，2012 年估計達新台幣 2,240 億元。台灣 LED 元件產業在產能規模上已成為全球前三大 LED 元件供應國。

國際綠能新趨勢 Latest Green Energy Trend in the World

The United Nations Environment Program initiated the "Green New Deal" in 2009 and submitted a green economy transition research in 2011. The UNEP report requested all member nations to appropriate 2% of the global green energy production value (now stands at about US$1,300 billion) for the green energy investment activities.

聯合國環境規劃署 (United Nations Environment Program) 於 2009 年倡議各國推動「綠色新政 (Green New Deal)」。2011 年提出「綠色經濟轉型研究報告」，建議應將全球生產總值的 2% (目前約為 1.3 萬億美元) 投資於綠色投資活動。

The following nations and their policies together with actions in the green energy are worth of much attention:

下列各國的政策與行動特別值得關注：

1. European Union mapped out the "EU Renewable Energy Act" by the end of 2008, designating the co-called "20-20-20" target. It requests

an increase of 20% renewable sources, the reduction of carbon dioxide (CO_2) by 20%, and an upgrade of energy efficiency by 20% in 2020.

1. 歐盟率先於 2008 年底通過「歐盟再生能源法案」，訂立所謂的「20-20-20」目標－於 2020 年前將再生能源提升到總需求量的 20%，同時亦將二氧化碳減量 20% 以及能源效益提升 20%。

2. The U.S. government passed an U.S. recovery and renewable investment act in February 2009, proposing a total investment of US$72.5 billion in the green energy and relevant constructions. It encourages the development of latest green energy and promises to cut the CO_2 emission by 17% in 2020, compared with 2005.

2. 美國政府於 2009 年 2 月通過的「美國復甦及再生投資法案」中，提出 725 億美元於綠能產業和相關建設；並特別獎勵先進綠能技術的開發與量產投資；另外，美國亦在 2009 年底承諾將 2020 年的二氧化碳排放總量比 2005 年減少 17% 的水準。

3. Mainland China expects to become the world's largest wind power generation nation in 2009. For this purpose, it plans to invest 500 billion RMB (Renminbi) in both the green energy industry and environmental protection infrastructures.

3. 中國大陸不但於「可再生能源法」及其長期發展規劃中，大力增加再生能源設立的目標，且於 2009 年成為全世界第一大的風力發電市場；亦在 2009 年的振興經濟發展中投入五千億人民幣於綠能及環保的基礎建設。

4. South Korea set up its own green energy industry strategy in 2009 by investing about 2% of its GDP within five years. It expects to become the world's 7th largest green energy nation before 2020.

4. 韓國在 2009 年訂立的綠能產業策略，明定於五年之內投入 2% 的國民生產總額，以期能夠在 2020 年之前成為全球第七大的綠能產

Unit 4　綠能事業新天地 ▶

Politics

Commerce

Jobs

Sports

Healthy

Society

Career

Life

業強國。

📎 重要單字暨新聞辭彙（Key Vocabulary & News Glossary）

- energy *(n.)* 能源
- solar cells 太陽能電池
- LED (light emitting diode) 發光二極管
- bio-fuels *(n.)* 生質燃料
- hydrogen power 氫能
- electrical vehicle 電動車
- low carbon 低碳
- module *(n.)* 模組
- Lausanne International Institute for Management Development of Switzerland 瑞士洛桑國際管理學院
- competitiveness *(n.)* 競爭力
- appropriate *(vt.)* 提撥
- map out 制定；安排
- carbon dioxide CO_2 二氧化碳
- Renminbi (RMB) 人民幣
- efficiency *(n.)* 效率
- infrastructure *(n.)* 基礎建設

📎 單字及句型範例（Vocabulary & Sentence Examples）

1. Most digital read-outs on laboratory instruments, calculators and watches use LED display. 實驗儀器、計算機、手錶的數字讀出大多是二極光顯示。

2. The city will appropriate funds for the new airport. 該市將撥款建造新機場。

3. He's already mapped out his whole future career. 他對自己未來的事業有了周詳的計劃。

4. These machines have increased our work efficiency many times. 這些機器使我們的工作效率提高了許多倍。

5. The current trend is towards informal clothing. 目前的趨勢是穿著比較隨性。

📎 問題與討論（Questions & Discussions）

Q 1. 台灣政府在綠能產業方面有做哪些努力？對此您有何意見？

Q.1　What efforts have been down by the government regarding the development of green energy industry in Taiwan, and what are yours comments?

Q 2. 未來太陽能及其他能源有可能逐漸取代核能發電？您願意支持並促進該項發展嗎？

Q.2　What if the solar and other energies replaces the nuclear power in the future? Will you support and promote it?

Q 3. 台灣綠能業者，在太陽能發電及 LED 產品方面，具有何主要競爭利基？

Q.3　Do you have any concepts about the competitive niche of Taiwan's solar cell and LED manufacturers in the world?

📎 主題對話範例（Dialogue Examples）

A：Taiwan is very competitive in the green energy business in the world marketplace.

B：I would like to know more about the latest development of green energy and its future prospects.

A：Both solar cells and LEDs are now two hectic green energy products in Taiwan.

B：The price of LED products is much expensive compared with traditional ones.

A：The "Green New Deal" announced by the UNEP has pushed many advanced nations for the promulgation of green energy policies.

B：Do you know the "20-20-20" green energy target made by EU?

Politics

Commerce

Jobs

Sports

Healthy

Society

Career

Life

同義字與名詞（Synonym & Terminology）
appropriate（提撥）⇨ allot ⇨ share ⇨ distribute ⇨ divide
promote(提升) ⇨ advance ⇨ work up to ⇨ move up
select（挑選）⇨ pick ⇨ choose
release（釋放）⇨ free ⇨ fire ⇨ relieve
vital(重要的）⇨ necessary ⇨ important ⇨ essential

英譯中練習：（參閱主題文章）

English ⇨ Chinese Translation Practice：(Refer to the theme article)

1. Solar cells, LED photonics, wind power generation, bio-fuels, hydrogen power and fuel cells, energy information/communications, and electric vehicles as strategic sectors to offer vital assistances.（英譯中）

....

....

2. Taiwan ranks as the world's third largest manufacturer in solar cells and the world's largest supplier in both LED modules and wind power electrical system.（英譯中）

....

....

3. Taiwan's green industry has now focused on solar cells and LED, with solar cells taking a share of 48.7% out of the total production value; and LED, with 46% in 2011, respectively.（英譯中）

....

....

4. European Union mapped out the "EU Renewable Energy Act" by the end of 2008, designating the So-called "20-20-20" target. It requests an increase of 20% renewable sources, the reduction of carbon dioxide (CO_2) by 20%, and an upgrade of energy efficiency by 20% in 2020.（英譯中）

....

....

Unit 05　如何從眾多的應徵者中脫穎而出？

（How to Reveal One's Talents Among Many Interviewed Candidates?）

📎 準備好自己成為老闆眼中的合適人選

讓主考官加深印象 Make Interviewer a Deeper Impression

As enterprises have started their recruiting plans for social freshmen, how to reveal one's talents among competitors has become an important issue for the interviewees.

由於企業已經開始針對社會新鮮人提出徵才計畫，如何在眾多的競爭對手中脫穎而出，已成為應徵者之重要課題。

The interviewer may raise a wide range of questions with the purpose to observe the interviewee's viewpoints, problem-shooting capabilities, or logical thinking during the interview. Thus, the interviewee needs the instant reaction to answer questions when each is tendered within 10 seconds. The answering time is suggested to last between about 20 seconds and two minutes.

在面試時，主考管可能提出各式各樣的問題，惟主要目的是想觀察社會新鮮人的眼界想法、解決問題能力及邏輯思維等。新鮮人臨場反應要夠快，最好能在問題結束的 10 秒內接話，回答時間大約以 20 秒到 2 分鐘為宜。

An interview is a kind of meeting conducted by employers to reconfirm the resume of employees. This offers the opportunity to understand new employees regarding their responses, oral expressions, working motives, attitudes, and a match of company culture.

Politics

雇主面試是一種有目的的會談，可能是履歷表的再確認，也可能是瞭解新受僱者的應對進退、口語表達、工作動機、態度以及是否適合符合該公司的文化特質等。

The enterprise will never hire employees without an interview is done. Based on the resume, it is a must to talk and review it—through "your previous behaviors and predict your future behaviors."
企業不可能在還沒有完成面試就進行錄用。在企業還未認識你時，僅能從你所提供的履歷與面試的對談中「以你過去的行為，來預測你如果被錄取之後的未來行為」。

"STAR" 的回話技巧 "STAR" —the Reply Skill

Coupled with the self-introduction, the basic etiquette is essential during the interview. It is important to grasp the contents of the reply. A reply skill called the "STAR" is referred as follows： "S" stands for "Situation," "T" for task (or mission), "A" for action, and "R" for result. "By using this skill, the interviewee enables to elaborate in an organized method and let the interviewer quickly understand his or her personal capabilities, including the way in handling things.
「面試除了基本的禮貌與條理分明的介紹自己之外，抓住企業想聽什麼內容是很重要的技巧。「STAR」的回話技巧，Situation 當時的情況是如何、Task 所扮演的角色或任務是什麼、Action 採取的行動是什麼、Result 事情的結果為何。把握這「STAR」「回答技巧，可以清楚表達自己在處理某一件事情的來龍去脈，利用重點條列式的說明，來讓面試官迅速瞭解你的做事方法與個人特色。

成功面試小技巧 Successful Interview Techniques

1. 誠實面對測驗 Face tests honestly
2. 三分鐘自我介紹 Self-introduction in three minutes

Commerce

Jobs

Sports

Healthy

Society

Career

Life

3. 仔細聆聽 Careful listening
4. 準備適當物品、作品 Prepare proper articles and work pieces
5. 精準的回答話術 Precise replies
6. 禮貌應對 Answer readily and politely

To submit good questions to the interviewer, for instance the challenge of the work and employee characteristics, has the opportunity to obtain bonus points. Before doing so, the background of the company must be first studied and let the interviewer understand the ambition of the interviewee.

向面試主管提出好問題是有加分的機會，例如可以詢問工作挑戰、理想候選人的特質及經歷，或先做功課了解公司背景後，詢問相關應具備的能力，讓面試主管了解求職者的企圖心。

Meanwhile, some "mine taboos" must be noticed during the interview. These include: to avoid negative answers, to avoid outside interferences, no chatting with the interviewer, and no questions about benefits or wages if you are not yet hired by the company.

另外，在面試中，有一些「地雷禁忌」也不可不知：避免負面的回答話術、避免受到外在的干擾、不要與面試官閒聊話家常、在還沒有確認是否錄取前，不要緊追著問公司福利或薪資。

企業需要什麼樣的人才
Which Kind of Talents is Needed by Enterprise?

Working attitudes (active and aggressive, dedicated, coordination), team works (cooperative spirit, human relationship), learning (strong learning, high potentials), stabilities (high stability, royalty), and specialties (good academic qualifications, intelligence test, language capability, working expertise) are five criteria in recruiting new staff.

工作態度（主動積極、敬業精神、配合程度）、團隊合作（合作精神、

Politics

Commerce

Jobs

Sports

Healthy

Society

Career

Life

人際處理）、學習能力（學習力強、可塑性高）、穩定性（穩定性高、忠誠度高）、專業能力（學經歷佳、智力測驗、語言能力、工作經驗）是五大徵才重點。

A good autobiography will bring you more advantages in the interview, at least for the social freshmen. As the company usually spares efforts in fostering new employees, it is a must to spend more endeavors in preparing your own autobiography.

一篇好的自傳更為自己加分，尤其對社會新鮮人而言。企業通常不願花費過多心力栽培新人，若想找到一份理想的工作，應該在自傳部分多加用心。

Despite the social freshmen are inexperienced in the work, they can point out their experiences and or certificates obtained in student clubs and how suitable you are for the job. The most important strategy is to emphasize the best selection of yourself alone, a best policy to win the opportunity for a granted interview.

社會新鮮人雖然沒有工作經驗，但可以在自傳中提及自己是否曾經參加社團、擔任幹部，或得到什麼獎狀與擁有哪些證照，同時要強調自己的優點與適合該項工作的原因。最重要的是要強調自己是最佳人選，如此，才有可能得到面試機會。

重要單字暨新聞辭彙（Key Vocabulary & News Glossary）

- talent *(n.)* 才能
- interview *(n.)* 面試
- interviewee *(n.)* 面試者
- interviewer *(n.)* 面試官
- recruit *(vt.)* 徵募
- social freshman 社會新鮮人
- logical thinking 邏輯思維
- instant *(adj.)* 立即的
- tender *(vt.)* 提出
- resume *(n.)* 簡歷
- review *(vt.)* 檢查
- predict *(vt.)* 預測

- etiquette *(n.)* 禮儀
- aggressive *(adj.)* 積極的
- specialty *(n.)* 專長
- autobiography *(n.)* 自傳

📎 單字及句型範例（Vocabulary & Sentence Examples）

1. Milo was the strongest candidate for the job.
   米洛在求職應徵者中具備最好的條件。
2. The new teacher made a good impression on the students.
   新教師給學生留下了一個好印象。
3. Most of the teachers there are recruited from abroad.
   那裡的大部分教師是從海外雇來的。
4. Opinions on various social questions differ from person to person.
   有關各種社會問題的意見因人而異。
5. None of them raised any objection. 他們誰也沒提出反對意見。
6. Some of these points will be elaborated in the following chapter.
   其中幾點將在下一章作詳細闡述。
7. She answers readily when called on. 她一叫到就會馬上作出回答。
8. He cannot brook interference. 他不能容忍他人的干涉。

📎 問題與討論（Questions & Discussions）

Q 1. 我有接到一家公司通知最近要參加面試，可是不知道是否會被錄用？

Q.1 I was informed by the company to attend an interview recently but I was wondering whether I will be hired or not?

Q 2. 參加面試新工作應該注意哪些事項？您可否提供有關這方面的好建議？

Q.2 What matters are needed attention for an interview of a job? Do you have any good suggestions in this regard?

Q 3. 企業到底需要哪些真正人才?

Q.3 Which kind of talents is needed by the enterprise?

📎 主題對話範例 (Dialogue Examples)

A：The interviewer may ask questions out of your specialty as a test for the knowledge of general sense.

B：If so, I have to prepare myself in case of any questions.

A：The employment is decided mostly by your answer to the interviewer.

B：The skill of reply is important especially when it is conducted in a short period of time.

同義字與名詞（Synonym & Terminology）

recruit（徵募）⇨ enlist ⇨ draft ⇨ muster ⇨ enroll ⇨ sign up

review（檢查）⇨ examine ⇨ inspect ⇨ survey

predict（預言）⇨ foresee ⇨ foretell ⇨ prophesy

aggressive（積極的）⇨ combative ⇨ belligerent ⇨ offensive

specialty（專長）⇨ specialization ⇨ major ⇨ concentration

📎 英譯中練習：（參閱主題文章）

English ⇨ Chinese Translation Practice：(Refer to the theme article)

1. The most important strategy is to emphasize the best selection of yourself alone, a best policy to win the opportunity for a granted interview.

（英譯中）

....

....

Politics

Commerce

Jobs

Sports

Healthy

Society

Career

Life

Part 4　談運動健身
Talks About Physical Exercises & Fitness

Unit 01 有益健康的健身運動
（Healthful Exercises for Fitness）

📎 讓自己活得更健康

提升健身效果

The benefit of physical exercises enables you to build up heart and lung functions, promote blood circulations, and strengthen immunity against diseases. What if you have only 20 minutes to move but you are in an obvious dehydration or the lack of sleeping? This achieves not any effects of exercises!

健身運動的好處可增強心肺功能，促進血液循環，及增強免疫力等。
但是，您所有能做的就是讓自己有二十分鐘去運動，當有明顯的像是
脫水或是缺乏睡眠的話，就無法達到運動健身的效果！

How to obtain a healthful exercise and improve fitness effects? The following secrets are introduced to enhance the effect of exercises.

如何作有益健康的健身運動或改善運動健身的效果呢？以下幾項訣竅，
教您如何提升健身效果。

選擇正確的運動位置 Select a Right Exercise Location

Mainly because of fresh air, most people agree to take physical exercises in outdoors rather than in fitness gyms. A research in the periodical"environment science and technology"reveals that outdoor exercises make people become more active. Dr. Kay Porter, an exercise psychologist and author of "the Mental Athlete", said that "Besides of a good mood, it makes your foot muscle become stronger."

很多人都會同意在狹窄的體育館裡跑步比不上在外面有新鮮空氣的地
方運動來的好。《環境科學與科技期刊》研究顯示，戶外活動會讓您

Politics

Commerce

Jobs

Sports

Healthy

Society

Career

Life

變的很活躍。運動心理學家和《精神運動員》作家凱‧波特博士說，「除了心情上有好處外，也讓腳部肌肉更強壯。」

找同好運動不競賽 Find Exercise Kindred Spirit But No Competitions

A research from Newton University noted that the effect of exercise is improved if you share the kindred spirit with others. Amie Hoff, an expert in nutrition and health, added that people in exercises are used to compete with others, and this "bad" habit should be eliminated. "Try your best in sports ground. And find a pair of fine shoes or sportswear to upgrade your faith in exercises."

牛頓大學的研究提出，有相同目標信念的運動同好可以提升您的健身運動效果。營養健康專家艾咪‧霍夫表示很多人都有把自己和其他健身同好互相做比較的「壞習慣」，這應該排除。「在運動場上盡力做到最好，並找一雙適合的運動鞋或是運動服，幫助您提升運動自信心。」

月經來時請溫和運動 Gentle Exercise When Having Woman's Periods

David Geier, a doctor at the sports medical department of University of Southern California, said that "the change of hormone, sometimes, makes the muscle of women become soft during their menses and creates a dangerous dilemma, especially on knees." He suggested gentle exercises be taken for the sake of better effects.

美國南加大運動醫學系的大衛‧吉爾醫師提及，「荷爾蒙的改變，在某個時候，女人的月經導致肌肉產生比較鬆散的變化，使得在比較危險的處境上，特別是膝蓋。建議在這時候請做一些比較溫和的運動以提升運動效果。

讓時間安排有條理 Ordered Time Arrangements

Most people go to fitness gyms in a hurry time, and this negative attitude affects the performance as you are not so concentrated on exercises. "The result of exercise focuses on experiences to maintain the health and life style."Make an ordered time arrangement to bring happiness of exercises.

大部分的人前往健身房做健身運動時都是急急忙忙的去，這負面的態度影響了表現，因為沒有集中您的心思在運動上面。「運動的結果其重點應該是享有維持健康身體和生活型態的經驗。」請安排好時間好好享受運動帶來的樂趣。

下午運動比早晨更好 Afternoon Exercises Are Better Than Morning

According to a report at "Physiology Periodical", exercises rebuild the daily biological clock of brain and it changes due to aging. Afternoon exercises have better benefits than morning, especially in the anti-aging. Christopher S. Colwell, a doctor at U.S. Los Angeles University Medical School, found out that the benefit of exercise in afternoon is better than morning after conducting a recent research.

根據新的《生理學期刊》報告顯示，運動可以重置產生大腦每日的生理時鐘，也會隨著年紀的增長改變，下午的時候運動會比較有好處，而且甚至提供抗老的好處。美國洛杉磯大學醫學院的克里斯多夫·康維爾博士也說，研究發現午後運動產生更多的好處，比在早晨做運動好。

邊聽音樂邊運動 Listing to music in exercises

It is easy to adjust your paces with rhythm of music and keep the brisk melody with exercises. Updating the music in your flash disc every week is a good way as new songs maintain you in a dynamic status. Refer to the digital music service at website: Rhapsody.com and check some music which is suitable for hearts in exercises.

當您邊聽音樂邊運動，您容易把自己的步伐和旋律對齊，保持旋律的輕快，每週更新您的音樂隨身碟也是個好方法，新歌會把您維持在有活力的狀態。可參考數位音樂網站 Rhapsody.com，其中有一些好的範例對心臟很好的運動適合的音樂。

正確飲食 Correct Diet

Try to avoid eating of any high carbohydrate food one hour prior to exercises as this may make dull reactions in exercises. And a cup of less caffeine coffee increases your dynamics and performances in sports ground. If you eat some snacks before resuming exercises two or three hours ago, you will not feel hungry in sports ground and make a pig of yourself after exercises.

運動前的一小時避免任何高碳水化合物的食物，因為這將會避免您在運動時有遲鈍的反應，並伴隨低血糖反應。運動前喝一杯含少量咖啡因的咖啡，會為您在運動場上多新增一些動力和表現。此外，運動前兩三個小時若能吃些小點心，在運動時場將不會感覺飢餓，但也請避免運動後大吃大喝。

保持正面態度；設定可達到的目標
Keep a Positive Attitude, Set Achievable Targets

A real target is set based on your lifestyle, and this also drives you to keep forward if the target is reached. Whether or not exercises are completed, the maintaining of a positive attitude is important as you can face it in calm.

基於您的生活型態設定實際的目標，您將感覺到，當達到您的目標時，這將會鼓勵您持續向前邁進。能夠完成運動量與否，維持正面的態度有無限的好處，您都可以從容面對。

暖身與天氣 Warming-Ups and Weather

Dr. Kevin McGrath, a U.S. immunity, asthma, and allergy expert, said that asthma, coughing, and tightened ribcage happen easily in the cold weather or dry air. Warming- ups will not result in asthma like the use of ventilators for 15 to 20 minutes before exercises.

美國免疫學，氣喘和過敏專家凱文‧馬格雷醫師表示，運動所導致氣喘，咳嗽和胸腔部位緊張，這更容易在寒冷的天氣下，乾燥的空氣發生。「運動前先暖身，比較不會導致氣喘，如同在運動前使用呼吸器十五到二十分鐘做暖身。」

運動後從疲憊中恢復體力 Recover Strength from Exercises

The human body needs a regular rest to recover strength from exercises, said Fabio Comana, a leader in National Sports Medical Center. "It requires rest, nutrition, sleeping, and stress management after exercises."Generally, the long muscle training such as Yoga requires 24 to 36 hours to recover strength in between twice practices. The recovery time takes about 48 hours or more if training is intense.

運動後，您的身體需要規律的休息來恢復體力。國家運動醫學中心的領導費比‧科瑪說「運動後需要休息，營養，睡眠和做好壓力的處理」。一般而言，肌肉持久訓練，例如瑜珈，兩次練習之間需要 24 到 36 小時的時間來恢復，更強烈的訓練需要 48 小時或更多來恢復。

✐ 重要單字暨新聞辭彙（Key Vocabulary & News Glossary）

- exercises *(n.)* 運動
- immunity *(n.)* 免疫力
- dehydration *(n.)* 脫水
- fitness gym (gymnasium) 健身房
- periodical *(n.)* 期刊
- psychologist 心理學家
- kindred *(adj.)* 同類的
- eliminate *(vt.)* 排除

- woman's periods 經期
- menses *(n.)* 月經
- dilemma *(n.)* 困境
- biological clock 生理時鐘
- rhythm *(n.)* 韻律
- asthma *(n.)* 哮喘
- allergy *(n.)* 過敏
- Yoga *(n.)* 瑜珈

✐ 單字及句型範例（Vocabulary & Sentence Examples）

1. We immediately realized that we were kindred spirits.
   我們馬上發覺彼此志同道合。

2. Their diet chiefly consists of grain and vegetables.
   他們的飲食主要是穀類和蔬菜。

3. Prior to the Revolutionary War, the United States was a British colony.　在革命戰爭前美國是英國的殖民地。

4. All work and no play makes Jack a dull boy.
   只工作不玩耍，聰明孩子也變傻。

5. The fracture caused him intense pain.　骨折給他造成了劇烈的疼痛。

✐ 問題與討論（Questions & Discussions）

Q 1. 您有每天做運動的習慣嗎？都做哪一類型之運動，每天做多久？

Q.1　Do you exercise everyday, and on what kinds of exercises? How long each time you do exercises?

Q 2. 可否談一下您喜歡做的運動項目，它們對您有帶來哪些好處？

Q.2 Would you like to talk about your favorite exercises, and what benefits have been brought to you from exercises?

Q 3. 運動對受瘦身有效嗎？您有否嘗試過此方法？

Q.3 Are exercises effective to lose weight? Have you tried the method in the past?

📎 主題對話範例（Dialogue Examples）

A：I like exercises, including all kinds of outdoor activities.

B：Do you exercise alone or have any companions?

A：Warming-ups are important to avoid athletic injuries.

B：Experts said that people should be careful when exercising in the cold weather or dry air.

A：Do you know the benefit of Yoga?

B：I have practiced the yoga class for one month and the curriculum is just great.

同義字與名詞（Synonym & Terminology）

1. exercise（運動）⇨ practice ⇨ use ⇨ train ⇨ drill
2. concentrate（集中）⇨ focus ⇨ think about
3. eliminate（消除）⇨ remove ⇨ discard ⇨ reject ⇨ exclude,
4. rest（休息）⇨ repose ⇨ pause ⇨ ease ⇨ relaxation
5. recover（恢復）⇨ regain ⇨ retrieve ⇨ rescue ⇨ reclaim
6. intense（強烈的）⇨ forceful ⇨ strong ⇨ dynamic ⇨ fierce ⇨ severe ⇨ rigorous

📎英譯中練習：（參閱主題文章）

English ⇨ Chinese Translation Practice：(Refer to the theme article)

1. The benefit of physical exercises enables you to build up heart and lung functions, promote blood circulations, and strengthen immunity against diseases.（英譯中）

   ....

   ....

2. A research in the periodical"environment science and technology"reveals that outdoor exercises make people become more active.（英譯中）

   ....

   ....

3. It is easy to adjust your paces with rhythm of music and keep the brisk melody with exercises.（英譯中）

   ....

   ....

4. Warming- ups will not result in asthma like the use of ventilators for 15 to 20 minutes before exercises.（英譯中）

   ....

   ....

Unit 02 "Linsanity" 林來瘋～ 林書豪的品牌精神與價值

("Linsanity"——the Brand Spirit and Value of Jeremy Lin)

📎 激勵人心的成功典範

林來瘋 Linsanity

"Linsanity" starts with the wave of popularity by Jeremy Lin in New York Knicks in February 2012. It is a new vocabulary composing of two words "Lin" and "insanity" thereafter.

林來瘋，英文原名是 Linsanity，指原紐約尼克的球星林書豪在 2012 年 2 月開始掀起的風潮。此字英文原來是以「Lin」（林），搭配「瘋迷熱潮」的英文單字「insanity」所組合出來的新詞彙。

品牌精神與價值 the brand spirit and value

A recent cover story from Forbes, the world's authoritative financial magazine, estimated that the brand value of Jeremy Lin would reach about US$14 million. A new coach was substituted in Knicks but the brand value of Jeremy Lin still soared rapidly.

世界權威財經媒體《富比士》雜誌估算，林書豪的品牌價值大約在 1,400 萬美元左右。儘管尼克隊已易新總教頭，林書豪的品牌價值仍在飆升。

JP Morgan signed a sponsorship contract worth US$300 million with Madison Square Garden (the home court of Knicks) and the birth of Jeremy Lin brand expects to create added values for the contract. Based on a voting by ESPN, the No. 17 T-shirt of Jeremy Lin accounts for the best selling among all NBA (National Basketball Association) T-shirts.

In New York, the popularity of Jeremy Lin outshines that of Derek Jeter, captain of New York Yankees in the U.S. Major League Baseball.
JP 摩根銀行同麥迪遜廣場花園球館（尼克隊主場）的贊助合同金額達三億美元，林書豪的橫空出世給這份贊助合同帶來了不少附加價值。林書豪的 17 號球衣目前仍是 NBA 聯盟最暢銷的球衣；而根據 ESPN 發起的投票結果來看，在紐約，林書豪的受歡迎程度甚至超過了美國職棒大聯盟紐約洋基隊隊長德裡克基特。

Jeremy Lin has brought several sponsorship contracts for Knicks ever since the "Linsanity storm." A PC company in Taiwan announced that it has become a commercial partner of Knicks as the Taiwanese company is allowed to insert its logo in the home court of Knicks. Before that, a tire-making company in Taiwan reached a same agreement with Knicks.
自從「林風暴」刮起後，林書豪給尼克斯帶來了不少贊助合同。台灣一家電腦公司宣佈，他們將同尼克斯成為商業合作夥伴，尼克斯將允許該電腦公司的 logo 出現在尼克斯主場場邊廣告牌上。而在此之前，還有一家台灣的輪胎公司也跟尼克斯簽訂了贊助合同。

As his first endorsement contract, Jeremy Lin reached an accord with Volvo recently. This is the first time that Volvo used a global spokesman and also the first time for Lin to represent himself as a brand ambassador.
林書豪還剛剛簽訂了自己成名後的第一份代言合同，他跟 Volvo 汽車公司簽訂代言合同。這是 VOLVO 第一次　用全球代言人，也是林書豪第一次以品牌大使的身分出現。

Meanwhile, a world-known carbonate drink giant plans to seize the China market by using the popularity of Jeremy Lin. A Chinese version advertisement for this purpose will be launched soon.
另外，某世界碳酸飲料巨頭公司也打算利用他的人氣來搶佔中國市場。中文版的廣告很快地開始上市。

It is not necessary for Jeremy Lin to become an all-star sports member in NBA or even the best back-fielder of Knicks. In consideration of the international influence of NBA, Jeremy Lin can earn huge brand values as long as he is an outstanding player in the playoff, plus his attitudes, charms, and backgrounds.

林書豪不必非得成為 NBA 全明星球員，他甚至沒有必要成為尼克斯最好的後衛。考慮到 NBA 在國際範圍內的影響力，以林書豪的態度、魅力、背景，他只需要成為一支季後賽級別球隊中的優秀球員，就可以擁有巨大的品牌價值。

林書豪基本資料 Data of Jeremy Lin:

出生日期 /Birth Date：1988 年 8 月 23 日 /Aug. 23, 1988

出生地點 /Birth Place：美國加州 · 柏羅奧圖市 /City of Polo Alto, California, U.S.A.

國籍 /Nationality：美國 /U.S.

登錄身高 /Registered Height：6 英呎 3 英吋（191 公分）/6 feet 3 inches (191cm)

登錄體重 /Registered Weight：200 pounds (91 公斤 /Kilograms)

學歷 /Record of education：

哈佛大學 (主修經濟學，副修社會學)

Harvard University (majored in economics; minored in social science)

NBA 職業生涯 /Professional career at NBA：

金州勇士 Godden State Warriors：2010-2011

休士頓火箭 Huston Rocket ：2011

紐約尼克 New York Knicks ：February, 2012

休士頓火箭 Huston Rocket：2012 until now

The Family of Jeremy Lin:

林書豪家庭：

Parents of Jeremy Lin came from Chunghwa County, Taiwan and both immigrated and married in the U.S. They have raised three boys with Jeremy ranking as the second birth order. Jeremy Lin and the family are all pious Christians.

林書豪父母來自台灣彰化縣，移民並在美國結婚。兩人育有三子，林書豪排行第二，全家督信基督教。

重要單字暨新聞辭彙（Key Vocabulary & News Glossary）

- brand *(n.)* 品牌
- insanity *(n.)* 瘋狂
- substitute *(vt.)* 代替
- Madison Square Garden
  麥迪遜廣場花園球館
- home court 主場
- added value 附加價值
- National Basketball Association
  (NBA)（美國）國家籃球聯盟
- outshine *(vt.)* 使黯然失色
- Major League Baseball (MLB)
  （美國）職棒大聯盟
- endorsement *(n.)* 背書
- reach an accord 達成協議
- brand ambassador 品牌大使
- seize *(vt.)* 搶占
- launch *(vt.)* 開始
- outstanding *(adj.)* 傑出的
- pious *(adj.)* 虔誠的

單字及句型範例（Vocabulary & Sentence Examples）

1. This brand of tea is my favorite. 這種茶我最愛喝。
2. He left New York in 1932 and we heard no more of him thereafter. 他一九三二年離開紐約, 自那以後再沒有聽到他的音訊。
3. He substitutes as our teacher of English. 他代任我們的英語教師。
4. Please sign your name in the space marked for endorsement. 請在標明簽署的地方簽名。
5. The enemy seized the town after a violent attack. 敵人猛攻後佔領了這個城鎮。

📎 問題與討論（Questions & Discussions）

Q 1. 您認為「林書豪精神」是什麼？為何它會引起世人廣泛之認同？

Q.1 What is the "Jeremy Lin spirit," and why it arouse identifications widely around the world?

Q 2. 您對於「林來瘋」這個字看法如何？它對於您有否代表任何意義？

Q.2 What is your opinion on the "Linsanity"? Does the word mean anything to you or not?

Q 3.「林書豪品牌」之商業價值據估已超過美金 1,400 萬元，對此您有何高見？

Q.3 The brand of "Jeremy Lin" is estimated to exceed US$14 million worth of commercial value. Do you have any comments on this issue?

📎 主題對話範例（Dialogue Examples）

A：The "Linsanity" represents the spirit of success that is pursued by most people.

B：I am so impressive about the spirit of Jeremy Lin and his pursuit of success.

A：The "Jeremy Lin spirit" is a success and the brand also brings many commercial values.

B：The commercial value of Jeremy Lin brand is beyond our imaginations.

A：Volvo invites Jeremy Lin as the spokesman mainly for sales potentials in China's car market.

B：Jeremy Lin signs the endorsement with other companies for the sake of promotion reasons.

同義字與名詞（Synonym & Terminology）

1. brand（商標）⇨ mark ⇨ label ⇨ burn ⇨ tag

Politics

Commerce

Jobs

Sports

Healthy

Society

Career

Life

2. substitute（代替） ⇨ replace ⇨ exchange ⇨ switch ⇨ shift
3. sign（簽署） ⇨ mark ⇨ endorse ⇨ seal ⇨ initial
4. endorse（簽名） ⇨ sign ⇨ approve ⇨ accredit ⇨ support
5. seize（抓住） ⇨ clutch ⇨ grasp ⇨ grab ⇨ grip ⇨ clasp ⇨ snatch
6. launch（開始） ⇨ start ⇨ introduce ⇨ spring
7. outstanding（傑出的） ⇨ important ⇨ great ⇨ eminent ⇨ famous ⇨ prominent
8. pious（虔誠的） ⇨ religious ⇨ devout ⇨ reverent ⇨ faithful ⇨ believing

✐ 英譯中練習：（參閱主題文章）

English ⇨ Chinese Translation Practice：(Refer to the theme article)

1. "Linsanity" starts with the wave of popularity by Jeremy Lin in New York Knicks in February 2012.（英譯中）

   ....
   ....

2. A recent report from the Forbes magazine estimated that the brand value of Jeremy Lin would reach about US$14 million.（英譯中）

   ....
   ....

3. A PC company in Taiwan announced that it has become a commercial partner of Knicks as the Taiwanese company is allowed to insert its logo in the home court of Knicks（英譯中）

   ....
   ....

4. In consideration of the international influence of NBA, Jeremy Lin can earn huge brand values as long as he is an outstanding player in the playoff.（英譯中）

   ....
   ....

Unit 03 傑出台灣女子運動員
（Outstanding Girl Athletes in Taiwan）

🔗 體壇閃亮的星星

曾雅妮──首位來自台灣之世界高爾夫球后（Yani Tseng──the World's First Empress of Golf from Taiwan）

Being a professional girl golf player from Taiwan, Yani Tseng has played the golf since she was five years old. Born on January 23, 1989 in Kweishan, a small township in northern Taiwan, she showed abilities of talents during her amateur career. Yani now stays in Orlando, Florida, the U.S.

曾雅妮是臺灣女子職業高爾夫選手，五歲就開始打高爾夫球。1989 年 1 月 23 日出生臺灣桃園縣龜山鄉，在業餘生涯時就展露頭角。她目前旅居美國佛羅里達州奧蘭多市。

In February 2011, Yani won the championship of ANZ women golf masters, ranking her the No. 1 in the world's women golf players (from the period of February 13, 2011 and up to March 18, 2013). She became the sixth empress of golf in history and the first Taiwanese athlete to post as the first place in the main stream sports of the world.

曾雅妮於 2011 年 2 月贏得 ANZ 女子高球名人賽冠軍後，在女性高爾夫選手排名登上世界第一（從 2011 年 2 月 13 日至 2013 年 3 月 18 日期間），成為史上第六位世界球后，也是第一位登上主流運動世界排名第一的台灣運動員。

Yani Tseng and the NBA basketball player Taiwanese-American Jeremy Lin were each selected by the Time magazine as one of "the 100th most influential persons in the world" in 2012. However, Yani Tseng's empress of golf title, which lasted for 109 weeks, was replaced by the U.S. golf player Stacy Lewis (born on Feb. 16, 1985 in Louisiana) in the LPGA Founders Cup held on March 18, 2013.

2012 年曾雅妮與台裔美籍 NBA 籃球員林書豪一同獲選為《時代》雜誌「年度全球百大最有影響力人物」，然而在 2013 年 3 月 18 日在創建者盃後，維持長達 109 周的世界第一寶座為美國選手史黛西・路易斯所取代。

In 2010, Yani Tseng was ranked as the top five girl tennis player in the world. She obtained four amateur grand slam championships beginning in 2003, including she outplayed the then most hot Korea-American player Michelle Wie (born on Oct. 11, 1989 in Honolulu, Hawaii) in the 2004 USGA Women's Amateur Public Link Championship.

曾雅妮至 2010 年世界排名第五。從 2003 年開始，接連獲得四個業餘的大滿貫冠軍，跌破許多人的眼鏡。（包含 2004 年打敗當時最具勝名也最被看好的韓裔美籍選手魏聖美得到 USGA Women's Amateur Public Link Championship 冠軍）。

Yani Tseng turned into a pro player in 2007 and kept creating many amazing achievements in golf, especially the winning of her first grand slam in LPGA McDonald Championship in 2006 when she was only 19 years old. And she gained the rookie of the year award from LPGA.

2007 年轉職業後，更是在世界高爾夫球壇不斷製造驚奇。2008 年以 19 歲之姿，贏得第一個生涯大滿貫 LPGA 麥當勞錦標賽，同年並獲得 LPGA 年度最佳新人獎。

In 2010, Yani won two grand slams in both Kraft Nabisco Championship and the Women's British Open, becoming the youngest player in LPGA history to win three grand slams. Thus, she was granted as the best player of LPGA in the same year.

2010 年再接連贏得納比斯科錦標賽以及英國公開賽兩個大滿貫冠軍，

成為 LPGA 史上最年輕贏的三大滿貫冠軍的得主。也因為這樣優異的表現，同年贏得 LPGA 年度最佳球員。

詹詠然——2006 年 台灣十大潛力人物體育競技類的得主（Yung-jan Chan——Winner of Taiwan's 10 Potential Athletes in 2006）

The tennis career of Yung-jan Chan was inspired by her father as she won champions in both 12-year and 14-year groups in a competition in Taiwan. Despite the devastating "921 earthquake" happened in central Taiwan in 1999, Chan's family continued to support her tennis career. She won the woman double play champion (juvenile group) in Australian Open Tennis Champions and the first place of the woman single play in Sri Lanka Tours held in February and August of 2004, respectively.

詹詠然的網球生涯是由她的父親開啟，她獲得全臺 12 歲組冠軍，之後又獲 14 歲組的冠軍。雖在 1999 年遭遇 921 大地震，家中仍然支持她繼續網球生涯。2004 年 2 月和 8 月，分別拿下澳洲網球公開賽 青少組雙打冠軍和斯里蘭卡女子巡迴賽女單冠軍。

In single plays, Chan beat Alla Kudryavtseva from Russia in the U.S. Open held in 2008. It was also the first victory for Chan to obtain her personal grand slam.

單打部分，詹詠然於 2008 年美國網球公開賽 首輪擊敗俄羅斯 選手 Alla Kudryavtseva，取得個人大滿貫賽單打會內賽第一勝。

In related news, Chan protested against the announcement of her representing as the Taiwan District, China when she attended a tennis tournament held recently in Ningbo, Zhejiang Province. "Please don't say that I'm from China, I am TAIWANESE, represent CHINESE TAIPEI, if you keep saying that, I'm afraid I'll need to protest about it!" Chan said.

相關消息，台灣網球好手詹詠然近日在大陸浙江寧波參加挑戰賽，當播報員稱她來自中國台灣區時，她勇敢表達自己是台灣人，「不要故意說錯我的國籍」。

Politics

Commerce

Jobs

Sports

Healthy

Society

Career

Life

"My last post was just saying that I'm from Chinese Taipei, as you can see on the draw it's TPE after my name, I only hope everyone can respect this, doesn't meter which country I go! I'm just a tennis player traveling all around the world, and try to make my tennis dream come true. There is no political thing in my travel bag," according to Chan.

詹詠然說「上一則貼文我並非想針對任何國家，也沒有要帶來任何不必要的情緒，我只是純粹在世界各地比賽，努力完成我的夢想。今天我不管身處在世界哪個角落，我都有權利要求把我代表的國家說的正確，我的名字後面的國家縮寫是 TPE 中華台北，只希望大家能尊重這一點！」

📎 重要單字暨新聞辭彙（Key Vocabulary & News Glossary）

- outstanding *(adj.)* 傑出的
- athlete *(n.)* 運動員
- professional *(adj.)* 職業的
- amateur *(adj.)* 業餘的
- masters 名人賽
- empress of golf 高爾夫球后
- main stream 主流
- sports *(n.)* 運動
- last *(vi.)* 持續
- outplay *(vt.)* 勝過
- amazing *(adj.)* 驚奇的

- LPGA (the Ladies Professional Golf Association) （美國）女子職業高爾夫球協會
- rookie of the year award 新人獎
- Women's British Open 英國女子高爾夫球公開賽
- Australian Open Tennis Champions 澳洲網球公開賽
- U.S. Open 美國網球公開賽
- tournament *(n.)* 錦標賽

📎 單字及句型範例（Vocabulary & Sentence Examples）

1. The pictures were taken by an amateur photographer.
   這些照片是一位業餘攝影師拍的。

2. It was amazing that the boy was able to solve the problem so quickly. 那男孩能這樣快地解完這道題 , 真是令人驚奇。

3. Our team won the championship in the basketball tournament.
我們隊在籃球聯賽中贏得冠軍。

4. The athlete won two gold medals in the Olympics.
這位運動員在奧林匹克運動會上獲得兩塊金牌。

5. A highly professional administrator. 一位非常內行的管理人員。

6. Outplay, to beat an opponent in a game by playing with more skill than they do. 〔比賽中〕勝過〔對手〕，擊敗。

7. The emperor looked ugly and the empress pale and pretty. 皇帝看起來很醜陋而皇后則蒼白美麗。

8. He always goes with the stream. 他總是順應潮流。

9. We were eager to hear the announcement of the winners of the race. 我們急於聽到賽跑優勝者名單的宣佈。

10. He did not attend the meeting yesterday. 昨天他沒有參加會議。

11. Our team won the championship in the basketball tournament.
我們隊在籃球聯賽中贏得冠軍。

📎 問題與討論（Questions & Discussions）

Q 1. 曾雅妮代表台灣在世界女子網球運動之最高成就，您認為將來後續有人嗎？

Q.1 Yani Tseng represents Taiwan's highest achievement in the world's women golf sports, do you think are there any qualified successors in the future?

Q 2. 曾雅妮從小就展露高爾夫球天賦，但您是否同意兒童太早作職業性訓練？

Q.2 Yani Tseng showed her golf talents since she was a child. Do you agree or not to conduct professional trainings so early, especially for children?

📎 主題對話範例（Dialogue Examples）

A：Yani Tseng is a good golfer and she won so many champions in LPGA and several international women golf tournaments.

B：Have you seen any golf games played by Yani Tseng? Do you have any impressions about the game?

A：Are you a golfer and what is your handicap?

B：Which is your favorite golf club in Taiwan or abroad?

A：Taiwan has not yet created too many tennis stars in the world, compared with foreign nations.

B：I used to play tennis when I was young but I quit now.

同義字與名詞（Synonym & Terminology）

1. outstanding（傑出的） ⇨ important ⇨ great ⇨ eminent ⇨ famous
2. amateur（業餘的） ⇨ dilettante ⇨ dabbler ⇨ non-professional
3. beat（打敗） ⇨ surpass ⇨ win ⇨ defeat, ⇨ trounce
4. tournament（錦標賽） ⇨ contest ⇨ tourney ⇨ game ⇨ sport ⇨ play

📎 英譯中練習：（參閱主題文章）

English ⇨ Chinese Translation Practice：(Refer to the theme article)

1. She became the sixth empress of golf in history and the first Taiwanese athlete to post as the first place in the main stream sports of the world.

（英譯中）

....

....

Politics

Commerce

Jobs

Sports

Healthy

Society

Career

Life

Unit 04 足球金童貝克漢
（Football Golden Boy Beckham）

📎令人稱羨的足球明星

貝克漢生涯簡介

David Beckham, the British football golden boy, announced that he would retire after this season is ended. This announcement terminates the brilliant professional football career of Beckham after 20 years and the 38-year-old football star said "it is the most right time." Beckham just won the champion for Paris Saint-Germain in the Ligue 1 of France.

英國足球金童貝克漢宣布，他將在本季結束後退休，結束他璀璨的 20 年職業足球生涯，38 歲的貝克漢表示：「這是最好的時機。」貝克漢才剛為聖日耳曼隊在法甲聯賽奪冠。

With his handsome and dashing appearance, Beckham is called "football golden boy" to represent the popularity in the world football.

貝克漢被稱為足球金童，英俊帥氣，是全球足壇最具人氣及代表性的球員。

個人資料：	（Personal Data）
全名 **(Full Name)**：	David Robert Joseph Beckham
Nicknames（綽號）：	Becks（小貝）、DB7、Frog Foots、咸爺（港澳地區稱呼 / called in Hong Kong & Macau）
生日 **(Birth Date)**：	1975 年 5 月 2 日 （38 歲 /years old）
出生地 **(Birth Place)**：	🏴 英格蘭倫敦 (London, England)
身高 **(Height)** ：	183 公分（約 6 英尺）/183 cm or about 6 Feet
位置 **(position)**：	右中場、組織中場（right midfielder, center midfielder）

Paris Saint-Germain has two more competitions left until the end of the season, but the final professional football career of Beckham will end on May 26, 2013. Beckham's handsome and dashing appearance represents the popularity of the world football. "The best way to leave is on the peak time," Beckham said. "All football players dream of leaving with champion titles."

聖日耳曼隊本季還剩下兩場比賽，今年（2013）5 月 26 日將是貝克漢球員生涯的最終戰。外型英俊帥氣的貝克漢毫無疑問是全球足壇最具人氣、代表性的球員。「這是離開最好的方式，在高峰時離開，」貝克漢說，「這是所有足球選手的夢想，以冠軍的身分離開。」

In the international football world, Beckham represented a team member of England National Team for 115 times, a record with no one to compete. He reached his professional peak in Manchester United as he attended a total of 394 matches, and helped "the Red Devils" to gain six champions in Premier League and one champion in UEFA Champions League.

在國際足壇上，貝克漢代表英格蘭國家隊出賽 115 次的紀錄，至今仍無人能比；他的職業巔峰期是在母隊曼聯度過的。他一共代表曼聯出戰 394 場，幫助「紅魔」六度奪得英超聯賽冠軍，獲得一次歐洲冠軍聯賽冠軍。

After leaving Manchester United, Beckham joined in Real Madrid of Spain and converted to Los Angeles Galaxy in the U.S. later. He was once leased to AC Milan of Italy and finally transferred to Paris Saint-Germain.

告別曼聯後，他還效力於西甲豪門皇家馬德里，再轉戰美國大聯盟的洛杉磯銀河隊，後曾租借至義大利的 AC 米蘭，最後就是目前的聖日耳曼。

Historically, Beckham is the only England football player who has obtained championships in four major national tournaments. And he is the only one that scored in the FIFA World Cup for three consecutive times.

他是史上唯一一位在四個國家的頂級聯賽中都獲得過冠軍的英格蘭球員，也是第一位在連續三屆世界盃足球賽都有進球的英格蘭球員。

"If I were told when I was a child: 'In the future, you will wear jersey of Manchester United, get champions, be the captain, represent as a national team member for over 100 times, and play in the world's largest football team.' I would say that you must be dreaming." "But all these have just come true because I was lucky," Beckham said.

"I don't think any other players are more popular than Beckham," Sven-Goran Eriksson, former coach of England National Team said. Beckham was the captain when Eriksson coached "the Three Lions" during the 2001-2006 period. "Beckham was always a focus whenever England Team goes to play, or at airports and hotels."

「如果在我小時候，有人告訴我：『你將來會穿上曼聯的球衣，獲得冠軍，成為隊長、代表國家出戰超過一百場，你還會在世界上最大的球隊踢球。』我那時一定會說：『你在作夢。』」貝克漢說，「但我很幸運，因為這些夢想我都實現了。」

「我不認為，還有哪個球員能比貝克漢更受歡迎。」英格蘭國家隊前主帥埃里克森（Sven-Goran Eriksson）也說，他在 2001 至 2006 年間執教「三獅軍團」時，貝克漢就是擔任隊長。「不管是每次英格蘭隊的比賽，還是在機場、在旅館，貝克漢永遠都是焦點。」

Beckham also leads a colorful life outside of the football field as he married Victoria Beckham, the past member of Spicy Girls (which are a British pop girl group formed in 1994) and gained commercial endorsement contracts. "Sports Illustrated" of the U.S. reported that Beckham recorded the highest income as a non-American athlete and

Politics

Commerce

Jobs

Sports

Healthy

Society

Career

Life

earned US$48.34 million last year. Beckham perceptually said that he wouldn't have today without the support of his family. He thanks the sacrifices of his parents to complete the dream, and also appreciates the support from his wife Victoria and their children.

不只是足球場上，貝克漢在場外也是多采多姿。他與辣妹合唱團（1994 成立之一英國流行歌曲女子團體）成員維多利亞結婚，商業合約、代言不斷，美國運動畫刊日前才報導，貝克漢是全世界收入最高的非美籍運動員，他過去一年共賺進 4834 萬美元，貝克漢最後也感性表示，如果沒有他的家人，就沒有今天的他。他感謝父母的犧牲，成就他的夢想，並感謝老婆維多利亞和小孩的支持。

📎 重要單字暨新聞辭彙（Key Vocabulary & News Glossary）

- football golden boy 足球金童
- announce *(vt.)* 宣佈
- brilliant *(adj.)* 璀璨的
- Paris Saint-Germain（法國）聖日耳曼隊
- Ligue 1 of France 法甲聯賽
- England National Team 英格蘭國家隊
- Manchester United 曼聯
- the Red Devils 紅魔（曼聯綽號）
- Premier League 英超聯賽
- UEFA Champions League 歐洲冠軍聯賽
- Real Madrid（西班牙）皇家馬德里
- Los Angeles Galaxy（美國）洛杉磯銀河隊
- AC Milan（義大利）AC 米蘭
- the FIFA World Cup 世界盃足球賽
- the Three Lions 三獅軍團
- Sports Illustrated 美國運動畫刊

📎 單字及句型範例（Vocabulary & Sentence Examples）

1. They announced that she would give one extra song. 他們宣佈說她將再唱一首歌。
2. She is a brilliant swimmer. 她是個技藝超群的游泳健兒。
3. He is a champion at writing familiar essays. 他是寫小品文的好手。

4. She always wants to be the focus of attention. 她老想成為人們注意的中心。

5. Parents often make sacrifices for their children. 父母親常常為子女作出犧牲。

問題與討論（Questions & Discussions）

Q 1. 您是不是貝克漢的粉絲？您為何喜歡他？

Q.1 Are you a fan of Beckham, and why you like him?

Q 2. 您喜歡看足球比賽嗎？您比較喜歡看哪一隊？

Q.2 Do you like football games? What is your favorite team?

Q 3. 您了解現在世界各國足球對現況嗎？有哪些隊或個人最近表現較突出？

Q.3 Do you know the existing situation of all football teams around the world? Which teams or players are most outstanding recently?

主題對話範例（Dialogue Examples）

A：Beckham has been the most popular football star in the world.

B：Beckham performed well when he was right midfielder in Manchester United.

A：I saw many impressive football games, especially in the World Cup.

B：The Italian Football Team won four champions in the World Cup.

A：My friend is member of the national football team.

B：The football has more fun in comparison with the baseball.

同義字與名詞（Synonym & Terminology）

1. announce（宣布） ⇨ proclaim ⇨ broadcast ⇨ report ⇨ state ⇨ declare

2. retire（退休） ⇨ resign ⇨ quit

3. brilliant（明亮奪目的）⇨ sparkling ⇨ bright ⇨ shining ⇨ clear ⇨ vivid
4. focus（集中）⇨ concentrate ⇨ adjust
5. terminate（結束）⇨ end ⇨ finish ⇨ close ⇨ conclude
6. popular（喜愛的）⇨ well-liked ⇨ dear ⇨ beloved ⇨ adored
7. peak（巔峰）⇨ top ⇨ crest ⇨ hilltop ⇨ summit
8. title(頭銜）⇨ tag ⇨ caption ⇨ designation
9. convert（轉換）⇨ change ⇨ transform
10. lease（租賃）⇨ rent ⇨ hire ⇨ let ⇨ charter
11. consecutive（連續的）⇨ following ⇨ successive ⇨ continuous

🖋 英譯中練習：（參閱主題文章）

English ⇨ Chinese Translation Practice：(Refer to the theme article)

1. Beckham's handsome and dashing appearance represents the popularity of the world football.（英譯中）

....

....

2. In the international football world, Beckham represented a team member of England National Team for 115 times, a record with no one to compete.（英譯中）

....

....

3. Historically, Beckham is the only England football player who has obtained championships in four major national tournaments. And he is the only one that scored in the FIFA World Cup for three consecutive times.（英譯中）

....

....

Politics

Commerce

Jobs

Sports

Healthy

Society

Career

Life

Unit 05 台灣旅美大聯盟棒球選手
（Taiwanese Baseball Players in U.S. MLB）

📎 球壇為國爭光的好漢

陳金鋒 Chin-feng Chen（Oct. 28, 1977-）

With several nicknames such as "Cannon Feng" or "Feng Brother," Chin-Feng Chen is an aborigine of Siraya in Tainan, one of indigenous peoples in Taiwan. He served at Los Angeles Dodgers and promoted to the Major League Baseball (MLB) on Sept. 14, 2002 when he was 24 years old, representing the first Taiwanese baseball player to appear in the U.S. baseball field.

陳金鋒外號「鋒砲」、「鋒仔」、「鋒哥」，台南市大內區西拉雅族原住民。他效力於洛杉磯道奇隊，於 2002 年 9 月 24 日升上大聯盟。他也是第一位在美國職棒大聯盟比賽中登場的台灣選手，當時年紀 24 歲。

In early 2007, Chen returned to Taiwan to join in the Chinese Professional Baseball League (CPBL) and he now serves at Lamigo team. He gained a plural contract, which was ranked as the highest income among all baseball players. Major contents of the contract included a six-year contract with an annual salary of NT$10 million in the first three years, and the pay of the remaining three years would be negotiated.

2007 年初，陳金鋒返台加盟中華職棒，目前效力於中華職棒 Lamigo 桃猿。曾是中華職棒球員中複數合約以及待遇最高的球員。簽約內容為：簽約六年，前三年薪資每年 1,000 萬新台幣 ，後三年再洽談薪水。

Politics

Commerce

Jobs

Sports

Healthy

Society

Career

Life

曹錦輝 Chin-hui Tso（June 2, 1981-）

As a former baseball player of CPBL, Chin-hui Tso served at Colorado Rockies, Los Angeles Dodgers, Kansa City Royals, and Brother Elephants of CPBL. He owns the blood of Amis Tribe and records as the first Taiwanese pitcher and strikes a first base hit in MLB.

曹錦輝為前中華職棒球員，曾效力於美國職棒大聯盟科羅拉多洛磯隊、洛杉磯道奇隊、及堪薩斯皇家隊與中華職棒兄弟象隊。擁有台灣原住民之一阿美族血統的曹錦輝，是台灣首位登上美國職棒大聯盟的投手及首位擊出安打的選手。

Tso was accused by prosecutors as a defendant in the CPBL match-fixing issue happened in 2009. He insisted that he has not involved in the fraud but admitted several contacts with betting leaders. Thus, Brother Elephants decided not to resume the contract with him. Together with his girl friend, Tso now runs a Sichuan beef noodle shop in Hualian, a city on the east coast of Taiwan.

在 2009 年中華職棒假球事件 中遭檢調單位約談並列為被告，曹錦輝堅持並未涉案，但坦承與賭盤的組頭多次接觸，象隊決定不予續約。目前他在花蓮市與女朋友開四川牛肉麵店為業。

王建民 Chien-ming Wang（March 31, 1980-）

Chien-ming Wang comes from Kuanmiao Township in Tainan City and guards as a pitcher. He served at New York Yankees, Washington Nationals, and Toronto Blue Jays but is now released as a free sport agent.

王建民生於台灣台南市關廟職業棒球選手，守備位置為投手。曾效力於美國職棒大聯盟紐約洋基、華盛頓國民、多倫多藍鳥，現為自由球員。

Chien-ming Wang is the first pitcher from the Asian region to win the playoff game in MLB. He is titled with a "winning pitcher of Asia" and keeps a record of 19 wins in a single season.

王建民是亞洲首位在季後賽拿下勝投的球員。他也是亞洲首位在大聯盟拿下『勝投王』的投手，以及亞洲投手在大聯盟單季最多勝投的紀錄保持人 (19 勝)。

郭泓志 Hong-chih Kuo（July 23, 1981- ）

A lefty pitcher and batter, Hong Chih-kou was born in Tainan City of Taiwan and served as pitcher at Los Angeles Dodgers, Seattle Mariners, and Chicago Cubs for about 14 years. He returned to Taiwan in 2013 and joined in Uni-Lions in October.

郭泓志生於台灣台南市，左投左打，守備位置為投手。曾效力於美國職棒大聯盟洛杉磯道奇，西雅圖水手隊，芝加哥小熊隊等前後約 14 年。他於 2013 年返台並於十月初加入中華職棒統一獅選手。

As the fourth pitcher from Taiwan, Kou took the plate on Sept. 2, 2005. He is the first Taiwanese baseball player to hit a home run in MLB and chosen for the Major League Baseball All Star Game.

2005 年 9 月 2 日在美國職棒大聯盟首度登板，是台灣第四位登上美國職棒大聯盟的棒球選手，也是第一位在大聯盟擊出全壘打及首位入選大聯盟明星賽的台灣選手。

It is reported that Kuo signed a three-year contract with Uni-Lions, with a record high price of NT$40 million, exceeding that of Chin-feng Chen and other active players in CPBL such as Cha Cha, captain of Brother Elephants. Kuo was very satisfied about the contract and said that playing baseball in Taiwan had been the wish since he was a child.

據了解，小小郭和統一獅這筆合約為期 3 年，總值超過新台幣 4000 萬元，也超越現役球員陳金鋒、及兄弟象隊長彭政閔 (恰恰) 所簽下的

Politics

Commerce

Jobs

Sports

Healthy

Society

Career

Life

3000 多萬元合約，是目前最大筆金額合約。郭泓志表示對合約和酬勞相當滿意，回台灣打球也是從小的願望。

胡金龍 Chin-lung Hu（Feb. 2, 1984-）

Chin-lung Hu comes from Tainan City and is the fifth Taiwanese baseball player in MLB. He also set a record of the shortest surname of "Hu" registered in MLB. He is the first Taiwanese player to make a successful steal base in MLB.

胡金龍台灣台南市 出身，為台灣第 5 位升上大聯盟 的球員，同時也創下大聯盟史上首位姓氏字母最少的球員 Hu。他也是第一位在大聯盟盜壘成功的台灣球員。

During his service at MLB, Hu rendered his service in New York Mets and Cleveland Indians. He returned to Taiwan for an entry draft held by CPBL in 2012 and became the No. 1 of the entry list since CPBL was established 24 years ago. He now serves as an outfielder at EDA Rhinos.

胡金龍於大聯盟時期效力於紐約大都會及克里夫蘭印地安人，他於 2012 年返國參加中華職棒舉辦之新人選秀，並成為中職 24 年的選秀狀元。現為義大犀牛隊外野手球員。

倪福德 Fu-te Ni（Nov. 14, 1982-）

Fu-te Ni used to play as a relief pitcher of Detroit Tigers. Before he joined in Detroit Tigers, he was a professional baseball player in CPBL.

倪福德曾是美國職棒大聯盟底特律老虎隊的中繼投手。在加入老虎隊以前，為中華職棒的球員。

Ni is the sixth Taiwanese baseball player and the fourth pitcher in MLB. He is the first Taiwanese player that is successfully transferred from CPBL to MLB.

他成為第六位來自台灣的大聯盟球員，和第四位投手。他也是首位成功由中華職棒轉戰美國職棒大聯盟的台灣球員。

陳偉殷 Wei-ying Chen（July 21, 1985-）

Born in Kaohsiung City, Wei-ying Chen is the first Taiwanese player that transfers from the Japanese professional baseball league to Baltimore Orioles and gains a plural year contract in MLB. He gained the title of No. 1 fielding percentage from the central league of Japan in 2009.
陳偉殷生於高雄市，是臺灣首位日本職棒轉戰美國職棒巴爾的摩金鶯隊的球員，他也是台灣首位在大聯盟獲得複數年合約的球員。他曾獲日本職棒 2009 年中央聯盟防禦率王。

According to unwritten rules of Taiwan's media, those local baseball players who are promoted to MLB are always nicknamed with the "X-boy." Thus, Wei-ying Chen is called the "Ying-boy" as the nickname. He follows the maxim：With utmost effort (for dear life),
臺灣媒體依自身潛規則：凡台灣球員升上大聯盟，一律稱之為 X 仔。因此，陳偉殷被稱呼為「殷仔」，其座右銘「一生懸命」。

📎 重要單字暨新聞辭彙（Key Vocabulary & News Glossary）

- the Major League Baseball (MLB)
  美國職棒大聯盟
- Los Angeles Dodgers
  洛杉磯道奇隊
- plural contract 複數合約
- Colorado Rockies 科羅拉多洛磯隊
- Kansa City Royals 堪薩斯皇家隊
- pitcher (n.) 投手
- home run 全壘打

- base hit 安打
- match-fixing issue 假球事件
- betting leaders 賭盤組頭
- New York Yankees 紐約洋基
- Washington Nationals 華盛頓國民
- Toronto Blue Jays 多倫多藍鳥
- free sport agent 自由球員
- winning pitcher 勝投
- Seattle Mariners 西雅圖水手隊

- Chicago Cubs 芝加哥小熊隊
- New York Mets 紐約大都會
- Cleveland Indians
  克里夫蘭印地安人
- steal base 盜壘
- taking the plate 登板
- Major League Baseball All Star
  Game 大聯盟明星賽

- entry draft 新人選秀
- outfielder 外野手
- Detroit Tigers 底特律老虎隊
- relief pitcher 中繼投手
- Baltimore Orioles 巴爾的摩金鶯隊
- fielding percentage 防禦率
- maxim 座右銘

Politics

Commerce

Jobs

Sports

Healthy

Society

Career

Life

單字及句型範例（Vocabulary & Sentence Examples）

1. He is the best pitcher I've ever seen. 他是我見到的最好的投球手。
2. a plant indigenous to New Zealand 一種紐西蘭原產的植物。
3. The government will not negotiate with the terrorists. 政府決不與恐怖分子談判。
4. She did not return home till eleven o'clock. 她十一點鐘才回家。
5. Aesop's fables illustrate moral maxims. 伊索寓言闡明了道德準則。

問題與討論（Questions & Discussions）

Q 1. 您最欣賞哪位台灣旅美棒球選手，原因何在？

Q.1 Who is your most favorite Taiwanese baseball player in Major League Baseball of the U.S., and the reason why?

Q 2. 王建民曾經是大聯盟『勝投王』，為何目前卻演變成自由球員？

Q.2 Chien-ming Wang used to be a winning pitcher in MLB, and why he has become a free sport agent now?

Q 3. 您認為台灣之職棒近年表現如何，未來前景可看好？

Q.3 How do you comment on the performance of CPBL in recent years and prospects of Taiwan's professional baseball in the future?

155

✎ 主題對話範例（Dialogue Examples）

A：Several Taiwanese baseball players have performed well in MLB in recent years.

B：There are so many games held in the playoff of MLB recently.

A：Most of my friends like to see the baseball game, especially the MLB of the U.S.

B：Many Taiwanese used to appreciate the performance of Chien-ming Wang in MLB but lost their money in betting.

A：With a record high salary, Hong-chih Kuo signed the contract and joined in Uni-Lions recently.

B：Kuo stayed in the U.S. professional baseball team for 14 years.

同義字與名詞（Synonym & Terminology）

1. indigenous（本土的）⇨ native ⇨ original ⇨ natural to
2. negotiate（談判）⇨ arrange ⇨ settle ⇨ mediate ⇨ intervene
3. professional（職業的）⇨ occupational ⇨ vocational
4. return（返回）⇨ revert ⇨ revisit ⇨ go back ⇨ come back
5. render（給與）⇨ give ⇨ present ⇨ grant ⇨ allow ⇨ allot
6. maxim（格言）⇨ proverb ⇨ saying ⇨ rule ⇨ law ⇨ code

✎ 英譯中練習：（參閱主題文章）

English ⇨ Chinese Translation Practice：(Refer to the theme article)

1. He served at Los Angeles Dodgers and promoted to the Major League Baseball (MLB) on Sept. 14, 2002 when he was 24 years old, representing the first Taiwanese baseball player to appear in the U.S. baseball field.（英譯中）

....

....

Politics

Commerce

Jobs

Sports

Healthy

Society

Career

Life

2. Chien-ming Wang is the first pitcher from Asia to win the playoff game in MLB. He is titled with a "king of winning pitcher" from Asia and keeps a record of 19 wins in a single season. （英譯中）

....

....

3. He is the first Taiwanese baseball player to hit a home run in MLB and chosen in the Major League Baseball All Star Game. （英譯中）

....

....

Part 5　談食品安全
Talks About Food Security

Unit 01 別吃壞了肚子～ 黑心食品中毒事件

（Don't Get An Upset Stomach—— "Black Heart" Food Events）

📎食品的衛生與使用令人擔憂

黑心食品 "Black Heart"（Seriously Risky） Food

The "black heart" (seriously risky) food is generally defined as follows:

1. To use raw materials or the use of materials in the manufacturing process that is harmful to the human body, and such commodities are mass produced for extravagant profits.
2. To put non-food additives for the production of inferior quality foods.
3. To alter the expiration date of food and sell to the consumers who are without the knowledge.

黑心食品一般而言泛指下列行為：

1. 指原材料或其生產過程中使用的材料對人體有害，卻還大量生產謀取暴利的商品。
2. 在食物中添加非食品添加物的材料製成的低品質食品。
3. 明知超過保存期限，仍故意變造商品標示，使不知情的消費者採購過期食品並食用。

The food security problem has long existed in every place around the world. Take Taiwan for instance, the island has been famous for its fine food and delicacies but several poisonous food cases are reported after "the plasticizer event" in 2011.

有關食品安全問題仍普遍存在世界各地。以美食文化著稱的臺灣而言，從 2011 塑化劑事件後，近年也陸續傳出有毒食品問題。

The "black heart" food has been an age-old problem, which actually has happened since the Industrial Revolution (1750-1830). Following the advanced development of science, the technique of making poison and fake food has improved significantly, making it an inevitable problem for people nowadays.

其實黑心食品由來已久，早在工業革命後就已發生。隨著科學日趨發展，讓有毒及造假食品的手法不斷升級，也是我們現代人無法逃避且須每天面對的問題。

2013 年臺灣食品安全問題事件 Taiwan's Food Security Incidents in 2013

In 2013, Taiwan encountered a series of illegal food cases which arouse the attention of public opinion. Most of the cases used industrial materials during the food processing (illegal food additives) and some were found to use false labeling in expired foods.

2013 年在臺灣發生了一系列引起社會輿論關注食品安全問題的食品產業違法事件。主要是其他工業用有害原料流入食品加工（違法食品添加物），以及被查出「過期食品」等商品虛偽標示事件。

A cabinet-level meeting under the Executive Yuan formally named the incident as the "illegal food additive incident".

中華民國行政院會議稱此事件的正式名稱為「違法食品添加物事件」。

Details of the incident are classified as follows:

統計所有台灣廠商的詳細事件分類如下：

· Expiration date products are sold as immediate ones or the use of overdue materials.

· 過期品當即期品販售，或以過期原料製作。

Politics

Commerce

Jobs

Sports

Healthy

Society

Career

Life

- Illegal use of industrial-level preservative, ethylenediaminetetraacetic acid disodium salt dehydrate, or EDTA-2Na.
- 違法添加工業級防腐劑——乙烯二胺四醋酸二鈉。

- Illegal use of industrial-level maleic anhydride to produce chemical starch.
- 違法添加工業級順丁烯二酸酐用以化製澱粉。

- Illegal use of industrial-level metanil yellow.
- 違法添加工業級色素皂黃。

- Illegal use of industrial-level salt as edible salt.
- 違法添加工業級鹽做為食用鹽。

- The content of preservative benzoic acid (C6H5COOH) exceeds the standards.
- 防腐劑苯甲酸,含量超標。

- The vegetable pesticide residuals such as Carbaryl and Profenofos exceed the standards.
- 蔬菜殘留加保利、佈飛松等農藥,含量超標

- The non-brewed soy bean sauce contains carcinogenic 3-chloropropane-1,2-diol and exceeds the standards.
- 非純釀造的醬油裡有致癌物單氯丙二醇,含量超標

- Eggs contain antibiotic Thiamphenicol and Florfenicol, which are carcinogenic and exceed the standards.
- 雞蛋裡有致癌性抗生素甲磺氯黴素與氯甲磺氯黴素,含量超標

政府對策 Government Measures

The Board of Foreign Trade (BOFT) of the Ministry of Economic Affairs (MOEA) proposes to regulate that exports of specified foods have to attach inspection approved certificates in the future. BOFT said that eight major food items including rice flour lath, meatball, Taiwanese tapioca, tofu pudding (Dou Wha), rice cake, taro ball (Yu Yuan), and sweet potatoes would need such proofs but the proposal would be finalized after seeking opinions from relevant governmental agencies.

經濟部國貿局擬針對特定食品在出口時必須附上合格檢驗單位的證明，才能出口。 國貿局表示，目前擬將粄條、肉圓、黑輪、粉圓、豆花、粉粿、芋圓、地瓜圓等 8 大類食品納入出口需檢附證明的項目，但還需與相關單位進一步討論後確定。

第三國對策 Countermeasures from the third nation

Singapore has now requested Taiwan to issue qualified certificates for exports to Singapore. The Southeast Asian nation also hopes to have a better understanding of latest policies adopted by Taiwan to cope with such food problems.

目前新加坡已要求台灣在出口至新加坡時需出具相關證明。同時也希望了解台灣對這類產品的最新措施。

惡名昭彰詐欺與爭議事件 Notorious and Fraud Cases

Edible oil products from Tatung, a food stuff company located in Chunghwa County in central Taiwan, have run into troubles recently! Many edible oils from the company are examined out with illegal adding of copper chlorophyll, which is harmful to human health. The company also blended its high level oil products with low levels, and its peanut oils and hot pepper oils were inspected to contain of not any peanuts or even zero hot pepper contents inside.

彰化大統食用油最近出包！該公司多項食用油被驗出違規添加銅葉綠素，對人體健康有害；及高階油品混攙低階油。而花生調和油與辣椒油更被查出完全沒有花生與辣椒成分。

Meanwhile, Tatung has a total of 74 items of edible oils which are packaged with vague labeling and contain copper chlorophyll. The Public Health Bureau of Taichung City has asked downstream hypermarkets and convenient stores to take down from the shelves of over 6,000 bottles. Company chairman Kao Cheng-li attributed the mixture of oil to the production of different oil products at the same time, but ranking officials at the Ministry of Health and Welfare said that the company has already involved in a livelihood fraud crime.

大統七十四種包裝標示不明或是混摻銅葉綠素的油品，台中市衛生局稽查下游賣場、超商等販售業者，要求下架共六千多瓶。雖然負責人高振利解釋是生產線同時生產不同油種發生混充，但衛生福利部稱業者已涉民生詐欺犯罪。

パン達人手感烘焙 Top Pot Bakery

The Taiwan-based Top Pot Bakery is a chain store which was founded in December 2010 and opened branches in both Hong Kong and China. This bakery boasted the "use of yeast starter without adding artificial (flavoring) essence," but it mixed synthetic essence when baking its European-style Taiwanese breads.

パン達人手感烘焙是台灣的一家連鎖麵包店於 2010 年 12 月開幕，並於香港及大陸等地均設有分店。該店之廣告標榜「天然酵母，無添加人工香料」；但製作歐風臺式麵包時，摻入人工合成製造出的香精。

Keith English Cottage, a performer in Hong Kong, doubted of Top Pot Bakery in the website, questioning that the company's products have added artificial essence. The Health Bureau of Taipei City soon inspected that there were nine artificial essences, including the legal food additives,

propylene glycol, and multiple edible pigments. The Health Bureau of
the New Taipei City also checked an emulsifier, or sorbitan fatty acid
ester, in yester from outside purchases of the bakery.

香港演奏家李冠集在網路上發表文章質疑胖達人的產品添加人工香精，
不久台北市政府衛生局稽查發現 9 項人工香料（含有合法的食品添加
物溶劑丙二醇及多種食用色素）；新北市衛生局亦查到外購酵母含乳
化劑（或稱脂肪酸山梨醇酐酯）。

消費者聰明的選擇 Wise Selection of Customers

Consumers are suggested to select food products with either GMP
or GHP marks. The Industrial Development Bureau of MOEA has
promoted the GMP mark, which is joined voluntarily by manufacturers
and is not enforced by the law, however.

消費者應選擇 GMP 或 GHP 廠商的產品。目前由經濟部工業局所推動
的食品「GMP」標章，是由食品工廠自願參加，而非法律規定強制實
施。

重要單字暨新聞辭彙（Key Vocabulary & News Glossary）

- mass produce 大量生產
- extravagant profits 暴利
- additives *(n.)* 添加物
- alter *(vt.)* 竄改
- expiration *(n.)* 期滿
- delicacies *(n.)* 美食
- poisonous *(adj.)* 有毒的
- plasticizer *(n.)* 塑化劑
- Industrial Revolution 工業革命
- inevitable *(adj.)* 無可避免的
- public opinion 社會輿論
- overdue *(adj.)* 過期的
- carcinogenic *(adj.)* 致癌的

- Board of Foreign Trade 國貿局
- notorious *(adj.)* 惡名昭彰
- fraud *(n.)* 詐欺
- hypermarket 大賣場
- convenient store 便利商店
- Ministry of Health and Welfare 衛生福利部
- chain store 連鎖店
- Industrial Development Bureau 工業局
- enforce *(vi.)* 強制
- eligible *(adj.)* 有資格的

單字及句型範例（Vocabulary & Sentence Examples）

1. They tightened security during the President's visit. 他們在總統訪問期間加強了安全防衛。
2. The lousy food upsets my stomach. 這糟糕的飯菜使我腸胃不適。
3. It is a risky undertaking. 那是一樁冒險的事情。
4. Do you know who defined man as a rational animal? 你知道是誰將人說成是有理智的動物的？
5. He has some extravagant expectations. 他抱有奢望。
6. Synthetic fabric is inferior to cotton fabric. 合成纖維織物不如棉織品好。
7. The tailor altered the coat to make it shorter. 裁縫把大衣改短了。
8. He is eligible for retirement. 他合乎退休條件。

問題與討論（Questions & Discussions）

Q 1. 黑心食品無所不在，您個人有採取任何防範聰明高招？

Q.1 The "black heart" food issues have existed in each corner of Taiwan. Do you have any wise measures against such products?

Q 2. 您會花錢購買即將過期或比較便宜但標示不清楚之商品嗎？主要考慮原因為何？

Q.2 Do you purchase products that are to be expired or cheaper but their labeling are so vague? What are your major considerations on such things?

Q 3. 您對大統食用油添加銅葉綠素及胖達人麵包添加人工香精等黑心食品案件事有何評論？

Q.3 Tatung added copper chlorophyll in its edible oils and the bread from Top Pot Bakery contained artificial essence. How do you comment on these black heart food incidents?

📎 主題對話範例（Dialogue Examples）

A：Taiwan is famous for a kingdom of delicious food in the world, but this title is fading out due to several "black heart" food incidents happened in recent years.

B：It is a must for the government to adopt more severe measures so as to stop the happening of such cases in the future.

同義字與名詞（Synonym & Terminology）

1. extravagant(過度的) ⇨ extreme ⇨ excessive ⇨ inordinate
2. inferior(低劣的) ⇨ lower ⇨ worse ⇨ subordinate
3. alter（竄改） ⇨ diversify ⇨ change ⇨ vary ⇨ modify ⇨ make different
4. bake（烘烤） ⇨ roast ⇨ broil ⇨ grill ⇨ barbecue ⇨ toast
5. poisonous（有毒的） ⇨ toxic ⇨ deadly ⇨ destructive ⇨ noxious
6. inevitable(無可避免的) ⇨ destined ⇨ fated ⇨ doomed ⇨ unavoidable
7. vague（模糊不清的） ⇨ unclear ⇨ indistinct ⇨ indefinite ⇨ dim
8. enforce（強制） ⇨ compel ⇨ force ⇨ oblige
9. eligible(有資格的) ⇨ qualified ⇨ fit ⇨ desirable ⇨ suitable

📎 英譯中練習：（參閱主題文章）

English ⇨ Chinese Translation Practice：(Refer to the theme article)

1. Following the advanced development of science, the technique of making poison and fake food has improved significantly, making it an inevitable problem for people nowadays.（英譯中）

....

....

Unit 02　茶與養身
（Tea and Health）

📎 健康的飲品

喜愛的飲料 Favorite Drinks

Dating back to thousands of years ago, tea has become a favorite drink for the public. Tea is tasty and also is an excellent natural health drink.

茶由藥用、食用，到成為我們喜愛的飲料，已有數千年之久。茶不但好喝，也是良好的天然保健飲料。

The Time magazine once selected tea as one of 10 healthy foods in the natural world. The Food and Agriculture Organization of the United Nations, the World Health Organization, and the American Society of Clinical Oncology sponsored and propagandized benefits of drinking tea in several large-scaled international conventions.

美國《時代雜誌》甚至曾特選「茶」為自然界十大健康食品之一。聯合國農糧組織、世界衛生組織和美國腫瘤學會也多次在大型國際會議中贊助並宣導喝茶對健康有益。

中西醫學證實喝茶對健康有益

Chinese / Western Medicine Verifies Tea Health

Most people consent that tea is good for health as the tea leaf contains abundant health-care contents, including catechin and their oxidative condensed compounds. And tea is rich in comparison with vegetables.

一般人認為喝茶對健康有益，這是因為茶葉的保健成份相當豐富，包括有兒茶素類及其氧化縮合物。其豐富性遠勝於一般蔬果。

The catechin (or theophylline) is known as functions of anti-oxidation, reducing cholesterol, and restraining blood pressure. Meanwhile, the caffeine component in tea represents about one third of coffee and possesses freshness, cardiotonic, emulgent, and hypermetabolism functions.

茶最為人知悉的保健成份為兒茶素類，除了有抗氧化，還有降低膽固醇與抑制血壓上升等作用。另外，茶之咖啡因元素，約為咖啡的三分之一，具有提神、強心、利尿、代謝亢進等作用。

減肥者宜飲烏龍茶、普洱茶、黑茶 Oolong, Pu'er, and Black Tea to Slim

As a kind of half-fermented tea, oolong contains almost no vitamin C but is rich in both iron and calcium, enabling it to promote digestive enzyme and resolve fats. It is distinct that black tea can suppress the increase of fat in the abdomen region, thus preventing heaps of adipose tissue. And Pu'er tea is an expert in deleting extra fats.

烏龍茶屬半發酵茶，幾乎不含維生素 C，但富含鐵、鈣等礦物質，有促進消化酶和分解脂肪的功效。黑茶對抑制腹部脂肪的增加有明顯效果，有防止脂肪堆積的作用。普洱茶更是消除多餘脂肪的高手。

接觸電腦者宜飲菊花茶、綠茶
Chrysanthemum Tea and Green Tea for Computer-Connected People

The white chrysanthemum in the tea can detoxify heat, hazardous chemicals, and radiation substances in the human body, a healing effect in both resistance and elimination. The vitamin in tea recovers and prevents the deterioration of eyesight.

茶中的白菊具有解毒的作用，對體內積存的暑氣、有害的化學物質和放射性物質，都有抵抗、排除的療效。而茶中的維生素則有助於恢復和防止視力衰退。

口有異味者宜飲綠茶、紅茶 Green Tea, Black Tea Cut Mouth Odor

The catechin in the green tea is ideal to withstand mouth odors. The black tea owns fewer catechin but its theaflavins has effects to remove mouth odor.

綠茶中的兒茶素對付口中異味有良好效果。紅茶含兒茶素甚微，但因含茶黃質，故也具有優異的除口臭效果。

老年人忌飲濃茶 The Elderly to Avoid Thick Tea

There are many benefits for the elderly to drink tea and this is helpful for their invigoration and digestion. Too much thick tea incurs constipation, high blood pressure, and indigestion, for example.

茶對老年人的好處很多，具有提神醒腦、促進消化等作用。但是，如果老年人經常大量飲用濃茶容易出現很多身體不適，如便秘、血壓升高、消化不良等。

不宜喝茶的人群 People Who Are Not Proper to Drink Tea

People who are suffering from insomnia (sleeplessness), fever from catch cold (influenza), gastric (stomach) ulcer, and pregnant women are not proper to drink tea. The caffeine in tea accelerates the speed of heartbeat and a burden of kidney, an unfavorable factor for the healthy of fetuses.

失眠者、感冒發熱者、胃潰瘍患者、孕婦等人群不宜喝茶。因為茶葉中的咖啡鹼能加劇孕婦的心跳速度，增加其心、腎負擔等，不利於胎兒的健康發育。

📎 重要單字暨新聞辭彙（Key Vocabulary & News Glossary）

- health drink 健康飲料
- natural world 自然界
- the Food and Agriculture Organization of the United Nations 聯合國農糧組織
- World Health Organization 世界衛生組織
- the American Society of Clinical Oncology 美國腫瘤學會
- international convention 國際會議
- consent *(vt.)* 同意
- cholesterol *(n.)* 膽固醇
- blood pressure 血壓
- suppress (vt.) 抑制
- propagandize (vt.) 宣傳
- oolong tea 烏龍茶
- Pu'er tea 普洱茶
- green tea 綠茶
- black tea 紅（黑）茶
- chrysanthemum tea 菊花茶
- fetus *(n.)* 胎兒

📎 單字及句型範例（Vocabulary & Sentence Examples）

1. Lester, the second son, was his father's favorite.
   二兒子里斯特是他父親的寵兒。

2. Would you consent to work for us? 你同意為我們工作嗎？

3. Even the grave old gentleman could not suppress a laugh.
   連那位嚴肅的老紳士都禁不住笑了。

4. Two Virginian Congressmen sponsored the bill.
   兩位弗吉尼亞國會議員提出這一議案。

5. When wine is fermented, it gives off bubbles of gas.
   酒發酵時發出氣泡。

📎 問題與討論（Questions & Discussions）

Q 1. 您平常喝不喝茶？您喜歡喝哪一類茶？

Q.1 Are you a tea lover? And what are your favorite teas?

Q 2. 中西醫都證實喝茶有益身體保健，您是否同意並遵行此建議嗎？

Q.2 Both Chinese and western medicine verifies that tea is helpful for health. Do you agree and obey the suggestion?

Q 3. 您知道有些人不適宜喝茶嗎？可否舉例說明原因為何？

Q.3 Do you know some certain people are not proper to drink tea? Could you identify the reasons?

📎 主題對話範例（Dialogue Examples）

A：Tea has so many benefits for health but do not drink too much if you have a gastric ulcer.

B：I prefer tea to coffee, and how about you?

A：The Time magazine selected tea as a natural health food.

B：I also like coffee and have about three cups a day.

A：Do you understand how tea is made?

B：I visited the factory to see the tea process in a local tour.

同義字與名詞（Synonym & Terminology）

1.favorite(喜愛的) ⇨ chosen ⇨ preferred ⇨ favored ⇨ selected

2.abundant（豐富的） ⇨ rich ⇨ lavish ⇨ luxuriant

3.sponsor（贊助） ⇨ underwriter ⇨ backer ⇨ promoter ⇨ supporter

4.ferment(發酵) ⇨ sour ⇨ change chemically

5. digest（消化） ⇨ absorb ⇨ ingest

6. suppress(抑制) ⇨ restrain ⇨ repress ⇨ inhibit ⇨ curb

7. incur(招致) ⇨ contract ⇨ catch ⇨ result in ⇨ bring on

8. proper（恰當的） ⇨ correct ⇨ right ⇨ fitting ⇨ decent

Politics

Commerce

Jobs

Sports

Healthy

Society

Career

Life

📎 **英譯中練習：**（參閱主題文章）

English ➪ Chinese Translation Practice：(Refer to the theme article)

1. Tea has become a favorite drink for the public. Tea is tasty and also is an excellent natural health drink.（英譯中）

   ....

   ....

2. It is distinct that black tea can suppress the increase of fat in the abdomen region, thus preventing the heap of adipose tissues.（英譯中）

   ....

   ....

3. People who are suffering from insomnia (sleeplessness), catch cold (influenza), gastric (stomach) ulcer, and pregnant women are not proper to drink tea.（英譯中）

   ....

   ....

Unit　03　你喝了一口好水嗎？

（Do You Drink Water Precisely?）

📎 一飲好水身強體健

水 Water

As far as the human kind is concerned, water is a principal structure consisting of a skin cartilage, organization, and organs. Each part of the body relies on water. The human body is nearly composed of water. How to introduce appropriate water into the body has become important regarding health care. Water represents about 80% weight of a newborn baby but the quantity of water decreases following the increase of age. The percentage of water stands at 60% of a grown male (standard weights) or at between 50% and 55% of female (standard weights).

對於人類來說，水是一個重要的結構組成的皮膚軟骨，組織，和器官。每一個身體的一部分依賴於水。人體幾乎是由水分所構成，如何讓水適當的導入體內，對於保養和健康是非常重要的一件事！剛生下來的小嬰兒，體重約有 80% 是水分，但隨著年齡的增長，體內的水分含量也會逐漸減少，例如成年男性（標準體重）是 60%，成年女性（標準體重）是 50~55% 是水分。

The reason behind the sunstroke is dehydration caused by insufficient of water. Accordingly, water is vital to the human body.

中暑的原因是體內的水分不足，所引發的脫水症狀，因此水分對我們人體來說是非常重要的。

一天喝 6~8 次，適量飲水
Appropriate Water Amount, 6-8 times per day

The main point of drinking water is "to drink one cup (about 150~250

Unit 3 你喝了一口好水嗎? ▶

Politics

Commerce

Jobs

Sports

Healthy

Society

Career

Life

ml) per time, plus six to eight times per day". Following the rule, the supply amount of water is about 1.5 liter each day.

喝水的要領就是「一次喝一杯的程度（大約 150~250ml），一天喝 6~8 次」。依照這樣的程度喝水的話，可以補充一日所需的水分量（約 1.5 公升）。

Specifically speaking, drink water at: right after getting up, breakfast time, lunch time, afternoon tea time, dinner time, taking a shower, and before going to bed.

具體的來說就是：

起床後馬上

早餐時

午餐時

下午茶時

晚餐時

要洗澡時

睡覺前

The internal body is very limited to handle the water quantity at each time. Thus, to drink a great amount of water in a sudden way is not good. This makes heavy burden of the body despite beauty effects.

體內一次可以處理的水量有限，所以為了想要補充一日的所需水量，一口氣大量飲水是 NG 的！即使對美容有效果，對身體卻是一大負擔。

睡覺前後一定要喝水 drink water before and after sleeping

It is effective to drink water before and after sleeping as people run off so much water in sleeping. A supply of 200 ml water right after getting up is needed. The vitality turns to be smooth in the morning if water is taken before sleeping.

喝水最有效果的兩個時間點，分別是睡覺前和起床後。其實在睡眠中，意外的流失很多水分呢！所以一起床馬上補充 200ml 的水分是很重要的。另外睡前攝取水分的話，隔天一早的氣血也會很暢通喔！

Aged people hate trips to the restroom at midnight and decline to drink water before going to bed. This may incur dehydration easily due to insufficient of water, and a special attention should be paid on this matter.

特別是年紀大的人，因為不喜歡半夜起床跑廁所，就不在睡前喝水，這樣很容易因為水分不足而引起脫水症狀，要特別注意！

空腹時飲水 Drink Water at an Empty Stomach

In order to absorb minerals in both mid-hard and hard water, the best time to drink water is at an empty stomach before meals. This move enhances the operation of mucous membrane in digestion organs and helps to absorb minerals in water.

為了吸收中硬水和硬水裡的礦物質，飯前空腹喝水是最好的。為了讓消化器官的黏膜運作以便吸收礦物質，空腹是喝水的最佳時刻。

Drinking of water stimulates both the parasympathetic nerve and internal organ operations. Small intestines absorb most minerals in water but not all of them if a great amount of water is taken in one shot. It is appropriate to drink a cup of water per time.

喝水會刺激副交感神經，促使內臟運作。雖然小腸會吸收水分中大部分所含的礦物質，但是如果一次大量飲水，礦物質會無法全部被吸收，因此一回一杯程度的量是最適當的。

喝常溫水 Drink Normal Temperature Water

In order to avoid a lower body temperature from water, the drinking of normal temperature water plays a key point. You may suffer from indigestion if you drink too much iced water. People who have heart diseases are not suitable to drink too much iced water. This may reduce the body temperature and incur burden of heart when iced water flows by the gullet near the heart.

為了不要讓體溫因為水的溫度而降低，飲用常溫的水是重點！特別是腸胃比較不好的人，如果一次喝大量冰水的話，小心會對腸胃有不好的影響。還有，心臟不好的人喝太多冰水，在心臟旁食道裡所經流的冰水，會導致心臟降溫而造成負擔。

流汗前喝水 Drink Water Before Sweating

Remember to supply water before taking a shower or exercises. During exercises, water is needed in about 15 minutes per time and the water temperature is suggested be lower than normal, or at about 6~13℃ .

在洗澡或運動前，請記得一定要補充水分。運動期間大約每 15 分鐘 1 次的程度喝水最佳。這個時候喝比常溫還要低溫，大約是 6 ～ 13℃的水是 OK 的！

在口渴之前，慢慢喝水 Slow Drinking Before Thirsty

When the moisture decreases to somewhat extent in the body, the blood will become viscous, leading to a symptom of sleepy or headache. Before the aforesaid symptoms have occurred, remember to supply water diligently!

當體內的水分減少時，血液會變得黏稠，引起想睡覺或者頭痛等徵狀。在這些徵狀發生之前，記得勤勞的補充水分吧！

📎 重要單字暨新聞辭彙（Key Vocabulary & News Glossary）

- precisely *(adv.)* 正確地
- principal *(adj.)* 重要的
- compose *(vt.)* 組成
- health care 保健
- vital *(adj.)* 極其重要的
- quantity *(n.)* 數量

- **amount** *(n.)* 總額
- **digestion organs** 消化器官
- **small intestines** 小腸
- **burden** *(n.)* 負擔
- **minerals** *(n.)* 礦物質
- **decline** *(vt.)* 婉拒
- **absorb** *(vt.)* 吸收
- **viscous** *(adj.)* 黏稠的

單字及句型範例（Vocabulary & Sentence Examples）

1. We all drank his good luck. 我們舉杯祝賀他的好運。
2. I'll tell you precisely how to do it. 我將確切地告訴你如何辦理此事。
3. Drinking is a principal cause of traffic accidents. 酗酒是交通事故的主要原因。
4. We know a lot about the structure of genes now. 如今我們對基因的結構有了較多的了解。
5. A university consists of teachers, administrators and students. 大學由教師, 行政人員和學生組成。
6. The villagers here rely on wells for their water. 這兒的村民用水全靠井。
7. The dove represents peace. 鴿子象徵和平。
8. Each of them got a percentage of the profits. 他們每個人都得到一部分利潤。
9. Your recent work has been below standard. 你最近的工作一直低於標準。
10. The questions put forward at the meeting are of vital importance. 會上提出的那些問題極其重要。
11. She declined their invitation. 她婉拒了他們的邀請。
12. A fever is a symptom of illness. 發燒是生病的症狀。
13. Cotton gloves absorb sweat. 棉手套吸汗。

📎 問題與討論（Questions & Discussions）

Q 1. 你喜歡喝礦泉水或僅是白開水？

Q.1　Do you prefer mineral water or only the boiled water?

Q 2. 你家裡有加裝自來水過濾器嗎？其功能如何？

Q.2　Have your house installed a filter for tap water, and what are their functions?

📎 主題對話範例（Dialogue Examples）

A：Water is important to human body and health.

B：We need an appropriate water amount of about 1.5 liter per day.

A：A normal person has to drink water for 6-8 times per day with one cup (150 ~ 250 ml) each time.

B：It is effective to drink water before and after sleeping.

同義字與名詞（Synonym & Terminology）

1. rely（依賴）　⇨ trust ⇨ confide ⇨ depend on ⇨ count on
2. quantity（數量）　⇨ amount ⇨ number ⇨ sum
3. lower(降低）　⇨ lessen ⇨ reduce ⇨ decrease
4. symptom(症狀）　⇨ indication ⇨ omen ⇨ token
5. absorb（吸收）　⇨ incorporate ⇨ engross ⇨ sponge

📎 英譯中練習：（參閱主題文章）

English ⇨ Chinese Translation Practice：(Refer to the theme article)

1. The reason behind the sunstroke is dehydration caused by insufficient of water. Accordingly, water is vital to the human body.（英譯中）

　...

　...

Politics

Commerce

Jobs

Sports

Healthy

Society

Career

Life

Unit　04　除油減脂妙方多
（Methods to Lose Weight）

📎 抓住個人合適的訣竅，和肥胖說再見

減肥永保苗條 To Lose Weight and Keep Slim Forever

Women always pay close attention to the topic of "lose weight". The fast lose weight bounces back easily, and only if a healthy method is adopted that keeps you slim forever.

「減肥」是女人永遠關注的話題。但是，快速減肥會容易反彈，只有健康的減肥方法才能幫助你永保苗條。

幫零食「瘦身」To "Slim" Snacks

High calorie snacks are a formidable enemy to lose weight. The selection of small packaged snacks can meet your appetites and reduce consumption of heats. Only if you control the quantity of snacks and they will no longer become obstacles of lose weight.

高熱量的零食是減肥的大敵，但選擇小包裝的零食，不僅能滿足你的口慾，還能幫助你減少熱量的攝入。只要控制零食的份量，它就不再是你瘦身的障礙咯！

有氧運動 Aerobics

Exercise is the best way to consume calories, and aerobics together with its power training enables to lose weight more effective. Commonly seen aerobics include bike-riding, swimming, jogging, yoga, and so on. Insist on a 30-minute aerobics per day do a lot of help in lose weight.

運動是最好的消耗熱量的減肥方法，而有氧運動與力量訓練能讓減肥效果更加明顯。常見的有氧運動包括騎自行車、游泳、慢跑以及瑜珈減脂等等。每天堅持三十分鐘的有氧運動對減肥有很大的幫助。

Politics

Commerce

Jobs

Sports

Healthy

Society

Career

Life

喝水的智慧 Wisdom on Drinking Water

Most people realize that more water drinking enhances metabolism and assists to lose weight. Drink a cup of water can exclude metabolite of former night out of the body and reduce the creation of excess flesh; and drink water before meals can increase the satisfaction and lessen the quantity of food.

很多人都知道，多喝水能促進新陳代謝，對減肥有很大的幫助！吃早餐之前喝杯白水能夠把前一夜體內的代謝物排出體外，減少贅肉的產生；餐前喝一杯水能增加飽腹感，減少你的食量。

When you feel weary or exhausted in the afternoon, you will be likely to over eat due to the mood. Drink water at the time is expected to lower the calorie consumption and this method of drinking water also helps to speed up the lose weight.

而下午是你覺得疲憊、倦怠的時候，容易因為情緒而吃得過多。這個時候喝水的話能減少熱量的攝入，這些喝水的方法都會幫助你加快減肥的速度哦！

辛辣的調味料 Spicy Seasonings

To add some spicy seasonings in cooking is another way to lose weight. Especially, pepper has functions to raise the body warmth and accelerate metabolism at the same time.

在做菜的時候添加一些辛辣的調味料是一個很好的減肥方法。尤其是辣椒，對於身體的加溫、提升基礎代謝功能都有很大的作用。

保持積極心態 Keep Positive Attitude

The success level of losing weight goes together with a positive attitude and psychological factor. Those who have positive attitudes are successful to lose weight and keep a good shape, avoiding the engorgement produced by a negative state of mind.

瘦身的成功程度和人心理的積極程度成正比。保持積極心態的人，更容易成功減肥，並在瘦身之後長期保持良好的形體，還能避免消極情緒帶來的暴飲暴食哦！

喝湯輕鬆瘦 Eat Soups to Lose Weight

Experts consider that soups can help food enter much closer to the gastric wall and increase the satisfaction by the central nervous system, thus reducing the absorption of less food. Remember soups must be made of light and avoid over greasy. Eating soups at the beginning of a meal is able to lower your appetite and reduce quantity of food.

專家認為，湯能使進入胃中的食糜充分貼近胃壁，增強飽腹感，從而反射性地興奮飽食中樞，因而減少食物攝入量。但要記住，湯要清淡，不要過於油膩。飯前喝湯能有效降低食慾，減少你的食量。

充足的睡眠 Sufficient Sleeping

The sufficient sleeping enhances metabolism, dispel edemas, and stimulate the growth hormone, thus turning fat into energy of the body and serving as a secret way to lose weight. If you are under a sleeping deprivation, your metabolism will become slower and makes you hungry—you are easily to eat more calories.

充足的睡眠會促進新陳代謝、消除浮腫、刺激生長激素，以指導身體把脂肪轉化為能量，是保持苗條的秘訣所在。而睡眠不足不僅會減緩你的新陳代謝，還容易讓你產生飢餓感，這樣你就更加容易吃進更多的熱量了。

晚餐吃得少 Fewer Meals at Dinner

Why fewer meals are effective to lose weight? This is because activities become deficient after dinner and calories will pile up and acquire

Politics

Commerce

Jobs

Sports

Healthy

Society

Career

Life

obesity if they are not consumed completely.

晚餐吃得少為什麼會有助減肥呢？這是晚上吃過飯後的活動量較少，攝入的熱量無法得到好的消耗就會變成脂肪堆積在身體內，容易造成肥胖。

控制飲食 Control Food

It is a must to understand your own food quantity and calories that are consumed, a success to control heat and lose weight. Read the food label to better understand calories and slow down the eating speed or eat 80% full in order to reduce the heat consumption.

要了解自己的食量以及攝入的熱量，這樣能幫助你控制熱量攝入而走向成功減肥之路。閱讀食物標籤能讓你更加清楚其熱量，而減慢吃東西的速度和只吃八分飽能減少熱量是攝入。

重要單字暨新聞辭彙（Key Vocabulary & News Glossary）

- lose weight 減肥
- slim (adj.) 苗條的
- formidable (adj.) 可怕的
- snacks (n.) 零食
- appetite (n.) 食慾
- calorie (n.) 熱量
- lessen (vt.) 減弱
- obstacles (n.) 障礙
- aerobics (n.) 有氧運動
- exclude (vt.) 排出

- dispel (vt.) 消除
- weary (adj.) 疲憊的
- exhausted (adj.) 倦怠的
- spicy (adj.) 辛辣的
- metabolism (n.) 新陳代謝
- sleeping deprivation 睡眠不足
- engorgement (n.) 暴飲暴食
- edemas (n.) 浮腫
- growth hormone 生長激素
- obesity (n.) 肥胖

單字及句型範例（Vocabulary & Sentence Examples）

1. Exercise gave her a good appetite. 運動使她胃口大增。

183

2. She was put on a diet of only 1600 calories a day. 她被限定每天只吃含一千六百大卡熱量的食物。

3. The heat will lessen during the evening. 晚上熱氣會減弱。

4. A rigid diet will make you slimmer. 嚴格節食會使你身材苗條。

5. How can we dispel their doubts and fears? 我們怎能消除他們的疑慮與恐懼？

📎 問題與討論（Questions & Discussions）

Q 1. 妳關心減肥問題嗎，有採取過哪些方法以及效果如何？

Q.1　Do you care for the problem of losing weight? What measures were adopted by you and their results are effective in this regard?

Q 2. 你覺得有氧運動會幫助減肥嗎，或是哪類型運動也可達到此預期之相同目標？

Q.2　Does aerobics is helpful to lose weight and what type of other exercises can reach the same target as expected?

Q 3. 飲食及睡眠影響體重之增減，您平常會注意這些問題嗎？

Q.3　Both food and sleeping are influential to gain and lose weight, do you pay attention to these problems usually?

📎 主題對話範例（Dialogue Examples）

A：I try to lose weight by taking exercises every day but it is not effective as expected.

B：You may try other methods to lose weight, like the control of food and drinking.

A：Having too much food, I gained weight recently.

B：I am not much for high calorie food, especially fired ones.

A：I like spicy food and people said that they are good to lose weight.

B：The surgical operation offers another way to lose weight but it is expensive and high risky, according to the news report.

同義字與名詞（Synonym & Terminology）

1. formidable（可怕的）⇨ difficult ⇨ hard ⇨ arduous
2. lessen（減低）⇨ abate ⇨ decrease ⇨ diminish ⇨ lower
3. dispel（消除）⇨ scatter ⇨ disperse ⇨ drive away
4. obstacles（障礙）⇨ barrier ⇨ obstruction ⇨ block
5. weary（疲倦的）⇨ tired ⇨ fatigued ⇨ weak

📎英譯中練習：（參閱主題文章）

English ⇨ Chinese Translation Practice：(Refer to the theme article)

1. High calorie snacks are a formidable enemy to lose weight. The selection of small packaged snacks can meet your appetites and reduce consumption of heats.（英譯中）

   ....

   ....

2. Exercise is the best way to consume calories, and aerobics together with its power training enables to lose weight more effective.（英譯中）

   ....

   ....

3. If you are under a sleeping deprivation, your metabolism will become slower and makes you hungry—you are easily to eat more calories.（英譯中）

   ....

   ....

Unit 05 健康食品我最愛
（Health Food Is My Favorite）

📎 吃出健康與自信

龐大商機 Huge Market Opportunities

It is estimated that Taiwan's health food market enjoys a business opportunity worth NT$100 billion per year. The local health food industry has appeared a "glory of Taiwan" recently.

根據業界推估，保健食品市場一年約有 1,000 億商機。保健產品最近出現了「台灣之光」。

The biotechnology of MIT (made in Taiwan) "cryptomonadales", a kind of alga product, has acquired multinational patent rights and three health food certificates, raising attention from the medical industry domestically. Alga experts conceded that the extract technology played an important breakthrough, plus a success of cooperation tie between the private sector and authorities concerned.

MIT 的藻類生技不但獲得世界多國專利，還拿到了三項健康食品認證，受到國內醫藥產業界的重視。國內專門研究藻類的專家對於這項產官的合作，認為萃取技術的突破也是一大功臣。

Algae are rich in protein, chlorophyll, carotinoid, and fatty acid, which have effects to reduce cholesterol in blood and adjust blood sugar, meeting the requirement of fellow countrymen. Algae, together with glucosamine, probiotics, and calcium were listed as four mainstreams in the health food market in 2011.

「藻類」因為本身含有豐富的蛋白質、葉綠素、類胡蘿蔔素和脂肪酸等成分，具有降低血中膽固醇含量及調節血糖的效果，迎合國人需求。

所以在 2011 年與葡萄糖胺、益生菌、鈣並列為市場四大主流之一。

The cryptomonadales tablets (or chlorella sorokiniana W-87) from the International Cryptomonadales Biotechnology (ICB) have been cultured and used for over four decades in Taiwan, and mass exported as food or nutrition supplements in the past. ICB was cited with its first certificate of health food having "function to adjust blood lipid" from the Ministry of Health and Welfare in 2005. A second certificate for "adjusting blood sugar" was granted in 2010 and the third "immunity regulation function" certificate on Sept. 9, 2013, respectively.

國際引藻公司研發的「引藻片（小球藻 W-87）」在台灣已有 40 多年的培養和食用歷史，長期大量外銷作為食品或營養補充品，且分別於 2005 年榮獲衛生福利部「調節血脂功能」健康食品認證、2010 年 9 月 9 日取得「調節血糖功能」健康食品認證、2013 年取得「免疫調節功能」健康食品認證。

As the first of its kind in the alga field in Taiwan, ICB passed the three health food certifications by the Ministry of Health and Welfare. Chairman Wang Shun-teh said that ICB planned to build up the world's largest algae biotechnology park, occupying a total area of 10 acres, in its headquarters located in the Changnan Technology Park, central Taiwan.

國際引藻公司順利通過衛生福利部三項健康食品認證，創記錄成為台灣藻類首家健康食品三認證商品。董事長王順德強調，將斥資打造全球最大藻類生技園區，目前已在彰南科技園區創建占地 10 公頃的引藻國際總部。

Wang boasted that his company has created several pioneering works in the field, and invited Dr. Henry Chang-Yu Lee (Nov. 22, 1938-), a Taiwanese-American and an international famous forensic evidence expert, as the brand spokesman. Beginning in 2006, Dr. Lee has

Politics

Commerce

Jobs

Sports

Healthy

Society

Career

Life

contacted and endorsed the product for seven consecutive years until now.

王順德表示，國際引藻締造許多業界創舉，更獲得國際鑑識專家李昌鈺博士代言其商品，李博士自從 2006 年起開始接觸引藻，至今已連續 7 年為「引藻片」代言。

Following Taiwan's new high aging index, the competition of health products in the elderly market has become increasingly fierce than before. To reach the utmost affect, the selection of products with precision and the use with an appropriate amount are essential.

隨著台灣老化指數達到新高，保健食品市場也趨向老年保養之競爭市場。如何正確選擇所需的產品，適量使用，才能發揮最大作用。

Statistics from the Ministry of the Interior show that about half-million out of 2.56 million people have suffered osteoporosis and the occurrence rate of osteoarthritis reached up to 80% as of the end of 2012. Most products in the market appeal to muscle and bone, accounting for 40% among approved health food made public.

根據內政部統計處 101 年底資料顯示，約 256 萬人當中，約有 50 萬人罹患骨質疏鬆症，退化性關節炎發生率也達 8 成。坊間訴求「顧筋骨」產品眾多，在公布的通過認證保健食品中，就有 4 成產品是這方面的保健訴求。

改善筋骨營養素材大不同
Different Nutrition to Improve Muscle and Bone

Dieticians said that calcium tablets, vitamin D formula products, dairy products, and soy bean buds from vegetable caffeoyl-esters are supplements to help the bone health of women from postmenopausal. The maintenance for the joints is suggested to take glucosamine, collagen, and MSM (Methylsulfonyl Methane).

營養師表示，骨骼保健素材常見包括鈣片及維生素 D 配方產品、乳製品、植物異黃酮類的大豆胚芽製品（幫助停經之婦女有助於骨質保健）都是補充的素材。而關節保養則有葡萄糖胺、膠原蛋白、MSM（甲基硫醯基甲烷）可攝取。

We are familiar with glucosamine which is applied for the initial staged osteoarthritis. The type II collagen, a major and necessary nutrition for the joint connective tissue and soft bone, enables to maintain a healthy soft bone and to repair soft bone after injured or swelling. MSM composes chondroitin sulfate needed by the joints and strengthens ligament cells, which also has functions to ease pains and anti-inflammation.

葡萄糖胺大家都較熟悉其適用於初期退化性關節炎者。第 II 型膠原蛋白是關節結締組織與關節軟骨最主要且必需的營養素，可以幫助維持軟骨健康並幫助修復受傷腫痛的關節軟骨；MSM 則可合成關節內所需的硫酸軟骨素，可強化韌帶細胞的強度，並且亦具有減緩疼痛、抗發炎的作用。

It is better to discuss with the doctor to confirm symptoms and required supplements before selecting certified health products and follow the dosage of commodities suggested. Meanwhile, curtail the daily drinking of cola, coffee, and tea, and take proper exercises to train muscles instead.

建議先與醫師討論，進一步確認症狀與需要補充的素材，再來選購有認證的保健產品，依照商品建議劑量來食用。除此之外，平日應減少可樂、咖啡及茶品飲用，適度運動，訓練肌力，如此才能擁有靈活的筋骨。

Politics

Commerce

Jobs

Sports

Healthy

Society

Career

Life

📎 重要單字暨新聞辭彙（Key Vocabulary & News Glossary）

- estimate *(vt.)* 估計
- glory of Taiwan 台灣之光
- biotechnology *(n.)* 生化科技
- alga (algae) *(n.)* 海藻（複數）
- patent rights 專利權
- concede *(vt.)* 承認
- extract *(vt.)* 萃取
- breakthrough *(n.)* 突破
- protein *(n.)* 蛋白質
- cholesterol *(n.)* 膽固醇

- glucosamine *(n.)* 葡萄糖胺
- blood sugar 血糖
- calcium tablets 鈣片
- nutrition supplements 營養補充品
- forensic evidence 法庭證據
- osteoporosis *(n.)* 骨質疏鬆
- osteoarthritis *(n.)* 退化性關節炎
- collagen *(n.)* 膠原蛋白
- curtail *(vt.)* 減少

📎 單字及句型範例（Vocabulary & Sentence Examples）

1. He keeps in the safe $3 million worth of diamonds.
   他在保險箱裡放著值三百萬元的鑽石。
2. The museum is the glory of our city. 這個博物館是我們城市的驕傲。
3. The first English patent for a typewriter was issued in 1714.
   英國第一臺打字機專利證書是一七一四年頒發的。
4. The medical-care cost is estimated to be one billion dollars.
   老年醫療保健費用估計為十億美元。
5. This substance is extracted from seaweed.
   這種物質是從海藻中提取的。
6. The candidate conceded that he had lost the election.
   這位候選人承認他已經在競選中失敗。
7. The government hopes to curtail public spending.
   政府希望縮減公共事業開支。

📎 問題與討論（Questions & Discussions）

Q 1. 您有訂期吃健康食品嗎？都是哪些功能之產品？

Q.1 Do you eat health food on a periodical date, and what function of these products?

Q 2. 醫生建議每天除三餐外，必須要吃不同維他命以補充營養。您是否同意此看法？

Q.2 Doctors said that different vitamins are necessary for nutrition supplements besides formal meals every day. Do you agree with the comment?

📎 主題對話範例（Dialogue Examples）

A：Women are easy to suffer osteoporosis, especially when they are getting old.

B：Osteoarthritis is commonly happened in the elderly.

A：Taiwan's national health insurance is a great policy, compared with other advanced nations around the world.

B：The medical-care for the elderly is important.

同義字與名詞（Synonym & Terminology）

1. extract（萃取）　⇨ elicit ⇨ obtain ⇨ get ⇨ bring forth ⇨ derive
2. suffer（忍受）　⇨ endure ⇨ bear ⇨ stand ⇨ undergo ⇨ tolerate
3. rich(豐富)　⇨ abounding ⇨ fertile ⇨ productive ⇨ prolific
4. raise（引起）　⇨ lift ⇨ increase ⇨ elevate ⇨ hoist
5. boast（誇耀）　⇨ brag ⇨ vaunt ⇨ crow ⇨ show off
6. pioneer（開拓者）　⇨ settler ⇨ leader ⇨ colonist ⇨ forerunner

Politics

Commerce

Jobs

Sports

Healthy

Society

Career

Life

📎 英譯中練習：（參閱主題文章）

English ⇨ Chinese Translation Practice：(Refer to the theme article)

1. Dieticians said that calcium tablets, vitamin D formula products, dairy products, and soy bean buds from vegetable caffeoyl-esters are supplements to help the bone health of women from postmenopausal.

   （英譯中）

   ....

   ....

Part 6　談社會新聞事件
Talks About Hot News

Unit 01 公寓大廈禁養寵物之我見
（No Pet-Rearing in Condominiums?）

🔗 保護動物之我見

立委擬提案修法 Legislation Amendments

More and more people are rearing pets but certain condominiums in Taiwan have prohibited inhabitants to do so. Local legislators and animal protection groups considered that such regulations have seriously infringed the living rights of pets.

現在越來越多人養寵物，但部分公寓大廈禁止住戶飼養寵物。立委及動保團體認為這樣的規範，嚴重侵害寵物居住權。

Yu-min Wang, a legislator of the ruling party Kuomintang, drafts a resolution to amend the Clauses 16 and 23 promulgated at" the Condominium Administration Act Building Administration Division"which forbids to keep pets inside condominiums. She also proposes to amend "the Animal Protection Law," and heightens the penalty against animal abuses.

執政黨國民黨立委王育敏將提案修改〈公寓大廈管理條例〉第 16 條、第 23 條禁止飼養寵物的條款。此外她也將提案修正〈動物保護法〉，對虐待動物者提高刑罰。

Statistics show that 26 families out of one hundred households, or over one fourth, in Taipei have pets, but the current law is unfriendly to the family with pets. Wang said that the number of people who own pets has increased significantly but rules such as "four legs of pets are not allowed to touch the floor when taking the lift" are not so friendly, for example. She urged that pet owners should be responsible of individual managements instead of adopting a ban.

根據統計，台北市平均每 100 戶中就有 26 個家庭有寵物，已超過 1/4，但現行許多法規卻對寵物家庭很不友善。王育敏表示，現今養寵物人數與日俱增，公寓大廈管理委員會卻常有「寵物搭電梯，四肢不得落地」等不友善規定，呼籲應是要求飼主做好寵物管理責任，而非用禁止方式。

Meanwhile, several condominium management committees even made regulations to rule out inhabitants to own pets. This move also deters people to adopt tramped animals, Wang lamented.

另外，有些公寓大廈管委會更可以制定規約，禁止住戶飼養寵物。這也讓很多想要飼養流浪動物的民眾都打消念頭，王育敏表示。

She added that the amendment will be proposed in the next session, regulating that the management committee should lift the ban against pets in condominiums. The new punishment for the animal mistreatment of first offender will be put behind the bar for one year, and a sentence of two years below for repeat offenders.

她說，下會期將提案修正〈公寓大廈管理條例〉，規範管委會不得以規約禁止住戶飼養寵物，並提案修正〈動物保護法〉，提高虐待動物刑責，初犯處 1 年以下有期徒刑，再犯則可處 2 年以下有期徒刑。

Jen-kang Huang, lieutenant chief of construction management division of the Construction and Planning Agency, the Ministry of the Interior （CPAMI）, said that the agency has not presupposed any standpoints. If the Legislative Yuan completes the amendment, CPAMI will work in cooperation in the future.

營建署建築管理組副組長黃仁鋼表示對立委的主張並沒有預設立場。並強調如果立院完成修法，營建署會配合執行。

動保團體 Animal Protection Groups

The Pet Life Protection Association called on that the people and animals should share the living space and distribution of resource ratios, thus reaching a harmonious co-existence. The Taiwan Society for the Prevention of Cruelty to Animals said that management of pet droppings is the problem to upgrade the education of pet owners.

寵物友善運動協會呼籲,民眾與動物應生活空間共享、資源比例分配,以達族群和諧共生;台灣防止虐待動物協會說,處理寵物如排泄物等問題,應是提升飼主教育。

The cruelty to animals is now subject to the punishment under the Clause 30 of the Animal Protection Law, noted Chung-yi Lin, head of animal protection division of the Council of Agriculture, the Executive Yuan （the Cabinet）. According to Ministry of Justice, a total of 24 cases were transferred to justice as of the end of June 2012 after the law was amended, and 17 cases were sentenced to prison or fined.

農委會動保科長林宗毅表示,目前虐待動物者,較常用動保法第 30 條作裁罰。而且據法務部的資料,從民國 97 年動保法修正到 101 年 6 月止,一共移送了 24 件,其中有 17 件受到徒刑或罰金的裁罰。

📎 重要單字暨新聞辭彙（Key Vocabulary & News Glossary）

- condominium *(n.)* 公寓
- inhabitants *(n.)* 居民
- ban *(n.)* 禁止
- infringe *(vt.)* 侵害
- living rights 居住權
- the Condominium Administration Act Building Administration Division 公寓大廈管理條例
- the Animal Protection Law 動物保護法
- clause *(n.)* 條款
- heighten *(vt.)* 提高
- penalty *(n.)* 刑罰
- abuse *(n.)* 虐待
- session *(n.)* 會期
- behind the bar 坐牢

- first offender 初犯者
- repeat offender 累犯
- tramped animals 流浪動物

- deter *(vt.)* 打消念頭
- Construction and Planning Agency 營建署

📎 單字及句型範例（Vocabularies & Sentence Examples）

1. Smoking is prohibited in the office building. 辦公樓內禁止抽煙。
2. Child abuse is widespread in this country. 這個國家虐待孩子的情況很普遍。
3. My friends urged that I（should）apply for the job. 朋友們力勸我申請那份工作。
4. Our plans are subject to the weather. 我們的計劃取決於天氣如何。
5. There are now stiffer penalties for drunken drivers. 現在對酗酒開車的處罰更嚴屬了。

📎 問題與討論（Questions & Discussions）

Q 1. 您有養寵物嗎？您如何照料牠們？

Q.1 Do you keep pets in your home and how do you take care of your pets?

Q 2. 您覺得公寓禁止養寵物的規定合不合理？為何？

Q.2 Is it reasonable or not to ban pets in condominiums? Why?

Q 3. 台灣在保護動物方面，未來有何需要再加強努力之處？試列舉出其中一二。

Q.3 What efforts should be made for Taiwan to upgrade its animal protection? Please make examples for one or two specific efforts.

Politics

Commerce

Jobs

Sports

Healthy

Society

Career

Life

🔖主題對話範例（Dialogue Examples）

A：Pets such as dogs and cats are adorable but sometimes they are noisy.

B：My neighbor's dog barks at passer-bys or pedestrians at night.

A：Do you agree with the regulation to forbid pets in condominiums?

B：Inhabitants have rights to enjoy good living environments without pets.

A：Taiwan has improved a lot in the animal protection law, compared with its neighboring nations.

B：Animal protection groups in Taiwan have spared no efforts to protect animals in recent years.

同義字與名詞（Synonym & Terminology）

1. ban（禁止）⇨ forbid ⇨ bar ⇨ disallow
2. infringe（違反）⇨ violate ⇨ break ⇨ trespass
3. propose（提案）⇨ offer ⇨ proffer ⇨ present ⇨ tender
4. amend（修正）⇨ change ⇨ correct ⇨ improve
5. urge（呼籲）⇨ push ⇨ force ⇨ drive ⇨ plead
6. share（分配）⇨ divide ⇨ proportion ⇨ apportion
7. heighten（提高）⇨ increase ⇨ add
8. deter(阻礙)⇨ discourage ⇨ hinder ⇨ prevent

🔖英譯中練習：（參閱主題文章）

English ⇨ Chinese Translation Practice：(Refer to the theme article)

1. More and more people are raising pets but certain condominiums in Taiwan have prohibited inhabitants to do so.（英譯中）

....

....

2. Some condominium management committees even ruled out the raising of pets by inhabitants. This also deters people to adopt tramped animals. （英譯中）

....

....

3. A total of 24 cases were transferred to justice as of the end of June 2012 after the law was amended, and 17 cases were sentenced to prison or fined. （英譯中）

....

....

Politics

Commerce

Jobs

Sports

Healthy

Society

Career

Life

Unit 02 你中了威力彩嗎？
（Did You Win a Welly Lottery?）

📎 彩券的威力

什麼是「威力彩」Welly（Power Ball）Lottery

Marketed on January 22, 2008, the Welly (power ball) lottery is a latest generation lottery with the highest award money among all types of public welfare lotteries issued by Taiwan Lottery Co. With a selling price of NT$100 per stake, the guaranteed prize was set at NT$250 million for the winner of jackpot.

「威力彩」是台彩新一代的彩券，2008 年 1 月 22 日上市，其獎金高於目前所有台彩的公益彩券。每注售價為新台幣 100 元，於推出當時頭獎保證獎金為新台幣 2.5 億元。

The Welly (power ball) lottery is special as it is played with two zones. The first zone has to pick up six mark numbers out from 1 to 38, and select another one mark number from 1 to 8 for the second zone. The seven numbers have to hit all marks to win the first prize.

威力彩玩法較為特別，分為兩區：第一區有 1~38 號，可任選 6 個號碼投注；第二區則有 1~8 號，可任選一號投注。而開獎則是第一區開出 6 個號碼，第二區開出 1 個號碼。頭獎為全部號碼皆對中。

Beginning in March of 2009, Taiwan Lottery has doubled the award money of first prize to start from NT$400 million, plus a raised stake of NT$10 million each time and ceiling up to NT$50 million if the first prize is absent. The award money for the third prize, fourth prize, fifth prize, sixth prize, and seven prize is fixed at NT$150,000, NT$20,000, NT$4,000, NT$800, and NT$400, respectively.

自 2009 年 3 月起，威力彩的獎金組成方式有所改變。頭獎中獎金額改為保證新台幣 4 億元起跳，如該期無任何人對中頭獎時，則頭獎金額每期加碼新台幣 1000 萬元，直至當期頭獎有人對中或頭獎保證累積金額達新台幣 5 億元為止。而參獎、肆獎、伍獎、陸獎和柒獎的每注中獎金額則分別改為固定的新台幣 15 萬、2 萬、4000、800 和 400 元。

Beginning in September of 2010, the highest prize was changed to NT$200 million and cancelled the raised stake of NT$10 million per issue. Meanwhile, a ninth prize of NT$100 was added for winners who hit any three mark numbers in the first zone but no marks in the second zone.

自 2010 年 9 月起，威力彩頭獎中獎金額改為保證新台幣 2 億元起跳，並取消頭獎金額每期加碼新台幣 1000 萬元的規定；此外並新增玖獎獎項，即第 1 區對中任三個獎號，但第 2 區未對中者，每注中獎金額為新台幣 100 元。

史上最高 1 注獨得 23.6 億
A historical high sweepstake NT$2.36 billion

On July 18, 2013, a sweepstake of NT$2.36 billion was drawn in a lottery station in Taoyuan City, Taoyuan County. The jackpot was a historical high in Taiwan's lottery history after the island implemented lotteries as an effort to upgrade social welfares on December 1, 1999.

2013 年 7 月 18 日威力彩頭彩飆 23.6 億元，頭獎一注獨得，在桃園縣桃園市的彩券行開出。頭獎總獎金與單注獎金都創公益彩券史上最高紀錄。台灣博彩從 1999 年 12 月 1 日開始發行，以提升社會福利為主要目的之一。

能買 74 輛藍寶堅尼 Able to Buy 74 Lamborghini Roadsters

The after tax sweepstake is about NT$1.89 billion, an amount which is able to buy three Taiwan's most expensive mega-mansions located in the Xinyi District in Taipei, or 74 Lamborghini roadsters. The money can also be employed to adopt 157,000 children in poverty, or NT$12,000 for each child per year.

頭獎稅後約 18.9 億元可買位在台北信義區、被譽為全台最貴的豪宅 3 戶，藍寶堅尼超跑可買 74 輛。如果認養貧童每年花 1 萬 2000 元，1 年可認養 15.7 萬名貧童。

🔗 重要單字暨新聞辭彙（Key Vocabulary & News Glossary）

- the public welfare lottery 公益彩券
- Welly（power ball）lottery 威利彩
- award money 獎金
- stake *(n.)* 賭注
- jackpot *(n.)* 頭彩
- raised stake 加碼
- ceiling *(n.)* 最高限額
- historical high 史上最高
- sweepstake *(n.)* 獨得
- mega-mansion 豪宅
- roadster *(n.)* 跑車
- adopt *(vt.)* 認養

🔗 單字及句型範例（Vocabularies & Sentence Examples）

1. A new ceiling has recently been fixed on pay. 最近對工資規定了新的最高限額。
2. We went to see a historical play. 我們去看了齣歷史劇。

🔗 問題與討論（Questions & Discussions）

Q 1. 您有中過威利彩嗎？您也會買其他彩券嗎？

Q.1　Did you win a Welly（power ball）lottery prize? Do you buy other kinds of lotteries?

Q 2. 如果您中了頭彩，您打算如何花那筆錢？

Politics

Commerce

Jobs

Sports

Healthy

Society

Career

Life

Q.2 How do you spend the money suppose to win the jackpot of lottery?

🔖 主題對話範例（Dialogue Examples）

A：I buy lotteries to try my luck and help disadvantage social groups at the same time.

B：Some people said that lotteries are only a cheating of money.

A：The guy is lucky to win a historical high jackpot in Taiwan's lottery history.

B：The stake is from pool resources of company colleagues, according to the report.

A：I would like to donate my money to those people who are in need of assistances if I win the first prize of lottery.

B：The jackpot has to pay a 20% tax and stamp duty surcharges.

同義字與名詞（Synonym & Terminology）

1. guarantee（保證） ⇨ promise ⇨ secure ⇨ pledge ⇨ swear
2. ceiling（最高限度） ⇨ top ⇨ limit ⇨ maximum ⇨ limitation
3. raise（增加） ⇨ lift ⇨ increase ⇨ elevate ⇨ hoist ⇨ boost

🔖 英譯中練習：（參閱主題文章）

English ⇨ Chinese Translation Practice：(Refer to the theme article)

1. The Welly（power ball）lottery is a new generation lottery with the highest award money among all types of public welfare lotteries issued by Taiwan Lottery Co.（英譯中）

....

....

Unit 03 交通違規要小心
（Be Careful of Traffic Violations）

📎 守護交通人人有責

酒駕取締更加嚴格 Clamp Down on Drunk Driving Becomes Stricter

Effective immediately, Taiwan has started a new traffic regulation since early 2013 and among which the clamp down on drunk driving becomes stricter. The drunk test for new hand drivers less than two years, professional drivers, and non-licensed drivers will be subject to a standard of 0.15 milligram and the alcohol concentration in blood is revised to 0.03%, down from 0.05%.

民國 102 年到來，交通新制上路立即生效，其中酒駕取締更加嚴格。主要針對剛領照上路不滿兩年的新手，以及職業駕駛跟無照駕駛，酒測標準下修到 0.15 毫克，血液中酒精濃度，也從 0.05% 降為 0.03。

Take a 60-kiliogram weight man for instance, he is supposed to exceed the standard by drinking only one and three-fourths of canned beer, compared with drink of three cans in the past. In this case, the maximum fine will be issued up to NT$60,000.

如果以體重 60 公斤成年男子來說，過去可能要喝到 3 罐罐裝啤酒的量才會違規，但現在只要喝 1 又 3/4 罐就會超標。如果違規的話，最高可開罰六萬元。

The drink of about one-third bottle of wine or one-tenth bottle of strong alcoholic will reach the ceiling standard of drunk test. The alcohol value in ginger duck and sesame oil chicken is 0.24 milligram, exceeding the new standard of 0.15 milligram. One quarter cup of 38℃ Kaoliang, a sorghum liquor, hits an awful high of 2.0 milligram.

Politics

Commerce

Jobs

Sports

Healthy

Society

Career

Life

紅酒量大約 1/3 瓶，烈酒更只要喝個 1/10 瓶，就會達到檢測值上限。
民眾冬天進補最愛的薑母鴨和麻油雞，只要喝幾口，對著酒測器一吹，
酒測值就達 0.24，已經超過新制定的 0.15，喝了四分之一杯的 38 度高
粱酒，一測更是嚇人，馬上飆高到 2.0。

If drunk test exceeds the standard, a ticket of between NT$15,000 and
NT$60,000 will be fined. To cope with the new standard, it is suggested
that never drink and drive, and do not touch any alcoholic drinks no
matter which is an alcohol or cooking rice wine.
如果酒測值超標，將開罰一萬五千元到六萬元。因應新制，不管是直
接喝，還是吃了摻酒料理都算喝酒，最好還是別開車上路不管是不是
直接喝。

「低頭族」Smart Phone Addicts

The smart phone addicted people have to be cautious after the new traffic
regulation is put into practice. Those car drivers and motorcyclists who
use mobile phones or Internet computer devices while driving will be
fined up to NT$3,000.
交通新制上路，「低頭族」要小心了。新增的交通法條規定，汽車或
機車駕駛人，只要在車輛行駛中使用手機或電腦等上網裝置，將被開
罰最多 3 千塊錢。

Most general public consent to seize smart phone addicts while driving
but believe it is hard to change the habits. The government has invested
to offer many traffic APPs so as to make the traffic smooth but the
promulgation of the new traffic regulation turns to be a contradictory,
however.
交通大隊出動抓「低頭族」，大多數民眾都認同，但也有低頭族認為，
習慣難改。更何況政府砸錢設計許多好用的交通 APP，就是要讓駕駛
人行車更方便，但現在多出這個規範，也有人感覺矛盾。

逾期罰鍰費 Overdue Fines

Taipei City issues about 1.45 million traffic tickets and collects a total fine of NT$2.2 billion per year, with overdue fines from motorcycles and cars representing a lion's share of 40%. If a parking fee of NT$20 is not paid within 15 days, an overdue payment of NT$300 plus a registered mail fare of NT$50 will be notified, totaling the fee to jump to NT$370.

台北市一年交通違規件數有 145 萬多件，裁罰收入高達 22 億多。其中最大收費來源，竟然是摩托車和汽車逾期罰鍰費，而且佔了四成。以一張 20 元的停車單來說，期限內 15 天沒有繳，郵差雙掛號寄發催繳單工本費 50 元，還有逾期的罰鍰 300 元，一口氣就跳到 370 元。

People complained that their parking bills have disappeared or pulled out by others, a controversy which makes the city government to earn more money. Never let the parking bill become overdue and spend the money not worth, they suggested.

民眾抱怨之前也常爆發停車單不見，或被拔走的爭議，逾期罰鍰讓市府停管處賺進滿滿鈔票。千萬別讓停車繳費單過期，白花冤枉錢。

🖉 重要單字暨新聞辭彙（Key Vocabulary & News Glossary）

- traffic violations 交通違規
- clamp *(vt.)* 取締
- drunk driving 酒駕
- effective *(adj.)* 生效的
- drunk test 酒測
- milligram *(n.)* 毫克
- new hand 新手
- non-licensed *(adj.)* 無照的
- alcoholic concentration 酒精濃度
- canned beer 罐裝啤酒
- wine *(n.)* 紅酒
- strong alcoholic 烈酒
- Kaoliang liquor 高粱酒
- cooking rice wine 料理酒
- smart phone addicts 低頭族
- internet devices 網路裝置
- seize *(vt.)* 抓住
- overdue *(adj.)* 逾期未付的

📎 單字及句型範例（Vocabularies & Sentence Examples）

1. They clamp down on pickpockets. 他們嚴禁扒竊。
2. A bill passed by congress becomes effective as soon as the President signs it. 國會通過的法案一經總統簽署立即生效。
3. Police punished her with a fine of NT$1,200 for speeding. 由於超速，警察罰了她 1200 元。
3. We had an awful earthquake here last year. 去年我們這裡發生了可怕的地震。
4. His rent payment is overdue. 他的房租過期了。

📎 問題與討論（Questions & Discussions）

Q 1. 您知道新制交通法規對酒駕處罰很重嗎？

Q.1 Do you know the new traffic regulation has adopted a stricter punishment on drunk driving?

Q 2. 您認為台灣酒駕問題嚴重嗎，新制交通法規可因此降低酒駕事件？

Q.2 Do you think the drunk driving is a serious problem in Taiwan, and is the new traffic regulation able to clamp down on such incidents?

Q 3. 您會如期繳交停車單獲交通違規罰款？

Q.3 Do you pay your parking fee or traffic tickets on time?

📎 主題對話範例（Dialogue Examples）

A：The new traffic regulations are expected to stop any drunk driving in Taiwan.

B：Sometimes, it is useful to stop drunk driving by punishment of a large amount of money.

A：The drunk driving is dangerous and it could be fined up to NT$60,000.

B：I never drink and drive for the sake of my own safety and others.

A：The city government should not have charged extra payments for overdue parking fees.

B：We should not use any mobile phones or Internet devices while driving cars or motorcycles.

同義字與名詞（Synonym & Terminology）
1. clamp（取締） ⇨ crack down ⇨ stop
2. effective（有效的） ⇨ useful ⇨ serviceable ⇨ operative
3. awful（嚇人的） ⇨ brutal ⇨ ruthless ⇨ terrible ⇨ horrible
4. seize（抓住） ⇨ clutch ⇨ grasp ⇨ grab
5. smooth(平順的） ⇨ level ⇨ flat ⇨ even

✐ 英譯中練習：（參閱主題文章）

English ⇨ Chinese Translation Practice：(Refer to the theme article)

1. Effective immediately, Taiwan has started a new traffic regulation since early 2013 and among which the clamp down on drunk driving becomes stricter.（英譯中）

   ....

   ....

2. The drink of about one-third bottle of wine or one-tenth bottle of strong alcoholic will reach the ceiling standard of drunk test.（英譯中）

   ....

   ....

3. To cope with the new standard, it is suggested that never drink and drive, and do not touch any alcoholic drinks no matter which is an alcohol or cooking rice wine.（英譯中）

   ....

   ....

Part 7 談職場進修學習與教育
Talks About On-The-Job Learning and Education

Unit 01　大學教育的省思與展望
（Reviews and Prospects of College Education）

🔗 現行教育的現況

大學教育 "Our Underachieving Colleges"

In his book "our underachieving colleges," Derek Bok, former president of Harvard University, raised his views and improvements regarding contents and qualities of the college education in the U.S. This serves as a reflection and reference for the higher education in Taiwan.

哈佛大學前校長伯克在本書提出了對美國大學的大學部教育內容與品質的看法與改進之道。值得台灣高等教育界的省思與參考。

Bok pointed out that students have carried out knowledge and mental habits from colleges rather than what curriculums they have attended, depending on how curriculums are taught and how good the teaching is. The memory of subject contents and the information will fade away quickly but their interests, values, and cognitive abilities are kept for a longer time. Thus, the teaching quality is much important than curriculum contents, and performs profound effect on students.

伯克校長指出，學生從大學帶走的知識和心智習慣，較少取決於他們上了什麼課，而是取決於課是怎麼教和教得多好。學生對學科內容資訊的記憶消逝得很快，但興趣、價值觀、認知能力以及經由自己的思考努力所獲得的觀念或知識，則會保留得較長久。因此，教學的品質遠比課程的內容與分量來得重要，對學生的影響亦更深遠。

During the period of 1971-1991, Bok posted president of Harvard University for 20 years and also was the acting president during 2006-2007. He was deeply experienced on the college education quality and teaching method in Harvard University as well as other U.S. universities, and worried about such issues.

伯克於 1971-1991 年擔任哈佛大學校長達 20 年，並於 2006-2007 年受命代理校長。對哈佛大學及其他美國大學的大學部教學品質及教學方法知之甚深，也極為憂心。

Derek Bok
300th Anniversary University Professor
Professor of Law
Harvard University President Emeritus
Harvard Kennedy School

Bok said that most professors have paid less attention to both the teaching quality and studies and seldom to improve their teaching methods and quality in favor of student benefits. This phenomenon not only happens in the U.S. but also in the higher education field around the world, Bok revealed.

他指出大多數教授甚少正視大學部的教育問題，也很少深入研究改進教學的方法及品質，讓學生真正受惠。這個現象，其實不只發生在美國，而是世界各國高等教育的普遍現象。

If the purpose of the college education is limited on the scope of knowledge development, it narrows the college education and hinders the foster of sentiments for students, according to Bok. The college education should pursue diversified targets, including capabilities such as communications, debates, morals reasoning, civic duties, varied livings, global societies, cultivating hobbies, and work preparing.

伯克校長也指出，若只把大學教育的目的限制在知識發展的範疇，是窄化了大學教育，並阻礙了大學培育學生重要情操的努力。大學部的教育應該追求多樣的目標，培養學生幾項重要的能力，包括溝通、思辨、道德推理、履行公民責任、迎接多元化生活、迎接全球化社會、拓展興趣以及就業準備等。

With the exception of work capability, the other seven capabilities are major reforms now listed in the general education in Harvard University. Bok identified that the college education should use the general education as its axis and not to sink down to a specialized or occupational educations.

除了就業能力外，其他七項能力，似亦呼應了哈佛大學最近通識教育改革所列舉的八大領域。易言之，伯克確實認同大學部的教育，應以博雅的通識教育為主軸，而不應淪為專業教育或職業訓練的養成。

The eight capabilities mentioned above are the theme topics discussed in the general education in recent years. Only college students own such capabilities can they open wide their careers and business developments in the future.

伯克所列舉之八項能力，其實也是近年來通識教育廣泛討論的核心議題，一旦大學生具備了這些能力，才能在未來的就業與事業發展，大開大闔。

Taiwan's colleges and universities have noticed the issue. Under the support of an "excellence teaching program" by the Ministry of Education, the teaching refinement, curriculum revolution, and encouraging students' learning motions are mapped out, an attempt to achieve a best teaching and learning result.

國內各大學亦已注意到這個問題，並且在教育部推動的「教學卓越計畫」支持下，正透過教師精進、課程改革、及激勵學生學習動機等方式，俾達到更佳的教學效果。

We are used to combine teaching and learning into a noun or verb. Actually, teaching and learning are two different actions and processes as teaching is only a means while learning is the main part.

我們習慣把「教學」兩個字合起來當成一個名詞或動詞。其實「教」與「學」是兩個不同的動作與過程，「教」只是手段，「學」才是主體。

📎 重要單字暨新聞辭彙（Key Vocabulary & News Glossary）

- college *(n.)* 大學
- reflection *(n.)* 反省
- higher education 高等教育
- curriculum *(n.)* 課程
- fade away 消逝
- cognitive agilities 認知能力
- profound *(adj.)* 深刻的
- president *(n.)* 大學校長
- benefit *(vi.)* 受惠

- phenomenon *(n.)* 現象
- hinder *(vt.)* 妨礙
- foster *(vt.)* 培養
- pursue *(vt.)* 追求
- diversified *(adj.)* 多樣化的
- debates *(n.)* 辯論
- general education 通識教育
- sink down 沉淪
- refinement *(n.)* 精進

📎 單字及句型範例（Vocabularies & Sentence Examples）

1. Superior courts may review decisions of lower courts.
   高等法院可以復審下級法院的判決。

2. References are given in full at the end of this article.
   本文末尾處有全部的參考書目。

3. All humans do have some kind of innate mental ability.
   凡是人確有某種天生的智力。

4. He never read these books, for he had long lost the habit of reading. 他從不讀這些書，因為他早就丟掉了閱讀習慣。

5. The sound of the footsteps faded away. 腳步聲漸漸消失。

6. Her parents' divorce had a profound effect on her life.
   她父母的離異對她的生活有很深的影響。

7. We benefited greatly by this frank talk.
   這次坦率的談話使我們獲益匪淺。

8. Concerts foster interest in music. 音樂會培養對音樂的興趣。

9. Age hinders me from moving about. 我年事已高 , 不能到處走動。

10. He is a bus driver by occupation. 他的職業是公車司機。

📎 問題與討論（Questions & Discussions）

Q 1. 您認為伯克對大學教育的論點如何？

Q.1 How do you comment on Derek Bok's opinions about the college education?

Q 2. 您認為台灣的大學教育品質如何，能否造就出學生之國際競爭能力？

Q.2 How do you comment on the quality of Taiwan's college education, and does it help students to create the competitiveness in the world?

Q 3. 您認為現在的大學文憑重要嗎？為何？

Q.3 Do you think the college diploma is important or not, and why?

📎 主題對話範例（Dialogue Examples）

A：Did you read the book "our underachieving colleges" by Derek Bok, former president of Harvard University.?

B：I agree with the observations Derek Bok has made on the college education issues.

A：The level of college education in Taiwan has declined significantly in recent years.

B：Some people commented that the higher education in Taiwan was not a success.

A：The Ministry of Education has mapped out an excellence teaching program.

B：I expect college students to spend more time in studying rather than in temporary jobs.

同義字與名詞（Synonym & Terminology）

1. fade（退色） ⇨ dim ⇨ pale ⇨ dull ⇨ bleach
2. profound（深刻的） ⇨ deep ⇨ great ⇨ extreme ⇨ intense ⇨ serious

3. benefit（好處）⇨ advantage ⇨ profit ⇨ gain
4. foster（培育）⇨ nourish ⇨ nurture ⇨ feed ⇨ cultivate
5. hinder（妨礙）⇨ stop ⇨ obstruct ⇨ impede ⇨ curb
6. pursue（追求）⇨ chase ⇨ follow ⇨ seek
7. debate（辯論）⇨ discuss ⇨ argue ⇨ reason ⇨ dispute

📎 英譯中練習：（參閱主題文章）

English ⇨ Chinese Translation Practice：(Refer to the theme article）

1. Derek Bok, former president of Harvard University, raised his views and improvements regarding contents and qualities of the college education in the U.S.（英譯中）

   ....

   ....

2. Thus, the teaching quality is much important than curriculum contents, and performs profound effect on students.（英譯中）

   ....

   ....

3. The college education should pursue diversified targets, including capabilities such as communications, debates, morals reasoning, civic duties, varied livings, global societies, cultivating hobbies, and work preparing.（英譯中）

   ....

   ....

Unit　02　烹飪有一套
（Are You Good at Cooking?）

📎 不可不知道的烹飪常識

8 種錯誤影響健康 Eight Mistakes to Influence Health

People purchase the most fresh and healthy foods from the supermarket but many of them waste nutrition needed in cooking. Nutritionists and food experts in the U.S. have listed eight mistakes that are often committed even by clever housewives, and submitted suggestions for healthier foods in the dinning table.

雖然人們經常從超市買最新鮮、最有益健康的食品，但很多人在烹飪時卻把我們真正需要的營養給白白扔掉了。為此，美國營養學家和食品安全專家，列舉了聰明主婦在烹飪方面也會常犯的 8 種錯誤，聽從他們的建議，你餐桌上的食物會變得更加健康。

錯誤一：一次採購過多蔬菜。
Mistake 1: Purchase too much vegetables each time

Experts said that vitamins and minerals in fruits and vegetables have begun to lose after they are plucked off and nutrition becomes less if storages are longer. A research found that about half of folic acid and 40% of xanthophyll in spinaches naturally run off when kept in refrigerators within one week. It is suggested not to buy too much food each time, and three times per week are available.

專家說「從採摘的那一刻起，水果和蔬菜中的維生素和礦物質就開始減少了。」如果你採購回來的蔬菜存儲時間越久，它們所含的營養就越少。研究發現，在冰箱保存大約一周後，菠菜中有一半的葉酸和 40％的葉黃素會自然流失。建議每次採購食物不要過多，一周買三次最為合適。

錯誤二：把食物貯藏在透明容器中。
Mistake 2: Keep food in transparent vessels

If the milk you drink is still packaged with plastic bags, it is suggested to convert it into boxes made of stiff paper. Researchers at Belgium said that riboflavin（vitamin B2）in milk suffers losses easily under the exposure of sunlight. U.S. food scientists also recommended not to mix milk with grains in transparent vessels as much as possible, a move to keep nutrition.

如果你現在喝的牛奶還是透明塑料袋裝奶，建議你考慮換成硬紙盒包裝的牛奶。比利時研究人員指出，牛奶富含的核黃素（維生素 B2）暴露在日光下易發生損失。美國食品科學家為此建議，盡量避免將牛奶和穀物放在透明容器裏，可以保留營養。

錯誤三：快炒大蒜。Mistake 3: Stir frying garlic

A research panel at the American Association for Cancer Research（AACR）said that crushed or sliced garlic should be laid aside for at least 10 minutes before cooking as garlic will trigger the enzyme, an anticancer chemical compound. Put 10 minutes then cook, giving it the time to fully form the chemical compound.

美國癌症研究協會營養學研究小組說：「把大蒜拍碎、切片，放上至少 10 分鐘後再烹飪。拍碎大蒜會引發酶並釋放出一種能抗癌的化合物；放上 10 分鐘再烹飪，就是要讓這種化合物有充足的時間全部形成。」

錯誤四：少用調料。Mistake 4: Few dressings used

Under the situation of no adding edible oil and salt, the use of more vegetable dressings and spices not only takes effect of seasoning but also protects people from suffering food position. Researchers at Hong

Kong University found that both lilac and cinnamon are antiseptic in the test for Escherichia coli, staphylococcus, Salmonella, and among others. Another research in the U.S. said that rosemary, thyme, nutmeg, and laurel leaves are abundant of anti-oxidants. Add half spoon of above dressings in each cooking is safe and healthy.

在不增加食用油和食鹽的情況下多用一些植物調料和香料，不僅能起到調味的作用，還能保護人們免受食物中毒之害。香港大學的研究人員在對 20 種常見調料所做的抗菌（包括大腸桿菌、葡萄球菌和沙門氏菌等）試驗發現，丁香、肉桂都具有很強的抗菌能力。發表在美國另外一項研究成果稱，迷迭香、百裏香、肉豆蔻和月桂樹葉也富含抗氧化劑。每次烹飪多加半匙調料，既安全又健康。

錯誤五：給水果多剝幾層皮。Mistake 5: Rind more fruit peels

Most fruit peels own higheranti-oxidants by two to 27-folds than their pulps, according to researches published on U.S. periodicals. Nutritionists suggested that potatoes and carrots be rinded by only a layer of their outer skin. If fruit and vegetable have to be peeled before eating, try to rind only the thin skin on the surface.

發表在美國雜志上的研究發現，多數水果表皮中進行的抗氧化活動比水果果肉中進行的要高出 2—27 倍。營養學家建議，土豆和胡蘿蔔的皮只要輕輕刮掉一層就夠了。如果有些果蔬必須剝皮才能入口，去掉盡可能薄的一層皮就可以。

錯誤六：把維生素和礦物質慢慢燉掉。
Mistake 6: Stew out vitamins and minerals

Generally, the boiling is an easy cooking without adding oil or lost of nutrition but this kind of cooking may lead to loss of 90% nutrition. Doctors at AACA said that "potassium and soluble vitamins will spill over with the mix of water." Add less water for stewing and use microwave for slow cooking or sautéing are able to decrease the lost of nutrition. Sautéing is suitable for deep green or orange color vegetables.

一般人認為，煮食是一種簡單的烹飪方法，不用加油，又不損失營養。但實際上，這種烹飪方法最多可導致 90％的營養成分流失。美國癌症研究協會營養博士說，「鉀和可溶性的維生素等混入水中就會溢出。」加入少量的水燉煮，用微波爐慢煮或爆炒，可減少營養成分的流失。爆炒則適用於深綠色或橙色的蔬菜。

錯誤七：有些食物該洗不洗。
Mistake 7: Some foods should be washed or not?

People would wash plums or strawberries before eating but not for bananas, oranges, or mangos. Bacteria on the surface of food may infect on hands or invade into inside of fruits when cutting apart. Use soap and wash hands at least for 20 seconds before taking fruits which are already peeled, an effective method to prevent the spread of germs.

吃李子或草莓的時候，我們都會先清洗一下。但吃香蕉、橘子或芒果的時候，很少有人把它們放進水沖洗。但停留在食物表面的有害細菌可能會沾染到手上，切開水果時甚至會侵入水果內部。手拿剝皮水果前用肥皂或溫水洗手至少 20 秒，可有效防止細菌蔓延。

錯誤八：食物搭配不當，營養減半。
Mistake 8: Improper foods, nutrition reduced by half

It should pay attention to a scientific collocation of different foods. If you eat beans and green leaf foods, eat some other foods with vitamin C such as peppers, potatoes, and strawberries at the same time so as to increase the absorption of iron. Tea or coffee will inhibit the absorption of iron by up to 60% during eating food. It is better to drink tea or coffee after finishing meals.

應注意不同食物間的科學搭配，吃豆類和綠葉食物時，同時吃一些含維生素 C 豐富的食物，如辣椒、土豆、草莓等，會增加鐵的吸收率。吃飯時喝茶或咖啡，最多可抑制人體對 60％的鐵的吸收。沒有徹底吃完飯，最好不要喝茶和咖啡。

🔗 重要單字暨新聞辭彙（Key Vocabulary & News Glossary）

- cooking (n.) 烹飪
- committee mistakes 犯錯
- transparent (adj.) 透明的
- the American Association for Cancer Research 美國癌症研究協會
- dressing (n.) 調料
- spice (n.) 香料
- seasoning (n.) 調味品
- food position 食物中毒
- antiseptic (adj.) 抗菌的
- fruit peels 果皮
- pulp (n.) 果肉
- periodical (n.) 雜誌
- bacteria (n.) 細菌（bacterium 的複數）
- inflect (vt.) 沾染
- germs (n.) 1 病菌
- inhibit (vt.) 抑制

🔗 單字及句型範例（Vocabularies & Sentence Examples）

1. I committed an error in handling the business. 我在處理這一業務時犯了一個錯誤。
2. Cups, basins, pots, bottles, casks, etc., are vessels that hold liquids. 杯、盆、罐、瓶、桶等都是盛液體的容器。
3. The Indians peeled the bark from trees to make canoes. 印第安人從樹上剝下樹皮做皮舟。
4. That is an improper usage of the word. 那是這個字的一種不禮貌的用法。
5. The flu virus infected almost the entire class. 全班幾乎人人都染上了流行性感冒病毒。
6. We cooked the fish in the microwave oven. 我們在微波爐中煮魚。
7. I ordered a steak at his suggestion. 我根據他的建議點了一份牛排。

8. The swimming pool is available only in summer. 這個游泳池只在夏天開放。這個游泳池只在夏天開放。

9. It is highly necessary to work out an emergency package. 制定一整套應急措施是非常必要的。

10. The priest converted many natives into Christianity. 這個牧師使許多土著居民改信基督教。

11. The newspaper's exposure of their crimes led to their arrest. 報上揭露了他們的罪行,這些人因而被捕。

12. Because of his poor nutrition, he has grown weaker and weaker. 他因為營養不良,身體越來越虛弱。

13. A spark triggered the explosion. 一粒火星引起了這場爆炸。

問題與討論(Questions & Discussions)

Q 1. 您喜歡烹飪嗎?做菜技巧如何?

Q.1 Do you like to cook, and how is your cooking skills?

Q 2. 您有學過做菜嗎?您對哪一種烹飪比較有興趣?

Q.2 Have you ever learned how to cook, and what kind of cooking you are interested in?

Q 3. 您同意美國營養及食品專家所列舉的八種常犯錯誤?您有無其他補充之看法?

Q.3 Do you agree with the eight mistakes listed by U.S. nutritionists and food experts? And you have any other supplemental opinions about the issues?

Politics

Commerce

Jobs

Sports

Healthy

Society

Career

Life

🖉 主題對話範例（Dialogue Examples）

A：I prefer cooking at home rather than eating out.

B：My mother taught me how to cook and I also learned from recipes.

A：Vitamins and minerals in fruits and vegetables have begun to lose after they are plucked off.

B： Never buy too much food each time and try to finish when they are fresh and nutritious.

A：I always wash fruits before eating mainly to avoid any insecticide residuals.

B：Most fruits in Taiwan are good but some contain with agricultural chemicals.

同義字與名詞（Synonym & Terminology）

1. commit（犯錯） ⇨ perform ⇨ pledge
2. vessel（容器） ⇨ container ⇨ receptacle
3. periodical（期刊） ⇨ magazine ⇨ journal ⇨ gazette
4. inhibit（抑制） ⇨ restrain ⇨ repress ⇨ suppress ⇨ curb
5. germ（微生物） ⇨ microorganism

📎英譯中練習：（參閱主題文章）

English ⇨ Chinese Translation Practice：(Refer to the theme article)

1. Nutritionists and food experts in the U.S. have listed eight mistakes that are often committed by clever housewives, and submitted suggestions for healthier foods in the dinning table.（英譯中）

   ....

   ....

2. Experts said that vitamins and minerals in fruits and vegetables have begun to lose after they are plucked off and nutrition becomes less if storages are longer.（英譯中）

   ....

   ....

3. Bacteria on the surface of food may infect on hands or invade into inside of fruits when cutting apart.（英譯中）

   ....

   ....

Politics

Commerce

Jobs

Sports

Healthy

Society

Career

Life

Unit 03　你的英文程度趕得上企業要求嗎?

（Is Your English Good Enough to Catch Up Enterprise Requirements?）

企業對員工的英語要求

全民英檢中級程度 GEPT Middle Levels

Employees with the good English capabilities are a plus to enterprises. English issued in foreign companies' interviews as "the good English" has become a basic criterion for the enrollment of employees. Enterprises need employees without international communication barriers in dealing with foreign letters, phone calls, and abroad meetings...

員工英文能力好，對企業只有加分！像是外商公司在甄選員工時，全程都用英語面試，「英文好」已經成為錄取的基本條件。包括對外書信、國際電話以及出國開會……，企業都需要沒有國際溝通障礙的員工。

A survey shows that as high as 64% of enterprises have now listed the English capability as a screening system for their employees, and about 68% of these enterprises have programmed their own tests. Generally speaking, employees are asked to meet the middle level of the General English Proficiency Test（GEPT）, or about a score of 550 in TOEIC（Test of English for International Communication）. Despite English has become increasingly important, the average English capability of employees in Taiwan is scored at only 56.79, failing to meet enterprise requirements.

根據調查顯示，有高達 6 成 4 的企業，會將英語能力列入招募時的篩選機制，其中 6 成 8 企業會自行規劃測驗，一般來說要求員工程度在全民英檢中級（約多益 550 分），然而諷刺的是，雖然員工英文能力越來越重要，不過企業幫員工英文打分數，平均才 56.79 分，根本就

Politics

Commerce

Jobs

Sports

Healthy

Society

Career

Life

不及格。

Thus, enterprises will hire foreign teachers for in-house trainings if employers expect to enhance the language capability of their employees, accounting for 45.26%. The subsidy to learn foreign languages in cram schools or language centers of college represents a share of 40.94%. Another 40.58% of enterprises offer on-line language learning classes or software.

也因此，當企業主若要加強員工外語能力訓練，會請外籍老師至企業內訓練，佔 45.26%、補助員工上補習班或大學推廣部課程，佔 40.94%、提供員工線上學習課程或軟體，佔 40.58%。

起薪及考績標準 因「英文能力」有所差異 Varied Starting Salary and Performance Evaluations Due To "English Capability"

Whether or not the standard of starting salary varies on the English capability? 43.58% of enterprises replied "no" or "no influence", and "yes" accounted for 27.77%. Is the evaluation of performance much higher due to a good English capability? The answer of "yes" was 12.21%. About 50% of enterprises would offer different salaries and performance evaluations on the basis of the English capability, which indeed affects the remuneration of employees.

至於問到企業主的起薪標準，是否會因為語文能力而有所差異？答否，沒有影響佔 43.58%，答是，起薪較高佔 26.77%。答是，考績分數較高佔 12.12%。約有 5 成企業主會因為員工英文程度，而給予不同的薪水及考績，英文程度的確直接影響到薪資待遇。

Whether or not enterprises have mapped out any advanced study programs to enhance the English capability of employees? 39.98% of enterprises responded "no," the in-house training class represented 26.65%, and subsidies for the purpose took a share of 25.69%. Most enterprises have not offered any advanced English classes for employees but 52% of enterprises have offered subsidies to study English at both inside or outside of the company.

再問到企業主是否針對提升員工英文能力，制定各種進修辦法？目前沒有佔 39.98%、公司有內部教育訓練課程佔 26.65%、提撥經費補助員工自行進修佔 25.69%。大部分企業沒有提供員工任何英語進修課程，但仍有 5 成 2 企業不論在公司內外部，都有進修津貼。

員工英文能力「糟」，4 成 2 企業好擔心
42% enterprise worry employees' "lousy" English

Which situations in daily general affairs need to use English? Foreign letters, e-mails, and faxes represent 65.19%, followed by international phone calls, with 60.98%. Abroad exhibitions, meetings, and customer visits appropriates at 57.02%.

而問到企業主每日工作庶務中，哪些情況需要用英語溝通？對外書信、E-MAIL、傳真往來佔 65.19%，國際電話溝通佔 60.98%。出國參展、會議及客戶拜訪佔 57.02%。

What is the attitude of enterprises in arranging employees to learn English? "Just encouraging," "requesting no results," and "nonintervention" account for 54.16%, and 23.53% of enterprises arrange training classes and adopt an assessment on learning result. Only 11.52% of enterprises set up a position to review the GEPT standards and ask the promotion and dispatched personnel to meet such requirements.

再問到企業主對同仁學習外國語言的態度？鼓勵學習就好、不要求成果、也不加以干涉佔 54.26%，安排培訓課程、並採取考試評量學習成果佔 23.53%。設立職位英檢標準、並要求升遷及外派需符合規定佔 11.52%。

The last question：Has the language problem incurred any troubles to the company? 42.38% said "never" but worried such situation would create troubles someday. "Happened in the past but is not a problem" accounted for 34.45%. "Never" and "no worry to happen problems" had a proportion of 21.37%.

最後問到企業主是否曾因員工語言能力不足，而造成公司營運的困擾？不曾有，但會擔心發生問題佔 42.38%。曾經有，問題不大佔 34.45%，不曾有，也未擔心會發生任何問題佔 21.37%。

As the English capability has become a tendency in enterprises, a standard operation procedure（SOP）must be set up, including interview mechanisms, advanced curriculums, English test certifications, and so on. This avoids employees not knowing what course to follow and provides a learning opportunity with employees who are poor in English but have the ambition to strive for the best.

企業要求員工英語能力已是必然趨勢，企業內部應制定一套「標準作業程序」，包括面試機制、進修課程、英文認證考試……等項目，才不至於讓員工無所適從，也給英文不好但有心上進的員工，一個學習英文的機會。

A high quality "application English school" within enterprises is suggested to build up to offer a natural way of learning English for employees, including internal training, outside training, or group competitions. Aided by the improvement of employees in English, sales performances and operations of the company are expected to upgrade simultaneously.

在企業內打造一個優質「應用英文學校」，讓員工在耳濡目染下自然學習職場英文，不論是內訓、外訓、分組競賽…等各種方式皆可。員工英文進步，公司業績及營運狀況自然也會提升。

Politics
Commerce
Jobs
Sports
Healthy
Society
Career
Life

🔗 重要單字暨新聞辭彙（Key Vocabulary & News Glossary）

- basic criterion 基本條件
- enrollment *(n.)* 錄取
- barrier *(n.)* 障礙
- GEPT（General English Proficiency Test）全民英檢
- TOEIC（Test of English for International Communication）多益
- in-house *(adj.)* 內部的
- cram school 補習班
- starting salary 起薪
- performance evaluations 考績
- remuneration *(n.)* 待遇
- vary *(vt.)* 變化
- respond *(vt.)* 回答
- subsidy *(n.)* 津貼
- proportion *(n.)* 比例
- dispatch *(vt.)* 派遣
- standard operation procedure（SOP）標準流程

🔗 單字及句型範例（Vocabularies & Sentence Examples）

1. What criteria do you use when judging the quality of a student's work? 你用什麼標準來衡量學生的學業？
2. They enrolled us as members of the club.
   他們將我們吸收為該俱樂部會員。
3. He dispatched an experienced worker to repair the damage.
   他派一個有經驗的工人去修理損壞的地方。
4. The Secret Service screened hundreds of students to select its agents. 特務機關仔細審查了數百名學生以選擇特務人員。

🔗 問題與討論（Questions & Discussions）

Q 1. 您們公司是否有提供員工加強英文訓練之津貼或其它協助？

Q.1 Does your company offer subsidies for employees to learn English or any other kinds of assistances?

📎 主題對話範例（Dialogue Examples）

A：The good English capability is a plus in applying jobs, especially in the foreign company.

B：Foreign companies usually use English in interviews and take the good English capability into consideration of their employees.

A：A few local companies have hired foreign teachers for in-house language training.

B：My company offers the subsidy to learn English in cram schools.

同義字與名詞（Synonym & Terminology）

1. barrier（障礙）⇨ barricade ⇨ obstruction ⇨ fortification
2. vary(變更) ⇨ change ⇨ differ ⇨ alter ⇨ deviate
3. respond（回答）⇨ answer ⇨ reply ⇨ retort ⇨ acknowledge ⇨ react
4. dispatch（派遣）⇨ send ⇨ transmit ⇨ forward ⇨ discharge
5. proportion（比例）⇨ ratio ⇨ measure ⇨ amount

📎 英譯中練習：（參閱主題文章）

English ⇨ Chinese Translation Practice：(Refer to the theme article)

1. Enterprises need employees without international communication barriers in foreign letters, e-mails, faxes, international phones, and abroad meetings.（英譯中）

....

....

Part 8　談樂活好自在
Talks about Happy and Free Living

Unit 01 台北文創園區
（Taipei Culture and Creative Parks）

📎 台北文創園區的發展與特色

三大文創園區 Three Large Cultural and Creative Parks

Taipei has owned three large culture and creative parks, including the Songshan Culture and Creative Park, the Huashan 1914 Creative Park, and the Taipei Information Park. The former two parks are now opened and the third one is scheduled to make its debut in the second half of 2014.

台北三大文創園區包括松山文創園區、華山 1914 文化創意產業園區，與台北資訊園區。前兩個文創園區已經設立，第三個文創園區預定 2014 年開幕。

As a predecessor of the Taipei Distillery, the Huashan 1914 Creative Park is a historic monument designated by the Taipei City Government. Beginning in 1999, it has started to serve as an arena of cultural activities for artists and writers, art exhibits for non-profit organizations and individuals, and music performances. Meanwhile, the park also establishes commercial facilities such as restaurants, shops, and galleries.

華山 1914 文化創意產業園區前身為「台北酒廠」，為臺灣台北市市定古蹟。在 1999 年後，成為提供給藝文界、非營利團體及個人使用的藝術展覽、音樂表演等文化活動場地。此外，園區內也有多間餐廳、店舖、藝廊等商業設施。

Eslite Living, a subsidiary under Eslite Books chain store, opened its main store in the Songshan Culture and Creative Park on August 15, 2013, with the target of combining culture creative spaces for sightseeing, exhibits, and movies. As Taiwan's leading book store chain,

Eslite Books expects to introduce over 100 local creativity brands into the park and estimates to create the revenue of up to NT$1 billion per year.

台北三大文創園區之一的松山文創園區內主要進駐廠商誠品生活松菸店於 2013 年 8 月 15 日開幕，結合觀光、展覽、電影院等文創空間，引進逾百家國內原創品牌，估計一年營收可達 10 億元。

The Eslite Living Songshan Store includes two basements and three floors, with a total business area of 7,200 pings. A hotel is planned to open in the fourth quarter of 2013.

誠品生活松菸店包含地下兩樓及地上三層，總營業坪數 7,200 坪。誠品生活同時規劃「誠品行旅」觀光飯店，預計第四季開幕。

The external appearance of 14-floor building is designed by It Toyoo（1941—）, a contemporary architect in Japan. With a design of shrinking back in elevation of each floor, the building reserves a green belt balcony, enabling to gaze at the distance view of Songshan historic spot, courtyard, and lotus flower pool, thus reflecting with the nature.

這棟有著些許弧度造型的 14 層大樓外觀是由日本當代建築大師伊東豐雄設計，建築立面逐層退縮而保留出的綠帶陽台，可眺望松菸古蹟群、中庭、蓮花池等，與自然相互輝映。

The Eslite Living Songshan Store allured over 100,000 people within 13 days after its opening. The tide of people extended from both Taipei 101 and Warner Vieshow Cinemas to cross the Zhongxiao East Road into the Civic Boulevard in the north and crowded in the Taipei Culture and Creation Building.

誠品松菸店於開幕 13 天內湧進超過 10 萬人次，讓往常以台北 101 大樓、信義華納威秀影城為主軸的人潮動線，跨過忠孝東路，往北延伸至市民大道，擠爆台北文創大樓。

The Eslite Living Songshan Store is the latest cultural arena developed by the Eslite Group. Eventually, the store expects to become an eye-catching sightseeing spot of Taiwan and sets as a foil to culture elements of Taiwan.

誠品生活松菸店是誠品歷經創作時間最長的一處新文化場域，最後期望可以成為觀光的文創勝地，結合併呈台灣與國際文化創意作品，襯托台灣文化元素成為觀光旅遊亮點。

BOT 招商，特許經營 50 年
BOT Investment, 50 Years Franchised Operation

In 2011, the Department of Cultural Affairs of Taipei City Government designated Songshan Tobacco Factory as No. 99 city monument and reserved historic sites such as office houses, cigarette-making facilities, boilers, and warehouses. Thus, a "double park" planning is finalized for the Songshan tobacco factory, occupying a total land area of 18 acres. With a space of 10 acres, the Taipei Sports Park, which annexes to the old tobacco factory in the west side of Kuanfu South Road, is now under construction of the Taipei Dome. The remaining eight acres and historic monuments are belonged to the Songshan Culture and Creative Park.

2001 年，台北市文化局正式將松山菸廠指定為第 99 處市定古蹟。將辦公廳舍，製菸工廠、鍋爐房，以及倉庫保存下來，自此確立松山菸廠「雙園區」的規劃，總面積達 18 公頃土地。菸廠西側緊鄰光復南路的 10 公頃土地，被劃為台北體育園區預定地，目前正在興建大巨蛋體育館。其餘的 8 公頃，包含古蹟在內，則被劃入松山文化創意園區。

Those historic monuments in the culture and creative park are protected under the cultural asset preservation law. To this end, the Department of Culture Affairs of Taipei City spent NT$600 million and three years to repair the old tobacco factory, together with a BOT(build-operation-transfer） project announced for the private investment. With a joint venture of NT$8.6 billion, Fubon Construction and Taiwan Mobile won the building construction and a franchised operation of 50 years in the park.

而在文創園區的部分，古蹟受《文化資產保存法》保護必須保留，台北市文化局花費台幣 6 億元，耗時 3 年，按照松山菸廠原有的建築藍圖加以整修。同時進行 BOT 民間投資招商。 2010 年，由富邦建設與台灣大哥大團隊組成的台北文創開發公司，以台幣 86 億元總投資金額，取得大樓興建及營運 50 年的特許。

紅點、iF 聚焦松菸 Reddot/iF Design Offices in the Park

Meanwhile, both iF and Reddot, the world's most two famous design houses from Germany, have already set up their offices in the Songshan Culture and Creative Park. A reddot museum also opened on August 30, 2013, making Taipei to follow Essen of Germany and Singapore to become the world's third city that has owned the museum.

「國際論壇」iF 與紅點這兩家全球最知名的德國設計公司，也陸續進駐。8 月 30 日，紅點設計博物館在松菸開幕，台北成為繼德國埃森與新加坡之後，全球第三個擁有紅點博物館的城市。

Politics

Commerce

Jobs

Sports

Healthy

Society

Career

Life

📎 重要單字暨新聞辭彙（Key Vocabulary & News Glossary）

- culture and creative park 文創園區
- debut (n.)初登場
- predecessor (n.)前身
- non-profit organizations
  非營利組織
- commercial facilities 商業設施
- gallery (n.)藝廊
- subsidiary (n.)關係企業
- brand (n.)品牌
- contemporary (adj.)當代的
- architect (n.)建築師
- allure (vt.)吸引

- Taipei 101 台北 101 大樓
- Warner Vieshow Cinemas
  華納威秀影城
- Civil Boulevard　市民大道
- foil (n.)襯托
- monument (n.)古蹟
- Taipei Sports Parts 台北體育園區
- Taipei Dome 台北巨蛋體育館
- BOT（build-operation-transfer）
  民間招商
- joint venture 聯合投資
- design house 設計公司

📎 單字及句型範例（Vocabularies & Sentence Examples）

1. The actress made her debut in the new comedy.
   這位演員在那齣新喜劇中首次登臺演出。

2. This brand of tea is my favorite. 這種茶我最愛喝。

3. a very creative musician. 極富創造力的音樂家。

4. The teacher posted the schedule of classes.
   教師將課程表公佈出來了。

5. the minister designate. 部長指定人選部長指定人選。

6. A member of congress works in the political arena.
   國會議員在政界活動。

7. The subsidiary is in France but the parent company is in America.
   子公司在法國，但母公司在美國。

8. His lecture is on contemporary American novelists. 他的演講是關於
   當代美國小說家的。

9. You can see the sea from our balcony.
從我們的陽臺，你可以看到大海。

10. The fine weather allures the ladies into the garden.
晴朗的天氣吸引女士們來到花園裡。

11. The ruins of the castle are an ancient monument, which the government pays money to preserve.
這一城堡廢墟是古代的遺跡，政府出錢加以保存。

12. The ruins of the castle are an ancient monument, which the government pays money to preserve.
這一城堡廢墟是古代的遺跡，政府出錢加以保存。

13. There was a crowd of people in front of the town hall.
市政大廳前有一群人。

14. The government eventually collapsed in 1970.
該政府終於在 1970 年倒臺了。

15. The bank has assets of over five million pounds.
這家銀行有五百萬英鎊以上的資產。

16. We have taken effective measures to preserve our natural resources. 我們已採取有效措施保護自然資源。

問題與討論（Questions & Discussions）

Q 1. 您曾拜訪過誠品松菸或是華山文創園區嗎，您覺得上述園區各有何文創特色？

Q.1 Have you visited Eslite Living Songshan Store or Huashan Culture and Creative Park? Do you think the two parks have their own culture and creation features?

Q 2. 聽說誠品松菸店已開設許多本土文創品牌和各項展覽及最新電影設施頗值得參觀？

Q.2 People said that Eslite's Songshan Store has opened several local culture and creation brands as well as exhibits and latest movie facilities, and they are worth visiting?

Q 3. 您喜歡台北文創園區及其設施所營造之樂活模式？

Q.3 Do you like Taipei culture and creation parks or the happy and free living style created by the facilities?

📎 主題對話範例（Dialogue Examples）

A：The Huashan 1914 Culture and Creative Park is the first of its kind in Taipei.

B：The Eslite Living Songshan Store expects to become a new scenic spot in Taiwan.

A：My friend held an art exhibition in the Huashan 1914 Culture and Creative Park.

B：Huashan Park is small but has much of fun, compared with Eslite Songshan Park.

A：The 14-floor building in the Songshan Culture and Creative Park was designed by a famous Japanese architect.

B：Do you know any other building works of Ito Toyoo in Japan?

同義字與名詞（Synonym & Terminology）

1. arena（活動場所）⇨ coliseum ⇨ amphitheatre ⇨ stadium
2. brand（品牌）⇨ mark ⇨ label ⇨ burn ⇨ tag
3. revenue（收益）⇨ income ⇨ receipts ⇨ profits
4. contemporary（當代的）⇨ present ⇨ present-time ⇨ present-age
5. allure（吸引）⇨ fascinate ⇨ attract ⇨ charm
6. preserve（保存）⇨ protect ⇨ keep ⇨ maintain ⇨ guard ⇨ defend

📎英譯中練習：（參閱主題文章）

English ⇨ Chinese Translation Practice：(Refer to the theme article）

1. As a predecessor of the Taipei Distillery, the Huashan 1914 Creative Park is a historic monument designated by the Taipei City Government. Beginning in 1999, it has started to serve as an arena of cultural activities for artists and writers.（英譯中）

   ....

   ....

2. As Taiwan's leading book store chain, Eslite Books expects to introduce over 100　local creativity brands into the park and estimates to create the revenue of NT$1 billion per year.（英譯中）

   ....

   ....

3. Eventually, the store expects to become an eye-catching sightseeing spot of Taiwan and sets as a foil to culture elements of Taiwan.（英譯中）

   ....

   ....

Politics

Commerce

Jobs

Sports

Healthy

Society

Career

Life

Unit 02 **寵物當家**
（Pets Rule!）

📎 各式各樣的寵物

寵物 Pets

Pets are raised for the purpose of amusement and companion. Cats, dogs, birds, and fishes are commonly seen and owned by people mainly to eliminate loneliness or to increase entertainment.
寵物是為了玩賞、陪伴，而飼養的動物。一般是指人為了消除孤寂或娛樂，其中貓、狗、鳥和魚最為常見。

Most pets are taken with good treatment by their masters and will not be used as food, but animal abuses are derived from pets sometimes. As the demand for pets has become hectic, several animals have encountered unnecessary death before they are delivered from the countryside to the bird trade market, for example.
大多數寵物在主人那裡會受到很好的對待，也不將寵用作為食用，但有時也衍生虐待動物問題。由於人們對寵物的需求很熱絡，導致市場的出現，但許多動物從野生到達市場如鳥類貿易市場之前，會導致不必要的死亡。

Usually, pets mean the class of mammals or birds as their cerebrums are much more developed, or equivalent to that of 3-5 years old children, making it easy to communicate with the human being. People can turn all animals into their pets, including fishes, reptiles, amphibians, and insects, which are animals with smaller sizes, however.
寵物一般是哺乳綱或鳥綱的動物，因為這些動物大腦比較發達，有的大腦能相當於 3 至 5 歲左右的幼兒的大腦，所以容易和人交流。但其

Politics

Commerce

Jobs

Sports

Healthy

Society

Career

Life

實人可以把所有種類的動物變成寵物，包括魚綱、爬行綱、兩棲綱甚至昆蟲，不過一般寵物都是體型比較小的動物。

The contents of pets have changed following the ecology transition that is acknowledged to people. Animals used to be raised as pets in the past are now no longer suitable due to the trade demand and the extinction issue. Under controlled activities, most pets are man-bred with the genera causing no threats to the wild groups.

寵物的內容也隨人們的認知的生態的變遷而變化，以前許多作為寵物飼養的動物，由於貿易需求而導致物種本身的瀕危，這些動物已經不再適合作為寵物。適合做寵物的物種往往是人工繁殖成熟，容易控制活動範圍，不會對野生種群造成威脅的種類。

法律定義 Legal Definition

Taiwan's animal protection law has defined pets as dogs, cats and other animals that are raised for pleasure or companion. It also specifies that pets are not allowed to be killed, traded, or fed for other economic purposes such as meat and fur.

臺灣動物保護法將寵物定義為：「指犬、貓及其他供玩賞、伴侶之目的而飼養或管領之動物。」並規定不得因「為肉用、皮毛用，或餵飼其他動物之經濟利用目的」而被宰殺、販賣。

動物寵物 Animal Pets

The genera in the following list can be raised for pets. But the raising of certain pets is not encouraged as the trade of certain genera has been hazardous to the survival of wild animals.

以下列出的是作為寵物飼養的種類，某些物種的貿易已對野生種群生存造成一定危害，並不鼓勵飼養。

哺乳類 Mammals

Dogs（Canis lupus familiaris）: Maltese, Pekingese, Shar Pei, Labrador Retriever, Golden Retriever, Cocker, Schnauzer, Chihuahua, Poodle, and Bulldog.
犬類：馬爾濟斯、獅子狗、沙皮狗、拉布拉多犬、黃金獵犬、可卡犬、雪納瑞、吉娃娃、貴賓狗、鬥牛犬等。

Cats（Felis silvestris catus）: American shorthair, British shorthair, exotic shorthair, Scottish fold, and Persian.
貓類：美國短毛貓、英國短毛貓、異國短毛貓、蘇格蘭折耳貓、波斯貓等

Mouse（Muroidea）, order of rodents: Cavia porcellus, little white mouse, gerbil, Siberian Chipmunk, Octodon, Pteromyini, and Golden Hamster（Mesocricetus auratus）.
鼠類，嚙齒目：荷蘭豬（天竺鼠）、小白鼠、沙鼠、金花鼠、八齒鼠、寒號鳥（鼯鼠）和金絲熊（黃金倉鼠）。

魚類 Fishes

金魚 Gold fish
錦鯉 Cyprinus carpio
熱帶魚 Tropical fish

鳥類 Birds

鴿 Dove
雞 Chicken

Psittaciformes: Melopsittacus undulatu, Ara, and Agapornis（also called love bird）.

鸚鵡類：虎皮鸚鵡、金剛鸚鵡、牡丹鸚鵡（又稱為愛情鸚鵡、愛情鳥）。

Songbirds: Alaudidae, Hwamei, Acridotheres cristatellus, and Serinus canaria.
鳴禽類：百靈、畫眉、八哥、金絲雀。

兩棲類 Amphibians

蛙 Frog
蟾蜍 Toad
娃娃魚 Chinese giant salamander（Andrias davidianus）
蠑螈 Fire-bellied salamander（Cynops orientalis David）
鯢 Cryptobranchus japonicusm（a kind of salamander）
蚓螈 Caecilian

爬行類 Reptiles

蜥蜴 Lizard
鬣蜥 Agama
蛇 Snake
龜 Turtle

Crocodilian: saltwater crocodile, Caiman latirostris, alligator, and Indian gharial.
鱷魚類：小灣鱷、寬吻鱷、短吻鱷、印度食魚長吻鱷。

蟲類 Worms

甲蟲 Beetle
蟋蟀 Cricket
蠶 Silk worm

蜘蛛 Spider
蠍子 Scorpion

其他用途 Other Functions

Working dogs can be divided into several categories in terms of market demands, for example, guide dogs help the blind to lead the way. Wolfhounds are tied to watch the door in front of farm houses. And these working dogs are generally regarded as pets.

工作犬因為市場需求所以種類很多，如導盲犬，專門幫助盲人領路；有看門犬，如農戶家門前栓的大狼狗等。這些工作犬通常也被視作是寵物。

機器人 Robots

Aibo, an electronics dog invented by Sony of Japan, can play with the children and lead the way for both the elderly and the blind person. Aided by the development of artificial intelligence, such robots can be employed with thinking and show considerations to people in the future. In electronics games, the physiological function of cats, dogs, fishes, or other pets are imitated and these pets also go through birth, aging, sickness, and death and need "feeding" and "taking care" by people.

機器人，如日本索尼公司開發的電子狗愛寶可以與兒童玩耍，也可以給老人或盲人領路。人工智慧的發展，未來這類寵物會有思想，會變得更加體貼人。電子遊戲程序，模擬真實的貓、狗、魚或其他寵物的生理狀況，這類寵物也會有「生老病死」，需要人的「餵養」與「照顧」。

📎 重要單字暨新聞辭彙（Key Vocabulary & News Glossary）

- amusement *(n.)* 玩賞
- companion *(n.)* 伴侶
- derive from 衍生
- hectic *(adj.)* 熱絡的
- definition *(n.)* 定義
- mammal *(n.)* 哺乳類
- reptile *(n.)* 爬行類
- amphibian *(n.)* 兩棲類
- exotic *(adj.)* 異國的

- insect *(n.)* 昆蟲
- ecology *(n.)* 生態
- extinction *(n.)* 絕種
- genera *(n.)* 類；種屬（genus 複數）
- hazardous *(adj.)* 危險的
- guide dog 導盲犬
- robot *(n.)* 機器人
- artificial intelligence 人工智慧
- imitate *(vt.)* 模擬

📎 單字及句型範例（Vocabularies & Sentence Examples）

1. The queen ruled her country for 20 years. 這位女王統治了她的國家二十年。
2. They used to breed fish in the reservoir. 他們過去一直在水庫養魚。
3. Many English words are derived from Latin. 許多英文字源於拉丁語。
4. Smoking is hazardous to your health. 抽煙有礙你的健康。
5. We saw pictures of exotic birds from the jungle of Brazil. 我們看到了來自於巴西熱帶雨林的各種奇異鳥類的照片。
6. Apes are in danger of extinction. 猿類正處於絕種的危險之中。

📎 問題與討論（Questions & Discussions）

Q 1. 您有養過寵物嗎？包括有哪些動物？

Q.1　Have you reared any pets, and what are they?

Q 2. 養寵物很貴嗎？您如何安排這些預算？

Q.2　Is it expensive to raise pets? And how do you arrange the budget?

Politics　Commerce　Jobs　Sports　Healthy　Society　Career　Life

Q 3. 您同意飼養瀕臨絕種之動物當作寵物嗎，理由安在？

Q.3 Do you agree with the raising of endangered animals as pets, and why?

📎 主題對話範例（Dialogue Examples）

A：Many friends of mine have reared pets, and dogs and cats are commonly seen.

B：I prefer to the raising of dogs to the raising of cats.

A：People who violate the animal protection law in Taiwan will be fined or sentenced to jail.

B：Most pets are adorable and should not be treated with abuses.

A：Do not buy or raise any endangered animals for pets.

B：It is our duty to protect the animal if we decide to raise them.

同義字與名詞（Synonym & Terminology）

1. derive（衍生） ⇨ get ⇨ obtain ⇨ acquire ⇨ secure
2. hectic（熱絡的） ⇨ feverish ⇨ heated ⇨ hot ⇨ burning
3. exotic（異國的） ⇨ foreign ⇨ strange
4. artificial（人工的） ⇨ false ⇨ pretended ⇨ unreal
5. imitate（模仿） ⇨ follow ⇨ trace ⇨ copy ⇨ duplicate

📎英譯中練習：（參閱主題文章）

English ⇨ Chinese Translation Practice：(Refer to the theme article)

1. Most pets are taken good treatment by their masters and will not be used as food, but animal abuse problems are derived from pets sometimes.（英譯中）

   ....

   ....

2. People can turn all animals into their pets, including fishes, reptiles, amphibians, and insects, which are animals with smaller sizes, however.（英譯中）

   ....

   ....

3. Aided by the development of artificial intelligence, such robots can be employed with thinking and show considerations to people in the future.（英譯中）

   ....

   ....

Politics

Commerce

Jobs

Sports

Healthy

Society

Career

Life

247

Unit 03　微笑單車熱潮
（U-Bike Upsurges in Taipei）

黃色腳踏車所帶動的休閒風

台北市府所提供的 U-Bike

In a response to the global trend of energy-saving, carbon-reducing, and an upgrade of metropolitan living quality, the Department of Transportation（DOT）of Taipei City Government has cooperated with Taiwan Giant to offer an all-round public bicycle leasing service known as U-Bike, a new type of short-distanced shuttle tool. With MRT as the core transportation, a total of 30 bike-leasing stops together with 960 units are installed along the sides of Biannan, Luzhou, and Wenhu Lines, extending to the life circle in Nankang District.

臺北市政府交通局為響應全球節能、減碳風潮,及秉持提升臺北都市生活品質之使命,與臺灣捷安特攜手合作,將全面拓展臺北市公共自行車租賃系統服務據點,新型態的短程接駁工具「U-Bike」。以捷運運輸為核心,沿途從捷運板南、蘆洲、文湖線至南港生活圈,增設 30 處租賃站,共 960 輛自行車的設置。

The expansion of U-Bike stops is expected to increase the utility rate of citizens, thus connecting with MRT system effectively. This effort also aims at offering a more convenient network of mass shuttle network in Taipei, said Lin Chih-ying, head of DOT.

交通局局長林志盈表示,期望藉由 U-Bike 據點的拓廣,增加市民的使用率,並與捷運系統有效連結。讓臺北市擁有更全面、更便捷的大眾接駁網絡。

DOT made public of its 30 new U-Bike stops in a press conference held recently. "Kiosk", a 24-hour service of automatic leasing equipment for

U-Bike, is also introduced.
交通局同時召開記者會公 30 處新設租賃據點。以及操作全新的 24 小時無人管理自動化的租賃設備 Kiosk(自動服務機）。

Taipei Mayor Hau Lung-bin(1952-) 　said that bike-riding has become a global trend in many metropolitan cities of the world, including Amsterdam of the Netherlands, Copenhagen of Denmark, and Britain's London, which just held Olympics Games, and they have owned sound public bicycle systems. As Taiwan's bicycle culture is getting ripe, Taipei expects to become a low-carbon and moving green city, Hau added.
臺北市長郝龍斌表示，騎乘自行車已在全球蔚為風潮，在許多成熟的國際大城市荷蘭阿姆斯特丹、丹麥哥本哈根、甚至剛舉辦完奧運的英國倫敦，都擁有完善的公共自行車系統。冀望在臺灣的自行車文化日漸成熟下，也能「讓臺北成為一個低碳移動的綠色城市」。

As an attempt to increase the utility rate, DOT allows users to lease U-Bike at place A and return it in place B, and an incentive of free membership fee is offered to join as U-Bike members, effective immediately. In order to meet biking requirements, each riding can enjoy a free mileage and no limitation of using times, plus a free charge in the first 30-minute riding.
交通局為提高使用率，除了提供甲地借乙地還的租賃服務外，更祭出大利多，即日起加入 YouBike 會員者，無需會費。可享有不限里程、不限次數，每次騎乘前 30 分鐘免費的專屬優惠，來滿足全方位的騎乘需求。

The existing 30 stops serves as only a beginning and the bureau plans to set up a total of 162 stops under three phases until 2014, when Taipei expects to own 5,350 units of U-Bike. It will always be available with the free riding service in each stop, according to Lin.
交通局長林志盈更說明，現階段的 30 個租賃點僅是一個開端，計劃在未來分三階段施行建置計劃，預計 2014 年臺北市區共將新增 162 處租賃站，擁有超過 5,350 輛的 YouBike 隨時待命服務民眾，歡迎大家一站接一站，免錢騎透透！

Liu Chin-biao, chairman of Taiwan Giant, noted that his lifetime mission was to build up a "bike island" for Taiwan. Being the world's leading bike brand, Taiwan Giant represents not only the No.1 bike manufacturer but also promotes more people to experience a bike culture in Taiwan. This solves both the traffic jam and the environmental issue at the same time. Today, the dream has come true in Taipei, and let U-Bike act as a most friendly public service in the world, Liu boasted.

捷安特公司董事長劉金標表示，自己畢生最大的使命就是建造臺灣成為「自行車島」。身為全球自行車領導品牌，捷安特不僅要臺灣成為自行車製造龍頭，也想讓更多人體驗新的自行車生活文化，同時解決惱人的塞車和環汙痛苦，今天，這一份理想與夢想將在臺北市實現，U-Bike 以作為世界最友善的公共自行車為目標。

In coordination with an overall improved biking environment and well-established MRT network in Taipei, the U-Bike is now in a better position to offer the mass transportation from the street deep into the lane and/or the alley, creating a new "two wheel" culture. "Taking cars is too fast while walking is slow. Only riding bikes can you keep a beautiful scenic view of life," Liu said.

配合全面改善的自行車騎乘環境，加上完備的臺北捷運路網，可讓大眾運輸從街道深入巷弄，創造新的「兩輪文化」。「坐車太快，走路太慢，只有自行車才能留得住人生美麗的風景。」

The U-Bike leasing system is equipped with two main facilities: one is the parking post and the other is "Kiosk" automatic service machine. Each parking post holds together with two bikes and a high-end precision locking design. The control panel is readable for the EasyCard and other electronics ticketing certificates, with which to lock and unlock a U-Bike. Four steps are followed to lease a U-Bike：enter → selecting a bike → riding → returning. It is easy to lease a bike.

YouBike 租賃系統擁有二個主要設備，一是停車柱，一是 Kiosk （自動服務機）。停車柱採一柱兩車、高精密電子鎖的設計，上方的控制器面板可讀寫 UBike 認證之悠遊卡等電子票證，自動將 UBike 上鎖或解鎖，民眾可以依租借四步驟：加入→選車→騎乘→還車，輕鬆租賃自行車。

Liu Li-chu, general manager of U-Bike Business Department, emphasized that the leasing process was simple. And the second generation U-Bike has three features：convenience, safety, and consideration. Adopting an "one size fits all" design, the new bike is comfortable for all people from the elderly to young users. Meanwhile, the generator of an environmental disc drum maintains the electricity at all time, thus ensuring a safe illumination in both front and back lights during riding. And the patented locking keeps the bike safe from burglaries. The general public is encouraged to take advantage of the incentive of 30-minumte free charge, thus enjoying the street view of Taipei City attentively, Liu said.

U-Bike 事業部總經理劉麗珠更強調，除了操作簡易的租賃程序外，第二代的 U-Bike 的車體更是擁有「方便、安全、貼心」三大特色，採用 One Size Fits all 的設計，不分男女老少都能舒適地騎乘；環保的輪鼓發電設計可隨時續電，在騎乘中點亮前後燈更安全；專利隨車安全鎖，隨時隨地都能安心保管自行車。她更指出，提供 U-Bike 會員前 30 分鐘騎乘免費之優惠，歡迎民眾多加利用，一同細細感受臺北街頭的美好！」

In related news, Hatano Yui(born on May 23, 1988 in Kyoto, Japan）, a famous and popular AV actress, visited Taiwan for the publication of her latest portrait album and caused a wave of unrest as she rode U-Bike

Politics

Commerce

Jobs

Sports

Healthy

Society

Career

Life

in Taipei recently. By spending a lot of works, the sponsor found the series number 3804 U-Bike which was once ridden by Hatano and gave a surprise with the same U-Bike during her stay on the island.

有關新聞，在台灣廣受喜愛的日本人氣女優波多野結衣（1988 年 5 月 23 日生於日本京都府），特地為了首發寫真書《天使波多野結衣：盛愛寫真》來台宣傳，日前她騎 U-Bike 微笑單車造成一股風潮，甚至引發一片尋找她所騎乘「3804」號單車，廠商耗費一番功夫與 U-Bike 協調同意，將原單車找到給波多野結衣一個驚喜。

🖈 重要單字暨新聞辭彙（Key Vocabulary & News Glossary）

- upsurge *(vi.)* 高漲
- metropolitan *(adj.)* 大都會的
- leasing *(n.)* 租賃
- shuttle *(n.)* 接駁
- MRT（Mass Rapid Transit）大眾捷運系統
- life circle 生活圈
- utility rate 利用率
- press conference 記者會
- mileage *(n.)* 里程
- traffic jam 塞車
- scenic view 風景
- EasyCard 悠遊卡
- illumination *(n.)* 照明
- burglary *(n.)* 竊盜
- AV actress AV 女優
- portrait album 寫真集

🖈 單字及句型範例（Vocabularies & Sentence Examples）

1. upsurge, a sudden increase 猛增，急劇上升。
2. She laughed in response to his jokes. 她聽了他的笑話大笑。
3. all-round--good at doing many different things, especially at many different. sports 【英】才能多方面的，（尤指體育）全能的。
4. Each student studies four core subjects. 每個學生學習四門基礎課。
5. The lease on this house expires at the end of the year. 這房子的租約年底到期。

6. He uses his own car for business purposes and is paid mileage.
   他用自己的汽車出差，並按行駛哩數支付費用。

7. We shuttled the passengers to the city center by helicopter. 我們使用
   直升飛機往返不停地將旅客運送到市中心。

8. He's going to install an air-conditioner in the house. 他要在這屋子裡
   裝冷氣機。

9. Can't you extend your visit for a few days?
   你們訪問的時間不能延長幾天嗎？

10. The store deals in objects of domestic utility.
    那家商店出售家庭用品。

11. Metropolitan buildings become taller than ever.
    大城市的建築變得比以前更高。

12. The time is ripe for a new foreign policy.
    採用新外交政策的時機已成熟。

13. The child has no incentive to study harder because his parents
    cannot afford to send him to college.
    這孩子沒有努力學習的動力，因為他父母供不起他上大學。

14. Please charge my account. 請記在我帳上。

15. The library's reading-rooms need better illumination.
    圖書館裡閱覽室的燈光不夠明亮，需要改進。

16. Burglary: the crime of getting into a building to steal things.
    入室盜竊（罪）。

📎 問題與討論（Questions & Discussions）

Q 1. 您有否加入 U-Bike 成為會員，並有經常騎乘微笑單車？

Q.1 Are you a member of U-Bike and ridden the bike regularly?

Q 2. 您覺得捷運站路線所附設的微笑單車對你方便嗎？你對目前北市政府之微笑單車有何批評？

Q.2 Is it convenient for you to use the U-Bike service along the Taipei MRT routes, and how do you comment on the facility now offered by the city hall?

Q 3. 報載北市微笑單車目前歸還車後 15 分鐘後才可續租，您覺得此新規定公平嗎？

Q.3 The newspapers reported that U-Bike is now available to lease again after returning it for 15 minutes. Do you think this new regulation is fair or not?

📎 主題對話範例（Dialogue Examples）

A：U-Bike has become a popular shuttle tool in Taipei.

B：Many people use U-Bike for their short distance transportation.

A：Taipei City Government should have set up more U-Bike stops along MRT routes.

B：Users are responsible for the public properties of U-Bike and are liable for damages.

A：Bicycle riders should pay more attention to the safety of pedestrians.

B：A new regulation governing safety of U-Bike riders will be announced soon.

同義字與名詞（Synonym & Terminology）

1. lease（出租） ⇨ rent ⇨ hire ⇨ let ⇨ charter
2. metropolitan（大都會的） ⇨ city ⇨ civic ⇨ urban ⇨ municipal
3. shuttle（來回移動）- ⇨ pass back and forth ⇨ go back and forth between
4. burglary（竊盜） ⇨ stealing ⇨ thievery ⇨ larceny ⇨ theft ⇨ robbery
5. scenic（雅緻的） ⇨ grand ⇨ breathtaking ⇨ beautiful ⇨ charming
6. portrait（肖像） ⇨ icon ⇨ profile ⇨ silhouette ⇨ effigy
7. album（紀念冊） ⇨ book ⇨ memory book ⇨ catalogue ⇨ anthology

Politics

Commerce

Jobs

Sports

Healthy

Society

Career

Life

📎英譯中練習：（參閱主題文章）

English ⇨ Chinese Translation Practice：(Refer to the theme article)

1. Taiwan Giant offers an all-round public bicycle leasing service known as U-Bike, a new type of short-distanced shuttle tool.（英譯中）

   ....

   ....

2. In coordination with an overall improved biking environment and well-established MRT network in Taipei, the U-Bike is now in a better position to offer the mass transportation from the street deep into the lane and/or the alley, creating a new "two wheel" culture.（英譯中）

   ....

   ....

3. By spending a lot of works, the sponsor found the number 3804 U-Bike which was once ridden by Hatano and gave a surprise with the same U-Bike during her stay on the island.（英譯中）

   ....

   ....

Unit 04 中國策略遊戲『麻將』
（China's Strategic Game──Mahjong）

📎 進入「麻將」的世界

麻將、麻雀 Mahjong, Mahjongg

Mahjong or Mahjongg is a strategic game which derives from China. The game is mostly participated with four players but it can be played by only two or three persons(often seen in Japan or Korea）.

麻雀、麻將、馬將或蔴雀是一種源自中國的策略遊戲。遊戲參與者以四人居多，但也有二人、三人等變種（在日本、韓國較為常見）。

Local rules of Mahjong are very different（especially in the method of scoring） but the basic target is same：by passing through a series of card changes and option rules for certain combinations to win and stop opponents to reach the same purpose at the same time. This game emphasizes on techniques, strategic uses, and calculations but involves in lots of luckiness sometimes. In comparison with the poker game, the combination of mahjong is complicated and need more probabilities to predict results.

麻將在各地的規則（尤其是計分方法）有很大不同，但基本目標都是通過一系列置換和取捨規則拼出某個特定組合的牌型，並阻止對手達成相同目的。遊戲側重技巧、策略運用和計算，但也涉及相當多的運氣成份。比起撲克，麻將的組合方式更為變化多端，需要通過複雜的機率分析才能預測結果。

Meanwhile, mahjong requires plenty rules to remember and its winning hand combinations are over poker. Among the Chinese communities in East Asia and the Southeast Asian region, mahjong is regarded as a mean of entertainment or gambling.

但麻將需要記憶的規則及胡牌型也比一般撲克牌戲要多得多。在東亞
與東南亞地區，特別是華人社區中，麻將常被當做娛樂或賭博手段。

Mahjong tiles are virtually the same and are an identical of Cantonese
style or its subsets. Cantonese mahjong has enjoyed the longest playing
history in Chinese, with cards dividing into three major categories.

麻將的牌張各地大同小異，但多與廣東麻將相同，或為其子集。廣東
麻將是迄今仍流傳的華人玩法之中，歷史最悠久者，其牌張分三類。

The first category is ordinal number cards(see attached chart）,
including three sectors : "dot tiles(shaped like a cake）," "bamboo/strip
tiles," and "character tiles." Every sector is numbered from 1 to 9 and
has four tiles each.(Three sectors total 108 tiles）.

第一類為序數牌（見附圖），分「筒子／餅」、「索子／條」、「萬
子／萬」三門。每門有序數從一至九的牌各四張（三門共 108 隻）。

The second category includes "wind tiles"： East, South, West, and
North and "dragon tiles"：White, Green, and Red. Each sector has four
tiles（and seven sectors total 28 titles）. The third category is "flower
tiles," including eight units：Plum, Orchid, Chrysanthemum, Bamboo"
and "Spring, Summer, Autumn, Winter." Thus, a full set of mahjong
has a total of 144 tiles. In ancient times, mahjong is made of bones,
bamboos, or ivories but it is mostly made of plastics nowadays.

第二類是字牌，包括「東、南、西、北」四款「風牌」及「中、發、
白」三款「三元牌」，每款四張（七款共 28 張）。第三類是花牌，有
「梅、蘭、菊、竹、春、夏、秋、冬」八隻。故全副麻將共計有 144
張。古代麻將有骨製、竹製或象牙製，現代麻將則多以塑膠製成。

In addition of tiles, a full set of mahjong also covers dice and other
dominos. For example, Japanese mahjong uses "chips"(for scoring） and

Cantonese mahjong has a piece of plastic tool called "banker" to identify the starting of each "round".

一副麻將除了牌張，還有骰子及其他道具，例如日本麻將有「點棒」（計分用），廣東麻將就有一件稱為「莊」的塑膠道具，用來識別莊家與顯示「圈風」。

Ordinal Number Tiles（each has four tiles）
序數牌（各四張）

dots / or cakes
筒子／餅

bamboos / strips
索子／條

characters
萬子／萬

Wind Tiles（each has four tiles）
字牌（各四張）

Politics

Commerce

Jobs

Sports

Healthy

Society

Career

Life

wind tiles / four luckiness tiles
風牌／四喜牌

arrow tiles / dragon tiles
箭牌／三元牌

Flower Tiles（one tile for each）
花牌（各一張）

歷史 History

Most people thought that mahjong was an old game but official documents were found in 1875, describing an American diplomat George B. Glover（July 8, 1827 － Oct. 4, 1885）, who donated a mahjong to the American Museum of Nature History. Another formal document to name the game as "mahjong" was recorded until 1894.

一般人以為麻將是很古老的遊戲，但文獻中首則麻將牌具記錄，要到 1875 年才出現，所描述的乃美國外交官吉羅福轉贈給博物館的藏品；首度有文獻將此遊戲名字記為「麻雀」，更遲至 1894 年。

麻將的發源地 Birthplace of Mahjong

The first mahjong book in English was written by Joseph Babcock, who conceded that mahjong might originate from Ningbo but others said that Fujian was the real place of origin. Stewart Culin（July 13, 1858 − 1929）, an American ethnologist and a famous traditional chess and card game researcher, said that the mahjong game was originally called "Chung Fat" only in Jiangsu and Zhejiang Provinces, according to the memorandum made by Sir William Henry Wilkinson（May 10, 1858 − 1930）

史上首部英語麻將譜的作者 Joseph Babcock 認為「麻將可能源自寧波，儘管亦有人指福建才是起源地」。著名的美國人類學家及遊戲研究者史都華・庫林 並無討論過麻將的起源地，但他引述另一著名的遊戲收集者務謹順爵士，謂當時的麻將遊戲（書中稱為「中發」"Chung fat"）僅限於江浙一帶，故其所述較吻合寧波起源論。

麻將術語 Terminology

After years of change, mahjong has owned local rules in each place. Common rules or behaviors are specified differently but some of them still kept those terminologies that are used in both Ming Dynasty（1368-1644）and Ch'ing（Qing）Dynasty（1644-1911）.

經過多年演變，各地不止有不同的麻將玩法。對共通的規則或行為，也冠以不同名稱，不過當中不少仍是明、清年代用語。

The following terminologies are used by individual mahjong players around the world.

以下列出各地玩家對部份術語的名稱。

打麻將 Play mahjong

莊家（莊）Banker

圈 Round

翻（台數）Fans

放銃 出衝（粵港澳／大陸吳語地區）／放槍（台灣）／放炮（大陸）
Chuck

生張牌、熟張牌 "raw" cards，A "ripe" cards

胡牌 To win（bingo, mahjong）

自摸 Selfmake（a winning hand）

聽牌（中國大陸吳地）／聽牌定口（台灣及中國大陸地區）／叫糊（粵
港澳）Waiting（to win）

門前清 A concealed hand（clear front door）

平胡 A winning hand without any flower tiles

清一色 Clear color of a kind

混一色 Mixed color of a kind

海底撈月 A selfmake with the last tile（Scoop up the moon out of the
sea）

大三元 Big Three Dragons

大四喜 Big Four Luckiness

📎 重要單字暨新聞辭彙（Key Vocabulary & News Glossary）

- mahjong (n.) 麻將
- strategic (adj.) 策略的
- option (n.) 選擇
- poker (n.) 樸克牌
- complicated (adj.) 複雜的
- probability (n.) 或然率
- tiles (n.) 麻將牌
- dots (n.) 筒（餅）子
- bamboos (n.) 索（條）子
- characters (n.) 萬（子）
- wind tiles 風牌
- flower tile 花牌
- diplomat (n.) 外交官
- donate (vt.) 捐獻
- anthropologist (n.) 民族學家
- bingo (n.) 贏／勝出

Politics

Commerce

Jobs

Sports

Healthy

Society

Career

Life

📎 單字及句型範例（Vocabularies & Sentence Examples）

1. How many options do we have? 我們有幾種選擇的可能呢？
2. poker, a card game that people usually play for money. （通常指賭錢的）撲克牌戲，紙牌戲。
3. That puzzle is too complicated for the children. 那個謎語對兒童來說太難了。
4. The probability of making a mistake increases when you are tired. 你累的時候犯錯誤的可能性就會增加。
5. She donated her books to the library. 她把自己的書捐贈給圖書館。

📎 問題與討論（Questions & Discussions）

Q 1. 您會不會打麻將，段數高嗎？

Q.1　Do you play mahjong and how is your playing skills?

Q 2. 你曾參加過家庭式麻將聚會嗎？

Q.2　Have you ever attended a family style mahjong game?

Q 3. 您認為麻將是遊戲或賭博？理由如何？

Q.3　Do you think mahjong is a game or gambling? What are your opinions?

📎 主題對話範例（Dialogue Examples）

A：Playing mahjong is a common gathering among friends in Taiwan.

B：I was invited by my friends to participate in a mahjong game recently.

A：People usually play mahjong for the gambling purpose.

B：Playing mahjong is a fun but the game should not involve too much money.

A：I used to play mahjong and lost money.

B：I quit playing mahjong and prepare to make exercises instead.

同義字與名詞（Synonym & Terminology）

1. option（選擇） ⇨ selection ⇨ adoption ⇨ acceptance ⇨ espousal
2. complicated（複雜的） ⇨ complex ⇨ elaborate ⇨ intricate
3. option（選擇） ⇨ choice ⇨ alternative ⇨ substitute
4. donate（捐贈） ⇨ give ⇨ contribute ⇨ present ⇨ bestow
5. emphasize（強調） ⇨ stress ⇨ punctuate ⇨ accent ⇨ italicize
6. technique（技巧） ⇨ skill ⇨ ability ⇨ faculty ⇨ talent
7. combination（組合） ⇨ assortment ⇨ grouping
8. entertainment（娛樂） ⇨ amusement ⇨ diversion ⇨ divertissement

📎 英譯中練習：（參閱主題文章）

English ⇨ Chinese Translation Practice：(Refer to the theme article)

1. In comparison with the poker game, the combination of mahjong is complicated and need more probabilities to predict results.（英譯中）

　　...

　　...

2. Among the Chinese communities in East Asia and the Southeast Asian region, mahjong is regarded as a mean of entertainment or gambling.（英譯中）

　　...

　　...

3. An American ethnologist and a famous traditional chess and card game researcher said that the mahjong game was originally called "Chung Fat" only in Jiangsu and Zhejiang Provinces.（英譯中）

　　...

　　...

Unit　05　戲如人生　人生如戲
（Drama is Life and Life is Drama）

📎 淺談戲劇

西方戲劇 Drama in Western Culture

The term "drama" comes from a classic Greek verb meaning "to act". Drama is the specific mode of writing represented in performance, and it is often combined with literature, music, and dance. Some dramas have been written to be read rather than performed.

戲劇這個單詞起源於古希臘的動詞，意為「表演」。戲劇是一種以表演來表達的寫作模式，並常和文學、音樂和舞蹈結合在一起。部分戲劇的創作則是以閱讀為主，而非以表演的模式進行。

A symbol of two masks are often associated with drama: one with the laughing face; the other with the weeping face. This symbol represents the traditional division between comedy and tragedy. The laughing face is the symbol of Thalia, the Muse of comedy, and the weeping face is the symbol of Melpomene, the Muse of tragedy.

在和戲劇相關的事物中，常能看到一個包含兩個面具的符號：一張笑臉，和一張哭臉。這個符號象徵喜劇和悲劇這兩個古典戲劇類別。笑臉是希臘神話中喜劇女神塔利亞的符號，而哭臉則是悲劇女神墨爾波墨的象徵。

According to Aristotle's Poetics, comedy is a representation of laughable people and involves some kind of blunder or ugliness which does not cause pain or disaster. Tragedy is a serious performance of incidents arousing pity and fear. The writing of comedy and tragedy presuppose collaborative emotion and collective reception of the audience, and its development is also directly influenced by this collaborative emotion and collective reception. The classical Athenian tragedy "Oedipus the King" is among the masterpieces of drama.

據亞里斯多德在《詩論》中所述，喜劇表現的是可笑的人群，以及他們所犯的錯誤或醜態，卻不造成痛苦或傷害。悲劇則是透過嚴肅的表演呈現事故，引起觀眾的憐憫或恐懼。喜劇和悲劇都是以影響觀眾的群體情感以及共同反應為前提，因此戲劇的發展也受這些群體情感及共同反應影響。古雅典的悲劇《伊底帕斯王》是戲劇的傑作之一。

東方戲劇 Drama in Eastern Culture

The major features of drama in eastern cultures are seen in three civilizations: China, India, and Japan. Chinese drama, also known as Chinese opera, is represented as both drama and musical performance. Its roots go back as far as the third century. There are several regional branches of Chinese drama, of which the Beijing opera from the northern region and of the Kunqu from the southern region are among the most notable.

東方文化中的戲劇主要出現在中國、印度、日本等三個文明中。中國戲劇也稱為中國戲曲，以同時演出戲劇及音樂的方式呈現。中國戲劇的歷史可追朔到公元三世紀。中國戲劇又依區域分為不同的派別，最有名的有北方的京劇和南方的崑曲。

The ancient India dramas were written in Sanskrit, tracing back to the first century, and is considered as the highest achievement of Sanskrit literature. Sanskrit dramas established stock characters, including hero, heroine, or jester. Some of the Sanskrit dramas were translated into German in the 19th century, which is said to influence Goethe's Faust.

古印度的戲劇則以梵文寫作，可追朔到公元一世紀，被認為是梵語文學中最傑出的成就。梵文戲劇創造出制式的角色，其中有男角、女角、及丑角。一部分的梵文戲劇在十九世紀被翻譯成德文，對哥德的《浮士德》造成影響。

Nogaku is one of the most important classical Japanese drama that combines drama, music, and dance into a complete performance. The performance technique was developed since the 13th century, and it is often passed down inside families, from father to son. Nogaku characters are often masked, with male actors playing both male and female roles. Like Chinese opera, Nogaku is still performed today.

能樂結合了戲劇、音樂、和舞蹈，是最重要的日本古典戲劇之一。能樂的技巧自十三世紀開始發展，常常在能樂世家中父子相傳。能樂中的角色常戴著面具，並由男演員飾演男性及女性角色。和中國的戲曲一樣，能樂在現代仍在演出。

戲如人生 人生如戲 Drama is Life and Life is Drama

In his work "poetics", Aristotle listed six parts of tragedy in order of importance, and they are: plot, character, thought, diction, melody, and spectacle. Plot is essential in a tragedy, and all other elements are subsidiary. A drama without a plot is like a man without a soul. A good drama not only presupposes the audiences' collaborative emotion, but also evokes it. Therefore a successful playwright, must be able to arouse emotion in the psyche of the audience.

亞里斯多德在《詩論》中依重要性的順序，列出悲劇應具備的六個部分：劇情、角色、思想、文藻、音樂、佈景。其中劇情是最重要的一部分，其他部分都是次要的。沒有劇情的戲劇，就像是一個沒有靈魂的人。一部好的戲劇不但要以影響觀眾為前提，更要能喚起觀眾的情緒。因此一個成功的劇作家必須要能激發觀眾的內在情感。

But what arouses the audience's emotion the best? Life experience, or better yet, life stories. Alfred Hitchcock once said that "drama is life with the dull parts cut out". It means that drama reflects life, but it's time-compressed with only the most memorable parts left in. Drama is carefully prepared life stories performed on stage.

Politics

Commerce

Jobs

Sports

Healthy

Society

Career

Life

但如何才能有效的激發觀眾的情感？生活故事可能比生活經驗效果更好。希區考克曾說過「戲劇就像人生，只是剪掉了無趣的部分」。這正說明戲劇反映了人生，只是萃取人生中最讓人難忘的部分而成。戲劇本身，就是把精挑細選的人生故事搬上舞台演出。

A famous quote from Shakespeare's "As you like it" would be "the whole world is a stage, and all men and women merely actors". If the whole world is a stage, then life itself is drama. There must be comedies and tragedies, and all actors have their entrances and exits. Drama helps people to understand the meaning of life.

在莎士比亞的劇作《如你所願》中有一句名言：世界是一座舞台，所有人不過是其中的演員。如果世界是舞台，則人生如戲。人生總是會有喜劇和悲劇，所有演員也必然會進場、離場。戲劇讓人了解人生的意義。

亞里斯多德與《詩論》 Aristotle's Poetics

Poetics, by Aristotle, is the earliest-surviving work discussing the theory of dramatic literary. The original work was divided into two parts - the first part addresses tragedy, and the second part focuses on comedy. However, the second part is lost today, and the discussion on tragedy becomes the core of this writing.

亞里斯多德的《詩論》是現存最古老的關於戲劇文學理論的文件。原作分為兩個部分：第一部分解釋悲劇，第二部分則專注於喜劇。但第二部分已失傳，因此相關討論皆以悲劇為核心。

According to Poetics, tragedy is a representation of a serious, complete action which has magnitude, in embellished speech, with each of its elements used separately in the various parts of the play and represented by people acting and not by narration, accomplishing by means of pity and terror the catharsis of such emotions.

《詩論》對悲劇的定義為一個嚴肅、完整、有一定長度的詮釋，以語言為媒介，透過各種戲劇的要素，以表演而非敘述的方式呈現給觀眾，並以引起憐憫、恐懼等感情為其目標的戲劇。

Classic tragedy is characterized by seriousness, and it usually involves a great main character whose fortune experiences a major reverse. Usually the reversal of fortune is from good to bad, as it effects the audiences with pity and fear. However, theoretically speaking, it can be from bad to good as well. According to Aristotle, when audience respond to the suffering of the character in the drama, the strong emotions will leave viewers feeling elated, in the same way people often claim that crying might make people feel better.

古典悲劇的特徵是內容嚴肅而尊嚴，通常涉及一個偉大的主角，其命運經歷過重大的逆轉。同常這種轉變是由好變壞，因為這會讓觀眾趕到憐憫和恐懼；但理論上來說，也可以是由壞變好的轉變。依亞里斯多德的看法，當觀眾對劇中角色的經歷感到悲痛時，這種強烈的感受反而會鼓動觀眾的情緒，就像在哭過之後人們會感到更好一樣。

📎 重要單字暨新聞辭彙（Key Vocabulary & News Glossary）

- drama *(n.)* 戲劇
- literature *(n.)* 文學
- tragedy *(n.)* 悲劇
- influence *(n.) (v.)* 影響
- character *(n.)* 角色
- melody *(n.)* 音樂
- emotion *(n.)* 情緒
- fortune *(n.)* 命運
- classic *(adj.)* 古典的
- comedy *(n.)* 喜劇
- regional *(adj.)* 區域性的
- plot *(n.)* 劇情
- diction *(n.)* 措詞
- spectacle *(n.)* 場面
- playwright *(n.)* 劇作家
- reverse *(v.)* 反轉

📎 單句及句型範例（Vocabularies & Sentence Examples）

1. A regional conflict may erupt into warfare. 區域性衝突可能演變為戰爭。
2. The media has a strong influence on public opinions. 媒體對輿論有很強的影響。
3. The melody is then taken up by the violins. 小提琴接著演奏主旋律。
4. Learn to control your emotions! 學著控制你的情緒！
5. Shakespeare is considered as one of the greatest playwrights of all time. 莎士比亞是古今最偉大的劇作家之一。

📎 問題與討論（Questions & Discussions）

Q 1. 你最喜歡的電視劇是什麼？我能在網上找到嗎？

Q.1　What is your favorite TV drama? Can I find it on the internet?

Q 2. 你知道蘇格拉底嗎？他是古希臘時代的哲學家。

Q.2　Do you know Socrates? He was a classical Greek philosopher.

Q 3. 你同意戲如人生、人生如戲這句話嗎？為什麼？

Q.3　Do you agree that drama is life and life is drama? Why or why not?

📎 主題對話範例（Dialogue Examples）

A：What's your plan for the coming weekend?
B：I don't know yet. I really need to find something to do.
A：We can watch TV dramas and comedies together. I just bought some DVDs online.
B：That would be great. Can I go to your place on Saturday evening?
A：Of course. Please bring me some soft drinks.
B：No problem. I'll see you on Saturday.

Politics
Commerce
Jobs
Sports
Healthy
Society
Career
Life

同義字與名詞（Synonym & Terminology）
1. specific（特定的）⇨ Particular ⇨ designated ⇨ given
2. symbol（符號）⇨ insignia ⇨ mark ⇨ token ⇨ emblem
3. blunder（錯誤）⇨ mistake ⇨ error ⇨ failing
4. emotion（情緒）⇨ sentiment ⇨ feeling ⇨ affection
5. technique（技巧）⇨ ability ⇨ skill ⇨ talent
6. fear（恐懼）⇨ afraid ⇨ dread
7. arouse（激發）⇨ evoke ⇨ stimulate ⇨ excite
8. perform（表演）⇨ act ⇨ play ⇨ show ⇨ demonstrate ⇨ stage

英譯中練習：（參閱主題文章）

English ⇨ Chinese Translation Practice:(Refer to the theme article)

1. According to Aristotle's Poetics, comedy is a representation of laughable people and involves some kind of blunder or ugliness which does not cause pain or disaster.（英譯中）

   ....
   ....

2. There are several regional branches of Chinese drama, of which the Beijing opera from the northern region and of the Kunqu from the southern region are among the most notable.（英譯中）

   ....
   ....

3. A famous quote from Shakespeare's "As you like it" would be "the whole world is a stage, and all men and women merely actors".（英譯中）

   ....
   ....

英譯中練習解答

Part 1　談政治情勢

Unit 1　梅克爾所領軍的歐盟

1. 梅克爾？是歐洲繼英國前首相柴契爾夫人後，最影響力的女性政治家暨領導人，也有人稱之為德國鐵娘子。
2. 梅克爾是她第一任丈夫的姓氏，離婚後保留下來。
3. 1989 年柏林圍牆推倒之後，她投入到蓬勃發展的民主政治運動中。
4. 歐盟近來打算對中國銷歐產品課徵整罰性關稅。太陽能板及部分通訊產品，廉價不合理，不公平競爭傷害歐盟業者。
5. 總部設在比利時首都布魯塞爾，歐洲聯盟（簡稱歐盟，European Union —— EU）是由歐洲共同體 （European Communities） 發展而來的，是一個集政治實體和經濟實體於一身、在世界上具有重要影響的區域一體化組織。

Unit 2　為何全球示威抗議的聲音不斷？

1. 此次大規模示威成為了自 1977 年埃及發生「麵包暴動」以來近 30 年內發生的規模最大的民主化的示威運動。
2. 因此導致大約 1.7 萬人被扣押，估計監獄裡的政治犯更高達 3 萬人。

Unit 3　中國之「一國兩制」

1. 此政策最早係由大陸前國家主席鄧小平首先提出，主要目的為實現中國和平統一目標，並針對台灣問題之基本解決方案。
2. 所謂『一國兩制』乃以『一個中國』為原則，同時強調「中華人民共和國是代表中國的唯一合法政府」。
3. 雖然香港和澳門已實行「一國兩制」，惟台灣民眾在中國統一或台灣獨立的問題上仍意見分歧。
4. 因此，台灣人民在短期間或可預計之未來，應該不會接受或實施所謂「一國兩制」。
5. 1949 年中華民國政府遷台時，中國共產黨起初採取「武力解放台灣」的方針。

Unit 4　小馬哥需要硬起來？

1. 馬總統也隨即召開記者會，指責王金平關說。

Unit 5　歐巴馬 vs. 曼德拉

1. 當曼德拉領導反種族隔離運動時，南非法院以「密謀推翻政府」等
   罪名將他定罪。

Part 2　談經貿發展

Unit 1　QE3 救市真有用？

1. 美國聯邦準備理事會宣布執行第三輪貨幣量化寬鬆政策（QE3）。
2. 前 Fed 經濟學家曼恩表示，Fed 希望經濟成長加速，尤其是增加更
   多工作機會，但 QE 在這方面的能力，實在有限。
3. 在 QE3 之後，而且在美元持續走貶的環境下，新台幣恐怕會維持相
   對高檔的價位。
4. 政府和民間仍要關注國內產業競爭力的提升並認真看待 QE3 長期帶
   來的影響，持續發展應有的努力。

Unit 2　您今天 Google 了嗎？

1. Google 自創立開始的快速成長同時也帶動了一系列的產品研發、併
   購事項與合作關聯，而不僅僅是公司核心的網路搜尋業務。

Unit 3　巴西未來的行情

1. 得益於豐厚的自然資源和充足的勞動力，巴西的國內生產總值位居
   南美洲第一，世界第六。
2. 19 世紀後期到 20 世紀前期，巴西接納了超過 500 萬來自歐洲和日
   本的移民並於 20 世紀 30 年代開始工業化。
3. 1998 年 11 月，巴西從國際貨幣基金主導的國際援助項目獲得了 415
   億美元的貸款，前提是調整財政政策和經濟結構。

4. 英國《經濟學人》雜誌更預估，巴西有機會再 2013 年就可超越法
   國，晉升為全球前五大的經濟體。

5. 從匯率的角度來看，巴西 Real 匯率長線還有大幅升值的機會，未來
   巴西幣再度跟美元等價的機率是非常高的。

Unit 4　App 令人好愛不釋手

1. 當某人說「A-P-P 給我」是指所謂使用 WhatsApp 即時通的軟體，這
   款免費簡訊軟體，目前在台灣非常相當受到歡迎。

2. 由於智慧型手機近年來已日漸普及，」App「 這個字眼已開始出現
   在我們的生活當中，就如同十多年前，個人電腦開始普及一般。

3. 「App」 在各廠牌智慧型手機中並不通用，這就牽扯到使用的 OS
   （作業系統） 是否一樣了。

4. 蘋果」App Store」目前已經吸引了全球近八萬位軟體開發業者，另
   一陣營」Android」系統也有兩萬餘人陸續投入應用軟體之開發。

Unit 5　柏南克～美國財政幕後操盤手

1. 出生於美國喬治亞州奧古斯塔，班・柏南克為美國猶太裔經濟學
   家，也是現任美國聯邦準備理事會（美國中央銀行）主席。

2. 2009 年，柏南克因為帶領美國度過大蕭條以來最惡劣的經濟危機中
   有傑出之表現，被《時代雜誌》評選為「年度風雲人物」。

3. 柏南克身為聞名的宏觀經濟學家，其主要研究興趣：貨幣政策和宏
   觀經濟史。

Part 3　談就業趨勢和就業率

Unit 1　你想創業嗎？

1. 數據顯示，台灣『創業家精神』全球排名第一，也是我國經濟發展
   的重要命脈。

2. 政府一定會給予全力支持。讓創業者創業有成，對國家社會做出最
   大的貢獻。

3. 透過被選拔出來的項目，藉以拓展海內外市場，並讓全世界看到台灣文化之美。

Unit 2 西班牙和希臘

1. 由於歐元區主權債務危機，使西班牙與希臘的勞工市場工作機會持續下降。致使這兩個歐盟國家的青年失業率同時也跟隨著不斷攀升。

Unit 3 台灣 vs. 南韓：薪資怎差這樣多？

1. 台灣新上班族每月平均起薪約 2 萬 4 千元，與去年相當。而薪資落在 1 萬 9 千元至 2 萬 5 千元中間，則佔大多數，有 5 成左右。
2. 調查顯示除了「22K」之外，「派遣」已經成為拉低台灣薪資的主要原因之一，自從 2008 年金融危機後企業開始採用此做法。
3. 諷刺的是，不只是民間企業愛用派遣，政府竟然才是全國最大派遣戶，而且還用低於合理薪資三到四成的超低價，讓台灣的薪資更進一步崩壞。
4. 根據英國人力資源分配方案供應商 ECA International 調查指出，預期台灣明年的調薪幅度大約是在 4%，相較於 2013 的 3.5% 略有增長調。

Unit 4 綠能事業新天地

1. 太陽光電、LED 光電照明、風力發電、生質燃料、氫能與燃料電池、能源資通訊與電動車輛為重點輔導的產業。
2. 台灣是全球前三大太陽電池生產大國、全球最大 LED 光源及模組供應國以及全球風力發電系統之供應商。
3. 台灣綠能產業以太陽光電與 LED 照明光電為主，在 100 年以太陽光電與 LED 照明光電為最多，分別佔總產值之 48.7% 與 46.0%。
4. 歐盟率先於 2008 年底通過「歐盟再生能源法案」，訂立所謂的「20-20-20」目標－於 2020 年前將再生能源提升到總需求量的 20%，同時亦將二氧化碳減量 20% 以及能源效益提升 20%。

Unit 5　如何從眾多的應徵者中脫穎而出？

1. 最重要的是要強調自己是最佳人選，如此，才有可能得到面試機會。

Part 4　談運動健身

Unit 1　有益健康的健身運動

1. 身運動的好處可增強心肺功能，促進血液循環，及增強免疫力等。
2. 《環境科學與科技期刊》研究顯示，戶外活動會讓您變的很活躍。
3. 當您邊聽音樂邊運動，您容易把自己的步伐和旋律對齊，保持旋律的輕快。
4. 運動前先暖身，比較不會導致氣喘，如同在運動前使用呼吸器十五到二十分鐘做暖身。

Unit 2　「Linsanity」林來瘋

1. 林來瘋是源於紐約尼克的球星林書豪在 2012 年 2 月開始掀起的風潮。
2. 《富比世》雜誌估算，林書豪的品牌價值大約在 1,400 萬美元左右。
3. 台灣一家電腦公司宣佈，他們將同尼克斯成為商業合作夥伴，尼克斯將允許該電腦公司的 logo 出現在尼克斯主場場邊廣告牌上。
4. 考慮到 NBA 在國際範圍內的影響力，以林書豪的態度、魅力、背景，他只需要成為一支季後賽級別球隊中的優秀球員，就可以擁有巨大的品牌價值。

Unit 3　傑出台灣女子運動員

1. 她成為史上第六位世界球后，也是第一位登上主流運動世界排名第一的台灣運動員。

Unit 4　足球金童貝克漢

1. 外型英俊帥氣的貝克漢毫無疑問是全球足壇最具人氣、代表性的球員。

2. 在國際足壇上，貝克漢代表英格蘭國家隊出賽 115 次的紀錄，至今仍無人能比。

3. 他是史上唯一一位在四個國家的頂級聯賽中都獲得過冠軍的英格蘭球員，也是第一位在連續三屆世界盃足球賽都有進球的英格蘭球員。

Unit 5　台灣旅美大聯盟棒球選手

1. 他效力於洛杉磯道奇隊，於 2002 年 9 月 24 日升上大聯盟。他也是第一位在美國職棒大聯盟比賽中登場的台灣選手，當時年紀 24 歲。

2. 王建民是亞洲首位在季後賽拿下勝投的球員。他也是亞洲首位在大聯盟拿下『勝投王』的投手，以及亞洲投手在大聯盟單季最多勝投的紀錄保持人（19 勝）。

3. 他是第一位在大聯盟擊出全壘打及首位入選大聯盟明星賽的台灣選手。

Part 5　談食品安全

Unit 1　別吃壞了肚子～黑心食品中毒事件

1. 隨著科學日趨發展，讓有毒及造假食品的手法不斷升級，也是我們現代人無法逃避且須每天面對的問題。

Unit 2　茶與養身

1. 茶成為民眾喜愛的飲料，不但好喝，也是良好的天然保健飲料。

2. 黑茶對抑制腹部脂肪的增加有明顯效果，有防止脂肪堆積的作用。

3. 失眠者、感冒發熱者、胃潰瘍患者、孕婦等人群不宜喝茶。

Unit 3 你喝了一口好水嗎？

1. 中暑的原因是體內的水分不足，所引發的脫水症狀，因此水分對我們人體來說是非常重要的。

Unit 4 除油減脂妙方多

1. 高熱量的零食是減肥的大敵，但選擇小包裝的零食，不僅能滿足你的口慾，還能幫助你減少熱量的攝入。
2. 運動是最好的消耗熱量的減肥方法，而有氧運動與重量訓練能讓減肥效果更加明顯。
3. 如果你睡眠不足不僅會減緩你的新陳代謝，還容易讓你產生飢餓感，這樣你就更加容易吃進更多的熱量了。

Unit 5 健康食品我最愛

1. 營養師表示，骨骼保健素材常見包括鈣片及維生素 D 配方產品、乳製品、植物異黃酮類的大豆胚芽製品（幫助停經之婦女有助於骨質保健）都是補充的素材。

Part 6 談社會新聞事件

Unit 1 公寓大廈禁養寵物之我見

1. 現在越來越多人養寵物，但部分公寓大廈禁止住戶飼養寵物。
2. 有些公寓大廈管委會更可以制定規約，禁止住戶飼養寵物。這也讓很多想要飼養流浪動物的民眾都打消念頭。
3. 從民國 97 年動保法修正到 101 年 6 月止，一共移送了 24 件，其中有 17 件受到徒刑或罰金的裁罰。

Unit 2 你中了威力彩嗎？

1. 『威力彩』是台彩新一代的彩券，2008 年 1 月 22 日上市，其獎金高於目前所有台彩的公益彩券。

Unit 3 交通違規要小心

1. 民國 102 年到來，交通新制上路立即生效，其中酒駕取締更加嚴格。
2. 紅酒量大約 1/3 瓶，烈酒更只要喝個 1/10 瓶，就會達到檢測值上限。

3. 因應新制，不管是直接喝，還是吃了摻酒料理都算喝酒，最好還是別開車上路不管是不是直接喝。

Part 7　談職場進修學習與教育

Unit 1　大學教育的省思與展望

1. 哈佛大學前校長伯克在本書提出了對美國大學的大學部教育內容與品質的看法與改進之道。
2. 因此，教學的品質遠比課程的內容與分量來得重要，對學生的影響亦更深遠。
3. 大學部的教育應該追求多樣的目標，培養學生幾項重要的能力，包括溝通、思辨、道德推理、履行公民責任、迎接多元化生活、迎接全球化社會、拓展興趣以及就業準備等。

Unit 2　烹飪有一套

1. 美國營養學家和食品安全專家，列舉了聰明主婦在烹飪方面也會常犯的 8 種錯誤，聽從他們的建議，你餐桌上的食物會變得更加健康。
2. 專家說「從採摘的那一刻起，水果和蔬菜中的維生素和礦物質就開始減少了。」如果你採購回來的蔬菜存儲時間越久，它們所含的營養就越少。
3. 停留在食物表面的有害細菌可能會沾染到手上，切開水果時甚至會侵入水果內部。

Unit 3　你的英文程度趕得上企業要求嗎？

1. 包括對外書信、e-mail、傳真往來、國際電話、出國開會…，企業都需要沒有國際溝通障礙的員工。

Part 8　談樂活好自在

Unit 1　台北文創園區

1. 華山 1914 文化創意產業園區前身為「台北酒廠」，為臺灣台北市市定古蹟。在 1999 年後，成為提供給藝文界等文化活動場地。
2. 身為台灣連鎖書店的龍頭，誠品書店期待引進超過 100 個地區的創意品牌進入園區，而且估計一年營收可達 10 億元。
3. 最後期望可以成為觀光的文創勝地，結合併呈台灣與國際文化創意作品，襯托台灣文化元素成為觀光旅遊亮點。

Unit 2　寵物當家

1. 大多數寵物在主人那裡會受到很好的對待，也不將寵用作為食用，但有時也衍生虐待動物問題。
2. 但其實人可以把所有種類的動物變成寵物，包括魚綱、爬行綱、兩棲綱甚至昆蟲，不過一般寵物都是體型比較小的動物。
3. 人工智慧的發展，未來這類寵物會有思想，會變得更加體貼人。

Unit 3　微笑單車熱潮

1. 台灣捷安特提供了整套的公共腳踏車租借服務，稱為 U-Bike, 一種新型態的短距離運輸工具。
2. 配合全面改善的自行車騎乘環境，加上完備的臺北捷運路網，可讓大眾運輸從街道深入巷弄，創造新的『兩輪文化』。
3. 引發一片尋找她所騎乘「3804」號單車，廠商耗費一番功夫與 U-Bike 協調同意，將原單車找到給波多野結衣一個驚喜。

Unit 4　中國策略遊戲「麻將」

1. 比起撲克，麻將的組合方式更為變化多端，需要通過複雜的機率分析才能預測結果。
2. 在東亞與東南亞地區，特別是華人社區中，麻將常被當做娛樂或賭博手段。

3. 著名的美國人類學家及遊戲研究者史都華‧庫林 並無討論過麻將的起源地，謂當時的麻將遊戲（書中稱為「中發」"Chung fat"）僅限於江浙一帶，故其所述較吻合寧波起源論。

Unit 5　戲如人生 人生如戲

1. 據亞里斯多德在《詩論》中所述，喜劇表現的是可笑的人群，以及他們所犯的錯誤或醜態，卻不造成痛苦或傷害。

2. 中國戲劇又依區域分為不同的派別，最有名的有北方的京劇和南方的崑曲。

3. 在莎士比亞的劇作《如你所願》中有一句名言：世界是一座舞台，所有人不過是其中的演員。

好書報報

心理學研究顯示，一個習慣養成，至少必須重複21次！
全書規劃30天學習進度表，搭配學習，
不知不覺養成學習英語的好習慣！

▲圖解學習英文文法 三效合一！
◎刺激大腦記憶◎快速掌握學習大綱◎複習迅速

▲英文文法學習元素一次到位！
◎20個必懂觀念 ◎30個必學句型 ◎40個必閃陷阱

▲流行有趣的英語！
◎「那裡有正妹！」
◎「今天我們去看變形金剛3吧！」

作者：朱懿婷
定價：新台幣349元
規格：364頁／18K／雙色印刷

要說出流利的英文，就是需要常常開口勇敢說！

國外打工兼職很流行，如何找尋機會？
怎麼做完整的英文自我介紹，成功promote自己？
獨自出國打工，職場基礎英語對話該怎麼說？
不同國家、不同領域要知道那些common sense？
保險健康的考量要更注意，各國制度大不同？

6大主題 30個單元 120組情境式對話 30篇補給站
九大學習特色：
■主題豐富多元 ■多種情境演練 ■激發聯想延伸
■增強單字記憶 ■片語邏輯組合 ■例句靈活套用
■塊狀編排歸納 ■舒適閱讀視覺 ■吸收效果加倍

作者：Claire Chang & Melanie Venecamp
定價：新台幣469元
規格：560頁／18K／雙色印刷

好書報報－生活系列

愛情之酒甜而苦。兩人喝，是甘露；
三人喝，是酸醋；隨便喝，要中毒。

精選出偶像劇必定出現的**80**個情境，
每個情境－必備單字、劇情會話訓練班、30秒會話教室
讓你跟著偶像劇的腳步學生活英語會話的劇情，
輕鬆自然地學會英語!

作者：伍羚芝
定價：新台幣349元
規格：344頁 / 18K / 雙色印刷

全書中英對照，介紹東西方節慶的典故，
幫助你的英語學習－學得好、學得深入!

用英語來學節慶分為兩大部分－東方節慶&西方節慶

每個節慶共**7**個學習項目：
節慶源由－簡易版、精彩完整版＋實用單字、閱讀測驗、
習俗放大鏡、實用會話、常用單句這麼說、互動單元...

作者：Melanie Venekamp、陳欣慧、倍斯特編輯團隊
定價：新台幣299元
規格：304頁 / 18K / 雙色印刷

用現有的環境與資源，為自己的小寶貝
創造一個雙語學習環境；讓孩子贏在起跑點上!

我家寶貝愛英文，是一本從媽咪懷孕、嬰兒期到幼兒期，
會常用到的單字、對話，必備例句，
並設計單元延伸的互動小遊戲以及童謠，
增進親子關係，也讓家長與孩子一同學習的參考書!

作者：Mark Venekamp & Claire Chang
定價：新台幣329元
規格：296頁 / 18K / 雙色印刷 / MP3

國際化餐飲時代不可不學！
擁有這一本，即刻通往世界各地！

基礎應對 訂位帶位、包場、活動安排、菜色介紹...
前後場管理 服務生Must Know、擺設學問、食物管理...
人事管理 徵聘與訓練、福利升遷、管理者的職責...
狀況處理 客人不滿意、難纏的顧客、部落客評論...

*120*個餐廳工作情境
*100%*英語人士的對話用語
循序漸進勤做練習，職場英語一日千里！

作者：Mark Venekamp & Claire Chang
定價：新台幣369元
規格：328頁 / 18K / 雙色印刷 / MP3

這是一本以航空業為背景，
從職員角度出發的航空英語會話工具書。
從職員VS同事 & 職員VS客戶，
兩大角度，呈現100% 原汁原味職場情境！

特別規劃→
以Q&A的方式，英語實習role play
提供更多航空界專業知識的職場補給站
免稅品服務該留意甚麼？ 旅客出境的SOP！
迎賓服務的步驟與重點！違禁品相關規定?！
飛機健檢大作戰有哪些...

作者：Mark Venekamp & Claire Chang
定價：新台幣369元
規格：352頁 / 18K / 雙色印刷 / MP3

用 News 英語增進表達力

作者	陳志遠◎著
特約編輯	焦家洵
封面設計	蔡曉曉
內頁構成	華漢電腦排版有限公司
發行人	周瑞德
企劃編輯	丁筠馨
校對	徐瑞璞・劉俞青
印製	世和印製企業有限公司
初版	2014 年 01 月
定價	新台幣 329 元

出版　倍斯特出版事業有限公司

電話／（02）2351-2007 傳真／（02）2351-0887

地址／ 100 台北市中正區福州街 1 號 10 樓之 2

Email ／ best.books.service@gmail.com

總經銷　商流文化事業有限公司

地址／新北市中和區中正路 752 號 7 樓

電話／（02）2228-8841 傳真／（02）2228-6939

國家圖書館出版品預行編目（CIP）資料

用 News 英語增進表達力／陳志遠著 .
-- 初版 . -- 臺北市：倍斯特 , 2014.01
面；　公分
ISBN：978-986-89739-8-5　（平裝）
1. 英語　2. 會話
805.188　　　　　　　　　　　102026529